Wayne,
Thank you for your interest in my newest novel.
Hope you like the hero, Brick N. he is a fictitious SAE Bro from UPS.
Wonderful to hear from you.
Next novel, Darkness over the Canal, is in the works —
Please enjoy "High Seas Darkness"

In the Bonds

Burr A   1/31/2015

HIGH SEAS DARKNESS

A
Brick Morgan
NOVEL

BURR B. ANDERSON

This is a work of fiction. The events and characters described herein are imaginary and are not intended to refer to specific places or living persons. The opinions expressed in this manuscript are solely the opinions of the author and do not represent the opinions or thoughts of the publisher. The author has represented and warranted full ownership and/or legal right to publish all the materials in this book.

High Seas Darkness
A Brick Morgan Novel
All Rights Reserved.
Copyright © 2014 Burr B. Anderson
v3.0

Cover Photo © 2014 thinkstockphotos.com. All rights reserved - used with permission.

This book may not be reproduced, transmitted, or stored in whole or in part by any means, including graphic, electronic, or mechanical without the express written consent of the publisher except in the case of brief quotations embodied in critical articles and reviews.

Outskirts Press, Inc.
http://www.outskirtspress.com

Paperback ISBN: 978-1-4787-3556-4
Hardback ISBN: 978-1-4787-3593-9

Library of Congress Control Number: 2014909977

Outskirts Press and the "OP" logo are trademarks belonging to Outskirts Press, Inc.

PRINTED IN THE UNITED STATES OF AMERICA

This book is dedicated to the memories of
Mike Anderson and Jack Taylor

Mike Anderson provided the author with behind-the-curtain insights into the world of musical bands and the life of professional musicians. In addition to being a superb trumpet player, Mike dedicated his life to teaching the skills of his lifework to the next generation.

Jack Taylor's interest in aviation started with his Naval Air training during the Vietnam War. After a forty-year business career, his passion for flight was not diminished. Jack's aeronautical wisdom provided a pilot's touch to this novel's time in the sky.

Acknowledgements

To the members of Anderson Literary Solutions LLC editorial committee: Nancy Anderson, Suzanne Durnford, Larry King, Carolyn Hash Shain, and Connie Zittel. You were so patient working with my drafts in a timely manner.

To Kyle Anderson, PhD, Kris Anderson, and Zach Anderson for helping your father with cyber-technology and computer science issues.

To Jodie Renner of Jodie Renner Editing. Your professional imput helped kickstart the editing process and made it possible for Brick Morgan to have balance in his crime-fighting life.

To Sigma Alpha Epsilon fraternity brothers Jim Clary, Dr. Bruce Logan, Dan Martin, Craig Mendenhall, Jerry Reilly, Craig Voegel, and Ken White. Each of your individual creativity provided me with wonderful ideas for plot design.

To the professional team at Outskirts Press and my publishing consultant Tina Ruvalcaba and author representive Colleen Goulet. I thank you for moving this novel through the many steps of publishing.

To Diana Schramer of Write Way Copyediting LLC. Your editing skills were nothing short of amazing. Not only did you help bring out my characters' special personalities, you also were able to make the *Matisse Under the Stars* a noble cruise ship.

To Katie Karim for your design work and maintenance of my author's website.

High Seas Darkness
Characters

Morgan Maritime Investigations, LLC
- ➤ Brick Morgan: Owner, Morgan Maritime Investigations, LLC
- ➤ Titus: Cyber Consultant to Morgan Maritime Investigations, LLC

Nobility Cruise Line, Inc.
- ➤ Sanan Jaidee: Bartender, Big Dipper Bar, *Matisse Under the Stars*
- ➤ Carolyn Luna: Passenger, *Matisse Under the Stars*
- ➤ Yvette Fuentes: Chief Security Officer, *Matisse Under the Stars*
- ➤ Raju Kumar Marwah: Deputy Security Officer, *Matisse Under the Stars*
- ➤ Deepak Mehta: Chief Security Officer, *Rembrandt Under the Stars*
- ➤ Nurse Mercardo: Medical Center Nurse, *Matisse Under the Stars*
- ➤ Robert "Rob" Spencer: Director, Fleet Wide Security
- ➤ Francesco Costanzo: Captain, *Matisse Under the Stars*
- ➤ Dakila Salazar: Cabin Steward, *Matisse Under the Stars*
- ➤ Kyle Throckmorton: Passenger, *Matisse Under the Stars*
- ➤ Dr. Pedro Ramos: Senior Medical Director, *Matisse Under the Stars*
- ➤ Dr. Jose Resende: Doctor, *Matisse Under the Stars*
- ➤ Rick Lansteiner: Art Auctioneer, *Matisse Under the Stars*
- ➤ Antonina Kartashov: Guest Artist, *Matisse Under the Stars*
- ➤ Officer Antonio: Chief Engineer, *Matisse Under the Stars*
- ➤ Inna Kozlov: Supervisor, Digital Experience, *Matisse Under the Stars*

United States Government
- ➤ Kryss Mitchell: Special Agent, Counterterrorism, Federal Bureau of Investigation

- Nathan King: Special Agent, Counterterrorism, Federal Bureau of Investigation
- Alexander "Ace" Zittel: Director, Federal Bureau of Investigation
- Elizabeth "Liz" Monroe: Deputy Director, Federal Bureau of Investigation
- POTUS, President of the United States
- Vic Bodner: President's Chief of Staff
- Herbert "Herb" Wallace: Assistant Director, National Security Branch, Counterterrorism, Federal Bureau of Investigation
- Michelle Murphy: Senate Minority Leader, United States Senate
- Martin Daniel: Speaker of the House, United States House of Representatives
- Maxine Johnston: Secretary of the Department of Homeland Security

Lashkar-e-Aalam
- Zaeem Hasan Al-Ajmi: Founder, Lashkar-e-Aalam
- Yusuf Al Omar: Terrorist, Lashkar-e-Aalam
- Jari Atwa: Head of Security, Lashkar-e-Aalam
- Faroug Hasan Ahmed: Chemist, Lashkar-e-Aalam
- Muhamed Bashir: Terrorist, Lashkar-e-Aalam
- Muhammad Bin Attash: Terrorist, Lashkar-e-Aalam
- Mullah Saleh Rahim: Terrorist, Lashkar-e-Aalam
- Zahir Ahmed Hahid: Terrorist, Lashkar-e-Aalam

Special Guest Characters
- Mark Whitfield: Nationally Renowned Guitarist
- Jim "Bud" Clary: Owner, Bud Clary Chevrolet, Longview WA
- Stephen Marchione: Owner, Marchione Guitars

Chapter One

Brick Morgan raised his finger to his lips and made eye contact with Chief Security Officer Deepak Mehta as they stood outside the door well below the waterline on the huge cruise ship. This was Mehta's cruise ship, but he deferred to Brick's expertise on matters involving security or smuggling. A silent countdown followed. Three . . . two . . . one . . .

Brick threw open the door, and they rushed into the reefer. As expected, they found two olive-skinned crew members on their knees pulling plastic bags of light-brown powder out of hollowed-out pineapples. Caught red-handed stuffing their shirts with smack, the drug runners jumped to their feet as if to fight.

The short, wiry one looked up at Brick's six-foot-four, muscled frame with eyes wide and then bravely rushed him. Brick smiled to himself. *Good chance these guys have never met a judo black belt before, much less a big black guy from the 'hood.* Brick effortlessly rolled the unsuspecting crew member over his right hip, slammed him onto the hard linoleum deck, and then jammed his size-thirteen boot into the crewman's neck.

The second man, the taller of the two, raised a piece of pallet board to knock Brick over the head, but Mehta tackled him to the floor.

Chuckling, Brick said, "Deepak, thank you. Thought you said you played soccer, not American football."

They subdued the two men by securing their hands behind their backs with plastic flex-cuffs and tossed them onto a pallet of lettuce. Brick propped them up against the cold boxes. Here down on deck three, the ship's insulated refrigerator made for a quiet, private interrogation room. And despite his appreciation for the law, Brick Morgan of Morgan Maritime Investigations LLC enjoyed taking down criminals without worrying about America's Miranda rules.

Brick pushed his face close to the scared smugglers. "So do they speak English wherever the fuck you're from?" His voice echoed in the metal-walled room. "Just where the fuck are you from anyway?"

The shorter one with slick black hair, wearing a kitchen apron, said in falsely broken English, "Mexico. *Sí!* We are from Mexico!"

Brick was certain that both jerks could speak English just fine if they were motivated. He stared at them for a full thirty seconds, formulating his plan of action. He needed to find out how many on the ship were involved in this smuggling operation, where the drugs were manufactured, the merchant who supplied the heroin-stuffed pineapples, and who in south Florida would take possession of the dope. He knew just how to make them talk.

Brick looked at the two captive crew members and asked with marked casualness, "Hey, have you guys met my partner, Stash?"

Both men raised their eyebrows and shook their heads.

Brick stood and placed one foot on the box of lettuce. "You with the apron, what's your name?"

"Miguel—Miguel Garcia."

"Mr. Garcia, Stash just loves puzzles. Finding concealed drugs isn't just a job to him; it's his calling. I mean he's a real animal when it comes to catching drug runners. In less than fifteen minutes, he tore through this reefer and found your dope. Now I'm not such a fan of the cold. But Stash? Working in this thirty-eight-degree temperature was an extra bonus for him."

The two men looked at each other in confusion.

"Oh, and that whole smack-in-the-fruit thing? Stash really eats that shit up. And I have to compliment you, too. If it wasn't for some chatter a friend of mine found about some Afghani heroin cruising into Florida on this ship, we probably wouldn't have thought to look here."

"We don't know anything about that! We're just kitchen helpers!"

Brick nodded and then spoke in a quiet, clear voice. "I apologize. My name is Brick Morgan. You probably already know Chief Mehta."

Mehta smirked, but the crewmen never took their eyes off Brick as he continued introducing himself.

"I investigate maritime crime. You know, things like assaults, theft, terrorism—and my partner Stash's favorite, drug smuggling."

The crew members exchanged worried glances. By this point, Brick knew they understood his words quite well. It was time for another introduction.

"Hey, Mr. Mehta, go ahead and get Stash. After the workout they gave him this morning, I bet he would love to meet these two. I'll let you back in."

Officer Mehta hurriedly left the room, the door closing behind him with a loud slam. The two men jumped. The one in the apron, Miguel, gulped as he looked up at the big commanding black man who now had them all to himself.

Brick's nonchalant chatter continued. "So, my friends—can I call you my friends?—I want three things from you. First, I'd like the names of everyone else on this ship involved in this smuggling ring."

The two glanced at each other with fear in their eyes.

"Then I want the name of the guy who pays you. And finally, I would really appreciate knowing just how you planned to get this tasty brown sugar off the ship. Please explain how this heroin made its way across the world. If it's part of a terror-funding scheme, that would be a big bonus and make this easier on all of us."

Miguel looked at the other man and then spoke up. "We know nothing! Nothing about terrorism! Some Indian guy in the engine room said he would pay us each one hundred American dollars to bring the bags in the pineapples to a trash can on deck nine." He nudged his conspirator for backup.

"*Sí!* Yes! The man said we could use the money for our families back home."

"Okay, well, I can understand that. Family is important." Brick saw the men starting to relax at his soothing words. He removed his foot from the crate of lettuce and began to turn away. "Oh, but wait . . ." Brick turned back and pulled Miguel to his feet. Reaching into Miguel's shirt, he pulled out a Ziploc bag filled with heroin. Brick's face betrayed no emotion as he pulled the shocked smuggler to him and stuffed the bag down the crew member's pants. He then grabbed another bag, ripped open the plastic, and poured some of the heroin over each of their heads.

Stunned at Brick's brazenness, one of them said, "You can't do this! You're an American! You have laws!"

Brick reseated the smuggler on the pallet of lettuce. "I know. I love the law. Stanford Law, actually. You might be impressed by that degree, but really, it's not that big a deal—especially since we're not even in America now. You see, you guys should have done this back in the Bahamas or at least waited until we got to Florida. Now that we've sailed into international waters, we're a lot of nautical miles away from those pesky rules and regulations of the United States."

Just then, a loud bang on the reefer door echoed through the room, followed by sharp barking and scratching on the door. The barking turned to deep growling, and the helpless smugglers looked at each other in horror. Brick banged on the reefer door twice, and the growling and clawing stopped.

"Gentlemen, please calm down. That's just my partner Stash. He's a tactically trained drug dog. He's schooled to claw and bite his way through any material to get to illegal substances like heroin and cocaine. Turns out he really doesn't like drugs at all. And you gotta know that his bite force is something crazy, like 238 pounds." Seeing the pair's eyes widen in fear, Brick knew he had them where he wanted them. "I once saw him tear right through a wooden crate and make a mess out a bunch of chickens stuffed with pot. You should have seen it. Feathers and skin and blood everywhere. Looked like a fucking bloodbath. And I know bloodbaths..."

Without warning, Brick became much less civil. Dragging the bound drug smugglers by their hair to just in front of the door, he banged again on the wall. Stash's bark came back to life even more vicious and vocal than before.

"So, assholes—can I call you assholes?—here's what's going to happen. When I open this door to let you meet our fine canine specimen, he's going to smell the dope that's all over you. That's really going to piss him off. He's gonna charge at you fuckers like a runaway train. I can't be sure if he'll go right for your balls before he chews his way from your little peckers straight through to your colons. But I know that he'll love sinking his sharp teeth into your ugly-ass faces while I sit here enjoying some fresh pineapple. The way I see it, that dog will not stop until you both resemble bloody piles of dead, mutilated chickens."

Eyes wide, they both started shaking, sweat pouring down their faces.

Brick cranked the door handle with his large hand. "I only want three answers. It's your call."

The men dropped to their knees, their hands supplicating. "No dog—*por favor*—*no perro!* Please! His name is Fawad!"

Chief Mehta took their captives to the ship's brig while Brick and Stash returned to the *Rembrandt Under the Star*'s security office. Deepak had suggested keeping the two men in the reefer for the rest of the trip back to Fort Lauderdale, but they decided to let the smugglers enjoy their final sailing in the cramped, windowless brig instead.

Brick rewarded Stash with five minutes of play with his reward towel. When Deepak returned, he seemed especially relieved when the Belgian Malinois returned to his kennel. He much preferred the large dog locked up. Brick couldn't help but smile at the man's phobia, even though he knew how intimidating these dogs could be.

"Deepak, I promise he's a big softie as long as you're not packing smack. A lot of this is a game to him. What drives Stash toward finding heroin or cocaine is the potential reward of playing tug-of-war with the white towel. When Stash trained in Europe, his trainers hid five different kinds of drugs in the towel and helped Stash relate their scents to playing tug-of-war."

"I wish you had told me this before, Mr. Brick. I would not have worn my white shirt today. I still don't know how he was able to find those pineapples. It would have taken us hours without him."

"His nose has two hundred million scent-receptor cells compared to five million in a human."

"If only he could smell terrorists, eh?" joked Deepak.

Brick shook his head. "Frankly, I don't think this is really terrorism. These guys are too dumb to be trusted with that kind of operation. And I can already tell that 'Fawad' is some alias. The FBI can have them when we dock, and I'll follow up with my contact when I get back home to Tacoma."

Brick reminded himself that he had just closed another case quickly and efficiently, even if the terrorist threat seemed like another false alarm. His ongoing contract with Nobility Cruise Line to augment the fleet's security teams came with a mandate to monitor for potential terrorist campaigns directed at the cruise line's ten ships. Brick enjoyed the challenge. When Nobility had first contracted Morgan Maritime Investigations on this case, they'd explained that their luxury ship, the *Rembrandt Under the Stars*, could be part of a smuggling ring operating between the Bahamas and south Florida. Brick's own investigation connected the drugs to Afghani heroin, which he hoped to tie to funding of terrorism.

Deepak interrupted Brick's thoughts with an attempt at reassurance. "At least we caught these drug bastards with their hands in the cracker jar!"

"*Cookie* jar," Brick corrected with smile. "But you're right, Deepak. A win's a win. I'm going to leave you to your paperwork while I get ready to disembark tomorrow morning. Don't worry. I'll be here to hand off Stash to my pals who loaned him to us. And I'll be sure to thank the captain for allowing him to join us on the operation."

As he headed up the stairs to the luxurious guest decks above the waterline, Brick reflected back to his tenure at the Seattle PD and his introduction to detection dogs. During his first six months in the east precinct as a patrol officer, he'd received a lot of crap from his fellow officers about his Stanford Law degree. They pegged him as a nerdy academic even though he looked intimidating in his blue police uniform. That all changed when Brick was dispatched to investigate a large man threatening people with a knife.

When Brick arrived, three other officers were already trying to talk down the knife-wielding suspect on East Pine Street. Brick walked right through the other officers, grabbed the suspect's wrist, removed the knife, and then used his right foot to flip the three-hundred-pound man to his face on the sidewalk. The east precinct then assigned him to the department's K-9 unit, and he became a handler for both tactical and drug dogs. It had been years since he'd walked a beat, but every so often, Brick called in a favor to his buddies so he could spend some quality time with dogs like Stash. Now a long way from home, Brick's beat saw him policing the entire seven seas, a challenge he enjoyed, with the freedom to choose his clients.

Back in his guest cabin suite, he packed his bag to disembark in the morning, looking forward to a few days off. After this week, he figured he finally deserved some quality time alone with his guitar and some real Seattle coffee. Content, Brick Morgan gazed out over the aqua blue water, watching the sun set on paradise.

Chapter Two

Look at those tits. Sanan Jaidee tried not to ogle as he watched the attractive American woman finishing her second Yellow Bird cocktail. He kept his left hand on the edge of the mahogany bar while his right hand reached deep into the pocket of his black slacks. The bartender's clammy fingers caressed the two roofies he had been patiently carrying for the right opportunity. This blonde passenger from the Cassiopeia deck had been enjoying her drinks at his bar for at least an hour by now. *More than enough time.*

"Mr. Jaidee, I think I'll have just one more Yellow Bird," said Carolyn Luna as she pulled out the tropical umbrella and took a final sip of the ship's drink of the day. She smiled absently and returned her gaze to the moon's reflection on the waves.

"My pleasure," replied Sanan as he fantasized about what was under her cashmere sweater.

Jaidee had been assigned the Big Dipper Bar for the last two months. The crew of the *Matisse Under the Stars* all considered it a prime assignment because of its location near the Galileo pool on the Constellation deck. The tips flowed like the mai tais so popular in Hawaii. But for Carolyn, he grabbed a cocktail shaker and filled it half full with ice. He added one-and-a-quarter ounces of light rum, three-quarters of an ounce of crème de banana, and one-half ounce of Galliano. Glancing up to make sure she wasn't watching, he discreetly crushed a roofie on his cutting board, used a bar knife to quickly scrape the drug into the drink, and then added two ounces each of pineapple juice and orange juice. After shaking it, he poured the spiked drink into a chimney glass filled with ice.

Jaidee signed his first contract with Nobility Cruise Line when he was only twenty-five. He had never before traveled outside of Thailand

and had only left Bangkok half a dozen times. It seemed like yesterday when he made his first airplane flight and traveled for twenty-four hours to Nobility's corporate offices in Fort Lauderdale, Florida. After being hired, Sanan completed his eight-week training on the *Monet Under the Stars* and remained onboard that ship, where, with his outgoing personality and clear command of English, he soon finagled his way to bar duty.

After his first cruise, he discovered that his good looks and above-average height—for an Asian, at least—made him popular with the ladies, particularly those American blondes who drank themselves into enjoying his company. He was only two inches taller than the average Thai, but that two inches had always given him a little extra self-confidence.

He handed Carolyn her Yellow Bird and said, "If I can have your cruise card, I can clear your tab." Carolyn took a sip of her drink and then reached into her handbag to retrieve her card. He subtly touched her fingers as she handed it to him. Sanan took her card and walked behind the bar to the busing station where he was out of view. He took a mini swipe reader from a hidden bag and swiped Carolyn's card, capturing three tracks of data from the ISO encoded magnetic stripe. When the green LED blinked, he unplugged the device, hid it behind some old bar supplies, and headed back to the bar.

"How does your Yellow Bird taste? I shook it over ice for exactly fifteen seconds—that is good luck in Thailand," he said, returning her card.

"I was in Bangkok for business about three years ago," said Carolyn. "There seemed to be lots of elephants everywhere," she added, a touch dismissively.

"Before I signed with Nobility, I had a job teaching elephants to juggle," whispered Sanan with a wink.

"Yeah, sure. You're just teasing me because I'm a little drunk," she whispered back.

As she sipped the drink, Sanan listened to Carolyn's explanation of how she came about traveling by herself. She explained that her best friend's mother fell and broke her hip just two days before the cruise left San Francisco. "So, Mr. Bartender, I'm traveling alone, and I plan on spending a lot of time here at the Big Dipper Bar. I might as well get my woney's morth, for her sake!"

Sanan realized with delight that either the alcohol or the drug was catching up with the American traveler.

"My friend Dianne and I selected the *Matisse Under the Stars* because of its fifteen-day cruise to Hawaii. When dis vacation's over, I'll start a six-month job remodeling a fifteen-thousand-square-foot mansion in Newport Beach."

"What kind of things will you do to that big house?" asked Sanan as Carolyn reached down to retrieve her purse.

"Move a few walls, carpet, and lots of pew naint. I think the walls of your bar are moving now. Thanks for the drinks. I think maybe I should have stopped after two. Point me to Cassiopeia 527—starlight, star bright, starboard side is on the right," she said with a slurred laugh. Carolyn carefully got off the bar seat and aimed herself toward the elevator to take her down three decks to her room on deck ten on the starboard side of the 135,000-ton ship.

Sanan Jaidee smiled after her. *Soon, you spoiled bitch*, he thought. *Soon . . .*

Chapter Three

Like many cruise employees, Sanan seethed with anger and bitterness. He resented the in-your-face contrast between the luxurious life of the passengers and the long hours and cramped quarters of the crew. The fact that crew members' passports were confiscated for the voyage so they couldn't leave made him feel that he had no control over his life. And then there was the filth. He despised the dirt of the crew's quarters more than he hated the sixteen-plus hours he was forced to work each day that left him too exhausted to start scrubbing his own quarters.

There was no escape. If the crew members complained, they were escorted off the ship at the next port, put on a plane home, and the airfare was deducted from their last paycheck. In pursuit of fabled opportunity—really, American money—Sanan had turned his fate over to the supervisors and the officers of the cruise line.

Tonight, he had been bartending for the last twelve hours and was scheduled to bus tables in the Gallery Grill and Food Court at six in the morning. But the Big Dipper Bar shift change would soon give Sanan a short window to express his disgust and rage at his situation.

When he left deck fourteen and went down the stairs to beneath the waterline, he left behind the world of plush carpets and polished mahogany and dropped into a pit of drab-colored walls and metal floors covered with peeling, faded linoleum. "I-95" was the name of the ship-length corridor running from the bow to the stern that the twelve hundred slaves of Nobility Cruise Line had to trudge along, exhausted, after their long, torturous work hours.

Sanan turned the Big Dipper Bar over to the next shift and furtively grabbed his hidden card reader. He quickly headed down to his cabin so he could change out of his bartender clothes. He shared his little cabin on deck two with a guy from the Philippines who worked in the *Matisse* art gallery. Two decks below the waterline, the cabin had no window, and they shared a tiny bathroom with the adjoining quarters. The cabin was too tiny for two, so it was lucky they often had opposing shifts. He had heard that the average American prison cell was larger and cleaner than the living quarters of a cruise ship employee. *Some of those fat, privileged guests are almost as big as our pitiful cabin,* Sanan thought, scowling.

Like many crew members, Sanan knew how to play dumb when it suited him. His supervisors never suspected him of nefarious behavior. While completing his first contract on the *Monet Under the Stars*, he had stolen some blank keycards from the purser's office and often enjoyed the access they provided. Now, he used his small encoder to transfer the data he had swiped from Carolyn Luna's magnetic strip. Sanan carefully put the new card in his pocket and hid the equipment in the battered suitcase stored under his bunk. Fueled by a surge of defiant energy, he turned off the cabin lights and walked up two decks to the crew's bar. A double Jack Daniels and Coke would feed his rage and set him up with a nice alibi.

Nobility Cruise Line operated ten ships, and each one was registered and flagged under Bermuda Maritime Operations. They gave all the ships names ending in "Under the Stars." Five of Nobility's ships were of the Bernini Class and the other five were of the larger Renoir Class. The *Matisse Under the Stars,* the newest of the Renoir Class, had dedicated decks eight through twelve to the comfort and pleasure of its thirty-two hundred guests. Each deck was named for a celestial constellation; deck number twelve, for example, was named the Aquarius deck.

No passenger on the *Matisse* had to walk far to find entertainment and libation in any of the nine exquisite lounges and bars. By contrast, the fourth deck bar used by the crew was a windowless repository of hand-me-down mismatched sofas, tables, and chairs. The one positive about the crew members' bar was that the booze was dirt cheap.

Sanan ordered a drink and found a chair as far away from the karaoke machine as possible. As usual, a group of Filipino waiters were competing over who was the next Frank Sinatra. Even though he had to wake up in five hours, Sanan's mind kept churning. That blonde from cabin C-527 would spend more money on her cruise than he would make in a year. The more he thought about how that woman lived so carefree, so spoiled, the more enraged he became about his life of servitude and near poverty.

Sanan had read that rape was a crime of rage more than it was a crime of passion or sex. He knew he could get laid almost anytime he wanted, but raping drunk American women would prove there was one thing in his life he could control.

Tonight, the company would not pull the strings. Sanan would be in full command of his destiny.

Chapter Four

As Sanan got up to leave the bar, his supervisor, Officer Cappelli, surprised him. "Jaidee, do you mind if I join you for a drink?"

"No, sir." *Damn. What the hell does he want?*

"I wanted to get by the Dipper tonight and ask you a question, but we had another stupid problem in the kitchen on deck five," continued the beverage officer.

"Sir, how can I help?" Sanan hoped his voice didn't betray his nervousness. He surreptitiously glanced at his watch.

"We're not hitting our bar numbers this cruise. And we missed our goal on the last cruise, too. We've got to get bar sales up."

"Yes, sir. I've been trying."

"Since a third of our revenue should be coming from beverage and liquor sales, we've decided to add another drinking event. We'd like you and José from the Sinatra Bar to be in charge of a special revenue event. What do you think?"

"That sounds great, sir."

"Good. We want to call it Martini University. The staff feels we can charge thirty dollars a head, and we hope to sell 250 seats. Get together with José, kick it around, and join me at lunch in the staff mess the day after tomorrow."

"Mr. Cappelli, I assume we'll have to create a whole new system for the guests to taste the drinks, like at the wine-tasting events?"

"Well, yes, obviously if we are going to charge them, we need to have the guests taste the martinis. You and José can work out the details." Officer Cappelli stood up, grabbed his beer, and walked over to a table of smiling officers in pressed white shirts.

Sanan suddenly realized that he had just tacitly consented to do Cappelli's job for him in figuring out how this event would work.

Typical of those fucking officers.

The *Matisse* brought in over nine million dollars in cabins for this fifteen-day Hawaiian cruise. The big three up-sell revenue opportunities were the casino, shore excursions, and liquor and beverage sales. The bar and lounge revenue goal for this trip was projected at almost two million. This Martini University event would probably add several thousand more dollars.

Sanan took a deep breath and ignored the last of his Jack Daniels. The good news, he realized, was he had a much stronger alibi for his location tonight. The bad news was he now had more work to do so the fat cats who owned Nobility could make more money. He looked at his watch and smiled. It was time to visit the American in C-527.

The *Matisse* maintained nearly thirteen hundred closed-circuit cameras and dedicated four members of the security team to the ship's video surveillance. These cameras covered all of the passenger areas as well as videotaping the crew areas and the sides of the ship

Sanan felt that he knew the location of all the cameras between deck four and cabin C-527, but just in case, he had a ball cap in his back pocket. Alternating between the staff stairs and the service elevators, he found himself at a crew service door that opened onto the starboard side of the Cassiopeia deck. He extracted the blue Boston Red Sox cap from his pocket and pulled it down, hiding most of his face. Cabins on the starboard side of the ship had odd numbers. The portside cabins were assigned even numbers.

Carolyn's cabin, C-527, was near the amidship. She'd probably paid extra for such placement. Sanan looked to the stern; the hall was clear. On his left, a middle-aged couple was walking away from him, passing the area where he assumed 527 was located.

Looks like the coast is clear. Keeping his head down, he stepped out into the starboard hallway, walked past two cabin doors, and found 527. Sanan carefully pulled the keycard from his pocket and pushed it into the cabin door reader. After hearing a click, he pushed down on the handle and stepped inside Carolyn's cabin.

There she was, sprawled across one of the two beds in her deluxe cabin. For a second, he worried that she might be dead. Had he given her too much? But when he heard her light snoring, he calmed down. Her cashmere sweater still clung to her shapely body, and one of her high heels had fallen to the floor. *When you dress like a whore ...*

The lights were still on, so she must have passed out as soon as she got in. Sanan checked the cabin. The sliding door to the balcony was closed and the curtain pulled. *Good.* Looking at her voluptuous body and expensive dress, he felt his hatred return. This woman had a room that was three or four times larger than his, but worse, it was clean. So revoltingly clean that it sparkled. His life below decks was buried in lies from Nobility. *This bitch was going to pay.* He turned off the cabin lights just in case she woke up and unzipped his pants.

Sanan's vicious crime lasted no more than five minutes. The effect of the date-rape drug was so strong that Carolyn never awakened during the attack. With a snap, he yanked off his condom and pulled his pants back on. He made no attempt to cover her nakedness. He liked the idea of her waking up with her dress in disarray and half of her body exposed.

Careful not to leave any prints or evidence, Sanan pulled his cap back on and quietly left her cabin. As he hurried back to the service area inside the Cassiopeia deck, he stuffed the hat in his pocket along with the used condom.

Within five minutes, he was standing back at the crew bar. He ordered another Jack.

Chapter Five

"*Kafar Huna Bhanda Marnu Ramro!*" shouted Raju Marwah as he paced back and forth in the small office that housed the ship's security department.

"Translate!" replied Yvette Fuentes, annoyed that he continued to announce himself this way.

"It is the motto of the Four Gurkha Rifles. It means, 'Better to die than to live like a coward,'" answered Raju as he headed to a chair by Yvette's desk.

"You're not a coward, Raju. Now let's finalize the department's training schedule."

Chief Security Officer Fuentes and her deputy security officer, Raju Kumar Marwah, had this same exchange about three times a week. Raju always reminded Officer Fuentes that he had been a Gurkha in the Indian Army for eight years and had been with Nobility twice as long as she. It was clear he felt he should have been promoted to the leadership position now held by Chief Yvette Fuentes on the *Matisse Under the Stars*. At least that was what he let everyone, including Yvette, know. But everyone also knew that the real reason for his attitude was that he couldn't stand reporting to a woman.

Yvette could see Raju had lost his focus on the task at hand. "Raju, stay with me. I want to get this schedule finished."

"Chief, it all starts with taxes. Taxes are the root of all evil."

"What do taxes have to do with our training requirements, Mr. Marwah?" Yvette was used to Raju's rants, but this was the first time she'd heard his opinion on taxes. She leaned back in her chair and let him ramble on.

"The flag on our stern is the flag of the Bahamas. If it weren't the Bahamas, it would be the flag of Panama or maybe the flag of Liberia."

Raju drew a simple shape of a ship and added a big flag on the stern.

"Raju, those are flags of convenience. Most cruise lines have their homeports and headquarters in the United States, yet they are registered in other countries. But you know that, right?"

"That's the point, Chief. That is how they avoid paying US federal taxes. Not only does Nobility escape taxes, they also skirt many of the United States labor laws. Because our cruise line does not have to follow labor laws, we have to work sixty- and seventy-hour weeks!"

When Raju threw his hands in the air, Yvette knew he was on a verbal roll. He was right, but she wasn't going to let him blame the crew members' long hours on a corporate tax issue. Every attempt by Congress to close some of the loopholes that allowed the cruise industry to make their billions had been stopped by the lobbying of the Cruise Lines International Association.

"Mr. Marwah, I think we should let Nobility's CPAs deal with the taxes. Right now, we need to schedule a test of the Long Range Acoustic Device equipment."

"All right, let's do that tomorrow. The gangway security demands should be at their lowest about fifteen hundred. We can send two of the Zodiac crews out. But you need to know, Chief, those crewmen will not want to participate."

"Why not?"

"They think the LRAD machine will shrink their nuts."

"Marwah, that's bullshit. Where did they come up with that crap?" Yvette wondered for a moment if Raju himself had started the rumor just to piss her off. "When I was a detective with the San Diego Police Department, they purchased an LRAD unit. I was involved in testing it, and I can assure you it's safe."

"Okay, but I'm just telling you what I heard."

"Raju, you remember several years ago when the cruise ship *Seabourn Spirit* was attacked by pirates? You know how useful the LRAD was in repelling the attackers who used two speedboats to fire automatic weapons and rocket-propelled grenades at it."

"I know it works, but the crew will still think that it will make them sterile."

"Why do they think that?"

"You know the high-energy acoustics it emits causes pain, nausea, and disorientation."

"Well, we need to do drills to be prepared for any terrorist attacks. Tell any volunteers we will award them an extra day off in the next two weeks." Yvette understood their apprehension, but she was certain it did not cause sterility.

Raju gathered up his training files. "Okay, boss. I'll have the LRAD test finished tomorrow."

An incoming call from the purser's office disrupted Yvette's focus on the LRAD test. At the same time, her emergency cell phone started beeping furiously.

"This is Fuentes."

"Ma'am, we have a passenger on Cassiopeia deck, C-527. She's hysterical, going nuts on us—claims she was raped in her cabin last night."

Chapter Six

Carolyn was shaking so much she could barely replace the phone in its cradle. She hugged herself, trying to stop the shaking and make sense of it all.

When she'd first woken up, she was totally confused and had no idea where she was. Once she realized she was on the ship and in her cabin, she was overcome with an unquenchable thirst. As she sat up to get out of bed, she knew something was terribly wrong.

She looked down. *What the—?* She was still wearing her bra, but her dress was pushed up to her armpits, and she was naked from the waist down. *Why were her panties off? What happened last night? She was sore, too. Did I get loaded and blackout or what?* She looked around. Her sweater and panties were in a bunch on the other cabin bed.

What the hell happened? As she swung her legs over the side of the bed, stood up, and pulled her dress down, a woman's worst nightmare entered her mind. *Oh my God!* Her brain screamed in panic as she ran into the little bathroom. She sat on the toilet and examined herself. Her vaginal soreness and a bruise on her inner thigh made her head spin. *"I've been raped!"*

She stumbled out of the bathroom and almost fell into the cabin's closet across from the bathroom. Finding a pair of sweatpants and a T-shirt, she put them on and then ran to the phone and dialed 911.

Yvette hung up from the purser's call and quickly dialed medical. "This is Officer Fuentes from Security. We have a report of a possible rape in C-527. I'm heading there now—get me a female nurse there fast!"

Yvette was lucky to catch an internal service elevator that took her directly to deck nine, where she took a direct route to the Cassiopeia deck. Just as she approached cabin 527, her department radio informed her that 527 belonged to a Carolyn Luna.

As Yvette knocked on the door, she announced, "Miss Luna, I'm the security officer. May I please enter?" When the door opened, Yvette saw the pain in Carolyn's eyes and knew that the *Matisse Under the Stars* had a big problem.

No sooner had Yvette entered Carolyn's cabin, a nurse from the medical clinic arrived. Yvette turned away and spoke as lightly as possible into her radio. "Raju, assign a single security detail outside 527. I'm declaring this cabin a crime scene. Make sure no one enters this cabin, especially housekeeping."

Seeing how unsteady Carolyn was, Yvette walked her over to the sitting area away from the bed, sat down with her, and spoke very softly. "My name is Yvette Fuentes, and I am here to help you. May I call you Carolyn?"

Carolyn's hesitation underscored the severity of the attack. "Yes. Are you a doctor?"

"No, Carolyn, I am the chief of security on this ship, and this is Nurse Elenor Mercado from our medical department. We are here to help. When you called the ship's emergency number, you said you had been raped. Please tell us what you remember."

For the next twenty minutes, Carolyn told them as much as she could remember, trembling as she spoke. She recalled drinking at the Big Dipper Bar on deck fourteen and then almost nothing until waking up in her cabin. Yvette had a dozen more questions, but they could wait a few hours.

"Carolyn, this is very important. First, we want to help you. Your health and safety are our primary concern. I want you to go with Nurse Mercado to the ship's hospital so we can check you out. Have you gone to the bathroom yet this morning?"

"I ... no." Carolyn started to cry.

Yvette comforted her with genuine concern. "It's okay to cry.

We're here to support you in any way we can. Will you hold off using the bathroom for ten more minutes until we get you down to deck four?"

"Yes, if we leave now." Carolyn wiped her eyes on her sleeve.

"Elenor, take her, her dress, and underpants, and make sure you throw nothing away. Be very careful with her dress. I'll be down in a few minutes with evidence bags. You're trained on using the kit, correct?"

"Yes, ma'am, very well trained."

Ten years ago it would have been rare to find a cruise ship that carried a sexual assault forensic evidence kit. Yvette had insisted that every ship in the Nobility Cruise Line fleet carry a minimum of five rape kits, and they even had testing equipment to detect residual gamma-Hydroxybutyric acid, ketamine, or Rohypnol, the most common date-rape drugs. When Yvette first joined Nobility, she was baffled that rape kits were not routinely available. Her tenacity paid off, and within a year, the kits were a compulsory supply.

Before Elenor escorted Carolyn to the medical center, she quietly explained to Yvette the procedure she had been trained to do. "Ms. Fuentes, I will collect a urine sample and then follow the protocol of evidence collection. Swabs will be collected of any fluids from her vagina, thighs, buttocks, and anus, and I will use a comb to collect any hair or fiber. The kit also has a special forensic nail pick for the collection of any debris from under her nails."

"Thank you, Elenor. If Carolyn remembers any more details of the attack, make sure you let me know."

Yvette stayed behind in Carolyn's cabin, making notes of the items and issues that needed follow-up. She also called the purser's office and located another cabin for Carolyn. Her new room would be an upgrade to a suite on Bootes, which was on deck eleven. Yvette knew that Carolyn would need the expanded space, as it was likely she would choose to stay in her cabin until she departed the *Matisse*.

HIGH SEAS DARKNESS

The next twenty-four hours would be hectic and critical. Yvette would need to inform the captain and place the dreaded call to Florida. Nobility's corporate headquarters still had enough old-school employees around to cause some pushback from any attempt to treat a victim fairly and with compassion. In the old days, the number-one goal was to get the victim to quickly sign a release that would help cover up any crime that could bring negative publicity to the cruise line—and then quietly drop the victim off the ship at the next port so word could not spread.

Yvette knew that the *Matisse* would dock in Honolulu the next morning, and thousands of passengers would be standing in lines to embark at their first of four Hawaiian ports. Before then, she would need to conduct another interview with Carolyn Luna and then photograph and inventory cabin 527 immediately.

Yvette looked at her watch and realized it was already 2:00 p.m. in Florida. She decided to go up to the bridge and brief the captain and call the incident in to Nobility's corporate office.

As she walked toward the cabin door, she spotted a small reflection on the carpet near the foot of one of the beds. She bent down to take a closer look. It appeared to be a small piece of foil or metallic packaging. Not wanting to wait for the time it would take to photograph the room, she used her phone to snap a picture of the small item. Then, using her fingernails like forceps, she picked it up and placed it in a piece of tissue.

Chapter Seven

Go with your instincts; trust your gut, Yvette thought as she reached for the phone to call Florida. Her Cal State Fullerton criminology education, coupled with years on the streets as a San Diego cop, was warning her to treat this case with kid gloves. She believed that Carolyn had been raped, but she also thought that Carolyn was not going to be a cooperative victim.

"Director Spencer, Yvette Fuentes on the *Matisse*. I hope I didn't call at a bad time." Yvette felt that she had a good relationship with her boss, as they had both joined Nobility after serving on large urban police departments. Rob Spencer had been a major in charge of criminal investigation for the Miami Police Department. When he reached fifty-five, he retired and became Nobility Cruise Lines' director of fleet security.

"Fuentes, every call today has been a bad call. An hour ago, I received a call from the *Renoir*. While the ship was in Greece, a member of the engineering department returned from some time ashore with three hundred units of oxycodone. And this morning I've been dealing with the *Cezanne* and the investigation of cash shortages in the purser's office. But how can I help my favorite Filipino chief security officer?"

"Rob, a passenger has reported that she was raped in her cabin last night."

"Oh no. What do we know so far?"

"Single woman, traveling alone. We are working through the protocol for onboard rape cases. Rob, this case has my fear meter on high alert."

"You and I have seen our share of sexual assaults. What's bugging you about this case?"

"We're running the toxicology test as we speak, but I would bet my

HIGH SEAS DARKNESS

San Diego PD pension that she was drugged. If it was a fellow passenger, that's bad enough, but if a crew member was involved, our liability will go through the roof. And one more thing. The passenger, Carolyn Luna, is going to be out for blood. My opinion is she has seen the elephant and heard the owl. She's a businesswoman from California."

"What I'm hearing you say is that this passenger is going to be aware of her rights and that we might also have a big publicity issue."

"And a large financial liability."

"Yvette, hang on a second. An e-mail just popped up on my screen from your ship."

"Please tell me it's not from Raju." Yvette waited while Rob digested the message from the *Matisse*. She leaned back in her chair and pondered how much easier her job would be if she didn't have to deal with the constant drama caused by her deputy chief.

"Yvette, you were right. Your buddy Marwah wants me to assign him as lead on the passenger-assault case. His e-mail is a little disjointed, but the crux is you are too emotional about this case because you are a woman, and he thinks the passenger might be faking. One more thing. Wait ... let me read it to you. 'Let martial note in triumph float, and liberty extends its mighty hand.'"

"That sounds like Raju. When he was in India, he learned English by listening to records of John Philip Sousa. When Raju talks, he is always adding band-music stuff."

"Okay, your job is to keep Raju controlled and away from me. And I also don't like band music."

"Got it, boss. Now back to the assault case. Passenger Luna is educated and owns a small business in California. She is distraught now, but I bet when the shock of the attack passes, there is going to be hell to pay. We need to get on top of this before we have a ship full of FBI and lawyers." Yvette was thinking about recent legislation that had passed the United States Congress, which meant more detailed recordkeeping and reporting procedures for crimes on the high seas. The Cruise

Vessel Security and Safety Act made it incumbent to promptly notify the FBI when a crime is reported or face a severe fine. She also knew that Rob would have his own definition of the word *promptly*.

"You want me to get Morgan out there?"

"Yes, as fast as you can. I know Brick Morgan can keep this from becoming a publicity nightmare. I'll try to keep Raju under control until then," Yvette said.

"Morgan should have just returned from a heroin-smuggling case on the *Rembrandt*. I'll give him a call and try to get him out to the *Matisse*. Sometimes I get a little nervous having Morgan work so many of these cases."

"What do you mean?" Yvette, Rob, and Brick all had backgrounds in large city police departments. In addition, Brick had a Stanford Law degree and had spent time with the United States Department of Justice.

"Don't get me wrong. The guy gets results. I just keep hearing that he gets very close to the line when he's interrogating some of these perps."

"Boss, the line gets real blurry when you're in international waters. I've never seen Morgan get seriously physical with a suspect. He's just good at creating psychological terror in their minds."

"Okay, but keep Nobility's name out of the press."

"Yes, sir," Yvette replied with touch of laughter in her voice.

"It looks like the *Matisse* will dock in Oahu in the morning. I'll see if I can pull off a miracle and get Morgan on the ship before you leave for Kauai. Once you and Brick agree on the crime specifics, I'll have to report the incident to the FBI. Are we cool?"

"Yes, we're cool. If you get any more e-mails from our wannabe John Philip Sousa, forward them to me. Raju does a great job of keeping his security team in line, but he tries real hard to throw rocks in the gears if it will discredit me."

"I know, I know. One more thing, Yvette. I am aware that you have the hots for Brick. Keep him out of your cabin. Is that going to be a problem?"

"No problem at all, Mr. Spencer." Yvette considered for a moment telling the head of fleet security that it was none of his goddamned business.

Chapter Eight

Brick tried to relax, though it was not in his nature. Even as the beautiful guitar music of Mark Whitfield filled his Tacoma, Washington, home, Brick's gut trembled. Something was coming. He could taste it on the wind off the Sound.

On schedule, the music system played "Ribbon in the Sky" and the rest of Whitfield's *Songs of Wonder* album as the morning wakeup music. Three years earlier, while working with Interpol in Washington, DC, Morgan had attended a Chris Botti concert. On stage with the trumpet player was one of the world's greatest jazz guitarists—Mark Whitfield.

While listening to a few more tracks from the album, Brick reached over and scrolled through a few e-mails on his iPhone. Not seeing anything urgent, Brick rolled his six-foot-four, thirty-eight-year-old body out of bed and headed to the Keurig coffee machine.

Before attacking his daily to-do list, Brick allowed himself a few minutes to gaze out his large kitchen window while drinking his coffee. The western exposure provided him with a spectacular view of Tacoma's famous Narrows Bridge. A little north from the Narrows he could see the outline of the picturesque city of Gig Harbor.

Glancing at his watch, Brick decided to go upstairs and do some of his judo body-conditioning exercises and then deal with those persistent bills. But before he was halfway out of the kitchen, his iPhone announced a text message. He looked at the phone and saw "Titus."

Brick had run into Titus about two years before. They both were on Sixth Avenue at Tacoma's Jazzbones listening to Everlast and eating sushi. She had obviously expected to find him there, but Brick had no idea who she was or how she could have found him. On her way out the door, Titus wrote her name and number on a napkin and pointedly dropped it in his lap. It simply read, "Hey, big guy. I am the best cybertech in the Northwest. Call me."

During the last two years, Morgan Maritime Investigations had made use of Titus's exceptional skills at least a dozen times. Brick only knew her by the name of Titus, as she claimed she did not have a last name. Brick had done a property search on her Fircrest address and found that her house was owned by an LLC, and the corporation's principal was just named Titus.

Maybe his earlier feeling of tension had something to do with Titus and her new assignment. He knew it was just a matter of time before the religious fanatics took their terrorism dog-and-pony shows to the high seas. Brick had assigned Titus the job of snooping around the cyber universe for any blog chatter that would indicate that al-Qaeda had a cruise ship on their radar.

"Titus, this is Brick."

"Hi, good-looking. Are you coming over to see me? I've been making progress on that special project you assigned to me six weeks ago."

"Sorry, but I've been home less than a day. How about tomorrow, first thing in the morning?"

"Tomorrow works."

"I'll call before I head your way. But tell me, what have you got so far?"

"You crazy? I never talk on the phone—you know that. Too many NSA ears. I'll see you tomorrow, chocolate bear. Ta!"

Brick couldn't help wondering what Titus had dug up for him. Not only was she a superb hacker, she also had good forensic instincts. After she dropped out of computer studies at Pacific Lutheran, she had landed at Boeing, where she'd worked as a computer security and information protection specialist for five years before setting up a private business out of her home near the Fircrest Golf Club. As far as Brick was concerned, Titus was the smartest person anyone could work with—that is, if you could get past the issue that she refused to wear clothes at home.

For a few seconds, Brick considered calling her back and changing the meeting to this afternoon. Or should he just stay here and attack all the damned paperwork? Just as he decided to find out what Titus had uncovered, Brick's phone started to play "White Rabbit" by George Benson. "Oh fuck," he said. The "White Rabbit" ringtone heralded his number-one client, the Fort Lauderdale headquarters of Nobility Cruise Line. *Not yet. I just got home.*

Brick pushed the "accept" button on his cell. "This is Brick."

"Hey, big guy, what's up? It's Spencer at Nobility."

"Hi, Rob. I'm enjoying my first day home in ten days—hope you're calling to congratulate me on my last assignment."

"That's it. You and the drug dog did so well on the *Rembrandt* that I want to send you to Hawaii."

"Oh yeah? What's happening there?" Brick smiled. He could do worse than big sunny beaches and tiny bikinis.

"The *Matisse* is on day five of a fifteen-day Hawaiian cruise. Tomorrow she pulls into Honolulu. Last night, we discovered a passenger who could be a victim of rape. Our chief security officer feels confident in her story and also thinks that this has the potential for serious repercussions. Can you help us out with this one?

"How can a Seattle ex-cop say no to a Miami ex-cop?"

"Great. How fast can you get to Oahu?"

"Where are we with the FBI?" Brick was hoping that he could get a jump on the case before the blue suits overran the ship.

"I want you to give me a head start on this before I call the suits. I am going to bring them onboard when the *Matisse* docks in Nawiliwili, Kauai, the day after tomorrow."

"Okay, I might be able to grab a private business jet this afternoon and meet the *Matisse* when she arrives in the morning. Is this big enough to blow your travel budget?"

"Okay, fine, Brick. I'll eat the cost of your jet. Just get there as fast as you can."

"Who's the chief security officer on the *Matisse?*" asked Brick, barely able to hold back a laugh.

"Damn it, Morgan, just a pretty Filipino ex-cop who wants to climb up on your seven-foot body."

Brick chose not to acknowledge his statement with more than a smile. "Mr. Director of Security, when you talk to the *Matisse*, tell them to locate a cabin suitable for my lifestyle."

"All right. Call when you get a feel for the situation. I'll keep the feds away as long as I can."

"Y'know, I shared an office with the FBI when I was assigned to Interpol," said Brick.

"I did not know."

"Yep, the Justice Department originally wanted to start me as a law enforcement coordination specialist, a G-8 position. Instead, I started as an assistant to the deputy of Interpol. We were under the direction of the Justice and Homeland Security. We had lots of guys on loan from the FBI. I tell you, man, Interpol's more screwed up than a kite in a hailstorm."

"How so?"

"For one thing, the policy of Interpol forbids it from dealing with political or religious matters," Brick said. "Then the leadership at the Justice Department decided to demonstrate to the Muslim countries that the United States was sensitive to their needs. So Interpol put out a dragnet for suspects whose only crime was insulting Islam. That was when I was told to keep my mouth shut and my head down."

"What did you do with those orders?"

"I decided that government work was not going to be a fulfilling career. I stuck around just long enough to lay the foundation of my own business in maritime investigation."

"Sounds like you made a good decision. Their loss and our gain.

Let me know as soon as you figure out what is going on with this rape case."

As Brick headed downstairs, he mentally formulated a list of what needed to be done, like cancel the meeting with Titus. But first he sent an e-mail to Yvette Fuentes, asking her to call him as soon as possible. He then called a fraternity brother from the University of Puget Sound. Even though Jim Clary, referred to as "Bud" by his close friends, had graduated in the sixties, Brick had met him while working on a committee to reinstate their fraternity chapter.

"Bud, Brick Morgan. Did I call at a bad time? You're not in a business meeting, are you?"

"Brick, you know that when you call I drop everything. What's up with 'Amazing Mr. Morgan' today?"

"I want to borrow your jet for a fast trip to Hawaii. Are you using it in the next twenty-four hours?"

"You're in luck, brother. We just got back from visiting the dealerships in Moses Lake and Yakima, so we'll be staying in Longview for the rest of the week. If you'd called two months ago, our Cessna Citation II wouldn't have had the range to make a trip to Hawaii. We've recently upgraded. Now we have a Cessna Citation Sovereign, and it has a range of twenty-eight hundred nautical miles."

"Awesome. Thanks a lot."

"I'll need about four hours to assemble the crew. Can you be in Longview about 4:00 p.m.?"

"Thanks, Bud, that's perfect. I told the cruise line this is going to be a big-ticket trip."

"I'll keep the receipts ready for them," joked Bud. "You'd better take the plane to Oakland first for a fuel top-off before you head to the islands. I'll even meet you at the hangar and make sure you have a supply of Nipps' great burgers and an appropriate red wine for your trip."

"Thanks again. See you in four hours." Brick hung up and went to his office to grab his go-bag. He had just opened his Eagle Escape and Evasion Bag when his cell phone rang again. It was Yvette.

"Chief Fuentes, I was expecting your call," Brick answered suavely.

"Brick, when can you meet the *Matisse?*"

"I'll be on board the minute your team hooks up the gangway. Tell me what you got."

"Her name's Carolyn Luna. She's thirty-two and is traveling alone."

"That's kind of unusual, isn't it?" asked Brick.

"She intended to travel with a friend, but a family medical emergency caused her roommate to back out at the last minute. She remembers having drinks on deck fourteen, and then everything is a blank until she wakes up this morning in her cabin. We've taken blood and urine tests, and a nurse is working through the protocols of a rape kit as we speak. As I told Rob, I think she could go ballistic when the shock wears off. She seems very aggressive. She was raised on the East Coast and has a bachelor's degree in fine arts from the New York School of Interior Design. She implied that she's had to deal with attorneys in her design business, and I felt her social style was aggressive."

"Okay, I think I have a feel for the case. I'll see you in the morning. Before I get there, in addition to your standard sexual-assault checklist, I need you to do a few more things. Have the medical technician test another urine sample later this afternoon for Rohypnol and make sure that they set the cutoff level at .02 nanograms per milliliter instead of .20. When you video and photo the primary crime scene, please take a bunch of black-and-whites in addition to the standard color shots. Do not let the victim have her toothbrush, and also get lots of swabs from the toilet. With respect to victimology, get a record from the purser of every purchase she made since she boarded. Try to develop a pattern of her lifestyle while she was on the ship."

"Got it. If I discover any new info, I'll send you a text."

"One more thing. Be careful. Sexual psychopaths are evil. They like to rape, and there is little difference between a rape and a rape-homicide. Oh, and I just thought of something else. Make sure you dust the balcony rail for prints before the salt spray degrades the evidence. Okay, I need to pack and find a fast ride to Hawaii. Morgan, out."

Brick quickly finished packing the last of his clothes in the small suitcase, including his brown suit, perfect for making him look more intimidating during interrogations. As he carried his suitcase and go-bag to the front door, he again had the feeling that Titus's project might open up a can of worms.

Chapter Nine

Special Agent Kryss Mitchell took his first sip of his fourteen-year-old Oban scotch on the rocks. He was so pissed that he didn't give a shit about the seventeen-dollar tab for the expensive drink. The FBI agent glanced at his watch and hoped his partner would arrive soon.

Taking another sip, he took in the carnelian chairs, tufted wall-coverings, and accent rugs that created a plush and sophisticated atmosphere in the upscale Off the Record Bar. Kryss liked the Hay-Adams Hotel because it was located across the street from Saint John's Episcopal Church, which many referred to as the Church of the Presidents. Located in the heart of Washington, DC, the luxurious Hay-Adams Hotel's classic Off the Record Bar was a meeting place for many of the nation's movers and shakers.

"Isn't this joint a little over our pay grade?" asked Nathan as he slid into the booth across from Kryss and his big wing chair.

"I'm pissed, and I'm buying," answered Kryss.

"I'm tempted to order a glass of Opus, but a cold IPA will do. Hey, man, we just spent half the day together. What happened since then that set you off?"

"Nathan, this job is bullshit. You and I have been busting our butts for two years trying to defeat terrorism, and then Zittel says everything is worksite violence or an overseas contingency operation. Zittel still will not classify Nidal Hasan as a terrorist."

"Look, Ace Zittel takes his orders from the White House, and you know the Fort Hood shooting is a can of worms," countered Nathan as he took a gulp of his beer.

"That's my point. Zittel, or Ace, as you like to call him, really believes in this crap of avoiding the terms *terrorism* or *terrorist*. Partner, I'm thinking about swimming upstream and having a meeting with

Wallace. Even one step up the chain of command may be able to make sense of this game." Kryss paused long enough to allow his partner of two years to jump in.

"Hey, calm down. Let's order another round." Nathan made eye contact with the server before he continued. "You aren't the only one frustrated, but it's better to just keep your head down and stay out of the line of fire. If you go public to someone like the executive assistant director of the National Security branch—bang!—Herb Wallace will run your position up the flag pole to the seventh floor. You might end up having a career-ending meeting with Deputy Director Monroe, or maybe even Director Alexander Zittel himself."

Kryss took a long pull on his second scotch. "You're better wired to Bureau politics than I am. Why would these smart people be in such denial about the real world?"

"Okay, I'm only going to tell you this so you don't do anything stupid. I've been dating a girl who works in the office of the deputy director—"

"You're talking about Director Elizabeth Monroe?"

"Yeah, though she's called Liz on the seventh floor. Sometimes 'Lady Liz.' But, Kryss, this stuff is very sensitive—Crypto, NATO, Top Secret. In 2000, there were 1,209 mosques in the United States. Last year, the number was over twenty-one hundred. Worldwide there are 1.6 billion Muslims, and 87 percent are Sunni Muslims. That leaves 13 percent Shia. By the way, a third of all the Shia Muslims live in Iran. Here's the problem, partner: a research company did a bunch of surveys and found that in the States, only 40 percent of Muslim Americans believe that Arabs carried out 9/11."

"What? You're saying 60 percent don't believe those guys from Saudi Arabia hijacked those planes?"

"Yep, and it gets better. There are about 2.7 million Muslims in the United States. Five percent, that is 135,000, have a somewhat or very favorable view of al-Qaeda, and 26 percent of Muslim American youth support suicide bombers. Now the good stuff: According to my source, the president, the secretary of the Department of Homeland Security, and our own FBI director feel that the expansion of militant Islamists cannot be stopped in the States. Those three feel that we cannot win the so-called war on terror. They have a secret plan to get in bed with those extremists and try to moderate, negotiate, and slow down their plans to bring Sharia law to parts of the States.

"You've gotta to be shitting me! They've given up and they're just going to roll over for these guys?"

"No. Their view is that because of our laws, constitution, and liberal attitudes, we just can't win. Their game plan is to get terrorism off the front page, downplay the 'us versus them' posture, and try to win over the majority of Muslim Americans who are more moderate."

"And your source says that Zittel is going along with POTUS and Homeland?"

Nathan nodded. "Yes. They think their plan is the only way to stop a full-court press by the radicals to completely take over North America."

"Fuck! What's the purpose of us staying with the Bureau and wasting our time doing all this counterterrorism effort if it's all a charade?"

"Kryss, things change. Remember, one day the general is running the CIA, and the next day he's out."

"What's the story about Ace Zittel? How did he get that nickname?"

"He went to the University of Pennsylvania, where he got a degree in electrical and systems engineering. That's how he got his job as a code guy at the NSA. I heard that in college our Alexander Zittel was very smooth with the opposite sex. The girls liked his six-foot-five looks, and he had a reputation for scoring every weekend. That's how he got the name Ace. And check out how he dresses—white shirts, always button down, with his 'AAZ' monogram above the shirt pocket. Next time you see him, look at his shoes. He only wears Gucci black brogue leather lace-ups or the

Gucci black moccasins that cost four to five hundred dollars."

"I guess it's good to be the king," Kryss said.

"Damn right."

Kryss took a moment to finish his scotch and then leaned back in the bar's big red chair. "I'll tell you what. I'm still pissed, but at least now I know why I'm pissed. I promise to be a good partner and not wander off the reservation—at least not this week." He looked up at Nathan and grinned. "Hey, think your friend can get me a date with Monroe?"

"Mitchell, you're scary. Let's get out of here."

Chapter Ten

"Oakland International Airport information, Bravo one-three-five-five Zulu weather. Wind three- zero-zero at five, visibility five. Five hundred few, one-thousand-two-hundred scattered, ceiling three thousand overcast, temperature one-five, dew point eight. Altimeter two niner eight seven. Runway two-nine and runway two-six left and right in use. VFR aircraft say direction of flight. All aircraft read back all hold-short instructions. Advise controller on initial contact that you have, Bravo."

After receiving the automatic terminal information service (ATIS), Captain Reed Benton called OAK Clearance Delivery. "Sovereign N804BC, IFR Honolulu, Information Bravo."

In response, the Captain heard, "Sovereign N804BC, Oakland Clearance, advise ready to copy."

"Ready to copy," replied Captain Benton.

"Sovereign N804BC is cleared to Honolulu International Airport as filed, fly runway heading, radar vectors BEBOP. Climb and maintain two thousand, expect FL 360 one-zero minutes after departure, departure frequency one-two-four point six-five, squawk two-seven-one-three. Hold for Oceanic clearance. Sovereign N804BC is cleared Oceanic to the Honolulu International Airport via the Oakland Five Departure, FL360, BEBOP at 1618Z."

The pilot read back his clearance, started the jet's engines, and called OAK Ground. "Sovereign N804BC, Kaiser, IFR Honolulu, Bravo."

Ground Control replied, "Sovereign N804BC cleared to taxi RWY two-niner via Tango and hold short of taxiway Uniform for runway two-niner."

Benton repeated, "Taxi RWY two-niner via Tango and hold short of taxiway Uniform for runway two-niner."

"Roger, cleared to taxi."

Slowly advancing the throttles, the captain reached the departure end of runway two-niner. Benton then switched to the tower frequency and called in.

The tower replied, "Sovereign N804BC cleared for takeoff runway two-niner, fly runway heading, maintain three thousand."

He replied, "Cleared for takeoff runway two-niner, fly runway heading, maintain three thousand," and switched his transponder code to 2713.

"Mr. Morgan, we will be busy for about ten minutes. We will give you a shout when we set the autopilot," announced Captain Benton. Brick watched through the open cockpit door while the captain continued to scan the jet's digital display and advance the throttles for takeoff.

After takeoff, the captain checked in with NORCAL departure and switched to San Francisco Radio or OAK Oceanic when advised by NORCAL.

Sovereign N804BC was now on its way to the Land of Mai Tais, as Brick liked to call it.

As promised, Bud Clary had been at the hangar when Brick arrived from Tacoma. Brick accepted from Bud the bottle of red wine and bag of Nipps burgers, and then the two spent ten minutes going over the interior of the new Cessna Sovereign. Brick was shocked at how roomy the lavatory was. Unlike a commercial airline toilet, a person could actually change clothes in it. Bud insisted that Brick give him the keys to his Audi so he could get a couple of kids from the fraternity chapter to drive down and deposit his car in his driveway.

It seemed they had only been in the air a short time when they made their landing at Oakland. The Kaiser Business Center at Oakland possessed a reputation for being one of the best quality centers for general aviation.

HIGH SEAS DARKNESS

Brick had read where the Cessna could carry sixteen-hundred gallons, or 10,720 pounds, of jet fuel. He watched the ground crew use the overwing ports to insure that the tanks were filled to their maximum.

Brick chose a forward left seat and adjusted the back to a semi-inclined position. He put on his Sennheiser PX 200-II headphones and scrolled for the perfect album. He stopped scrolling when he found Whitfield's *True Blue* album. Selecting "Immanuel the Redeemer," he closed his eyes and almost did not notice when the two Pratt & Whitney Canada PW306C turbofan engines applied their combined 11,400 pounds of thrust to the business jet.

As the Sovereign adjusted to a westerly heading at thirty-six thousand feet, Brick awoke. He realized that he had fallen asleep and was barely aware that they had taken off from Oakland. The pilot, noticing that he was awake, left the copilot in charge of the cockpit, walked back into the cabin, and took a seat next to Brick.

"Anything we can do to help make your flight more comfortable?" said Captain Benton.

"Can't believe I fell asleep. Where are we?"

"Mr. Morgan, we are at Mach .72, which is 475 miles per hour and little less than three hours out of Honolulu."

"That's good. Mr. Clary gave me a bag of burgers. Are you guys hungry?"

"I assume they're from Nipps? Then that's a yes. I was just heading to the galley to make a little coffee. Can I make you some?" the captain asked.

Brick got up from his seat. "No. I'll just open the bottle of wine Bud gave me."

"You are a little tall for this cabin, even though at sixty-six and sixty-eight inches, it's considered large for a business jet," remarked Captain Benton.

Pulling his case file from a side pocket in his go-bag, Brick settled back into his tan leather seat, adjusted it to a more upright position, and pulled the high-gloss woodwork table from its slot on the portside of the elegant jet. Brick had found a wine glass in the bar, so he arranged his hamburger, wine, and work file on his new workspace. His mind traveled back to his days with the Seattle PD when he ate cold pizza on long stakeouts on rainy Seattle nights. *Yep, things are good*, he thought.

As Captain Benton returned from the galley with his burgers and coffee, he paused a moment by Brick's chair. "Mr. Clary said we should expect that you will carry on this trip. After I give the copilot his dinner, would you share your thoughts on the best handgun to pack?"

"Sure," replied Brick. "I've got no secrets, Captain."

"Please, call me Reed."

When he returned, Brick explained his background with the Seattle PD and his time with the Justice Department. "My main carry is the old reliable Glock 23. I feel the .40 calibers are fine. I have friends who insist I should have a .45 or go .357 Magnum, but I feel my marksmanship plus a quality hollow point will get the job done. The Glock is only 6.85 inches and weighs only twenty-one ounces and only thirty-one ounces with a thirteen-bullet mag. My other favorites will surprise you. It's too long to be an ankle backup, but I'm big enough that I can hide it in my back. Any guesses?"

"Maybe one of the new 380 compacts?" guessed Reed.

"No, a Ruger 22 Long Rifle Lite Rimfire pistol. It's long, 8.5 inches, and the barrel length is a cool 4.4 inches. You wouldn't believe how accurate it is, and with a load of CCI Long Rifle Velocitor forty-grain hollow points, it will get the job done."

After asking about Brick's choice of ammo for his Glock, Reed returned to the cockpit, and Brick returned to his dinner and homework.

An hour out of Hawaii, Brick put away his work and leaned back in his comfortable seat. This time he selected *Led Zeppelin IV* and was asleep before "Black Dog" was finished. Dreams are unpredictable, and while flying at thirty-six thousand feet, Brick Morgan's subconscious was flickering between a naked Titus and her computers and making love to Yvette on a massage table in the ship's spa.

Fifteen hundred miles away, Yvette arranged to meet with Carolyn Luna in her new suite.

"Carolyn, I want you to know that we have made arrangements for one of the nation's top investigators to meet the ship tomorrow and help us find the person who sexually assaulted you. His name is Brick Morgan, and I have worked with him before."

"Officer Fuentes, I was wondering if it would be better if I just get off this ship in Honolulu, contact the police there, and then fly home."

"You can do that, and we will, of course, pay for your flight home. But what I would recommend is that you give it one more day. You can always get off the ship in Kauai, and we will make arrangements to get you home. I would really like you to meet Investigator Morgan. The faster we can gather all the information and evidence, the greater are the chances that we will catch the bastard that assaulted you. Will you consider staying with us one more day? I have great confidence in Brick's ability to help you. If you are in the States, it will be more challenging to complete the investigation."

"I'll think about it."

Yvette lowered her voice and leaned a little closer to Carolyn. "Can you close your eyes for a moment and try to walk me through your visit to the Big Dipper Bar last night? I know we asked you this before, but with your permission, I would like to go over the details one more time."

"I'll try," she said weakly. "I sat on one of the middle bar stools at that bar. Both seats next to me were empty. There was a couple from London there when I arrived. I said hello, but they weren't very friendly at first. I ordered a drink. A little later, they asked me where I was from. The bartender was a nice guy—had a weird name, I can't remember it. After the couple from London left, I ordered another drink."

"Do you remember what you were drinking?"

"Yeah, a Yellow Bird. I had three."

"Are you sure that you had three?" asked Yvette.

"Absolutely sure," replied Carolyn. "I remember playing with the two straws while the bartender was making the third drink. I was trying to push one end of the straw into the other end. When the third drink came, I pushed that straw into the other two and made this long straw. I was a little drunk, so I tried to drink the Yellow Bird from this triple-length straw. The only other things I remember are a couple of guys joining the bar and the bartender saying something about elephants. If my memory's correct, I was really starting to spin, so I left. I assume I went to my cabin then."

"Do you remember which way you went down to your cabin?"

She shook her head. "No, I'm sorry. I'm a blank after that."

Yvette stayed another few minutes and then left when the nurse came up from medical to check on her patient.

When Yvette returned to the security office, Raju promptly met her at the door.

"Hurrah for the flag of the free / May it wave as our standard forever / The gem of the land and the sea! / Raju should be chief of security!"

"God, enough, Mr. Music Man. What did the marching band find out at the purser's office?"

"The record shows that passenger Luna bought only two drinks at the Big Dipper, Ms. Fuentes."

Chapter Eleven

The ship's Internet was painfully slow this afternoon. Once Yusuf finally reached the Gmail site, he entered his username, "baseballfan999." He then entered the password and was ready to send a message to Zaeem Hasan Al-Ajmi. As he typed, he kept looking at the cabin door, hoping that the strange room steward would not interrupt again.

"Z.H.A., I will deliver the present the day we leave the islands, God willing. Will report each day after delivery. May Allah, the one and only God, bless you. Y.A.O." He then clicked on the cancel button and selected "save draft" instead of discarding the e-mail.

Yusuf Al Omar was humbled by the trust and confidence that had been bestowed on him by the leader of Lashkar-e-Aalam, Zaeem Hasan Al-Ajmi. Without hesitation, Yusuf would give his life for him and the group's cause. Yusuf and Zaeem had spent many nights sipping sweet tea and refining the mission of Lashkar-e-Aalam. They both acknowledged that the core group, al-Qaeda, had been severely crippled by the CIA drones and the persistent infidels. Today, al-Qaeda mostly provided inspiration and propaganda. The key to perpetuating the establishment of a global Islamic caliphate was through other jihadist elements, such as Lashkar-e-Aalam. The goal was to excise the United States from the Muslim world, and that started with the removal of Israel from Arab lands.

Both Yusuf and Zaeem knew that if they could attack and punish America, the weak-stomached Americans would abandon their support of the Zionist nation. That was Lashkar-e-Aalam's mission: inflict damage on America's men, women, and, of course, children, until they broke down and insisted that Israel leave the sacred and holy lands of Islam.

Yusuf's cabin was located on deck twelve, the Aquarius deck, one deck below the *Matisse*'s food court. He thought that it would be a perfect time to get some food and also study the layout of deck fourteen. But before he could leave his cabin, he needed to perform the *asr*, or the afternoon prayers.

He used the remote to scroll through the ship's channels until he found the one that displayed the navigator's ship position. He then wrote down the current heading of the *Matisse*. Returning to his computer, he found www.qiblalocator.com and determined the correct *qibla*, or direction to Mecca, for his afternoon prayer. He always performed the five daily prayers facing Kaaba, the central shrine in Mecca's Great Mosque.

Yusuf then performed the ablution, or cleansing. He washed his face, including his mouth and nostrils, and both hands; wiped his head; and then carefully washed his feet.

While Yusuf attended to his prayers, the leader of Lashkar-e-Aalam was holding a meeting in North Africa. Ten minutes north of Gao, Mali, Zaeem Hasan Al-Ajmi finished his project review with his chief scientist, Faroug Hasan Ahmed. After Faroug exited the room, Zaeem got up from his colorful pillows and retrieved his laptop. He opened the site for Gmail and entered the username "baseballfan999." After he entered the password, he found himself rewarded with Yusuf's e-mail draft. Zaeem clicked to read it and then deleted the unsent message.

The compound of Lashkar-e-Aalam had been established long before other militant Islamists had brought the world's attention to Mali. Zaeem felt that his group's global mission was greater than participating in tedious land battles in North Africa. Lashkar-e-Aalam, meaning "Army of the World," was established after Zaeem relocated from the Pakistan city of Multan, located in the Punjab province.

Faroug assured him the test on the great ship *Matisse* would be a

HIGH SEAS DARKNESS

success and would move their group one step closer to the main attack that would bring the great satan to its knees—an act of terrorism that would dwarf September 11, 2001. What then took nineteen hijackers, they would accomplish with only five members of Lashkar-e-Aalam.

Chapter Twelve

The *Matisse Under the Stars*, using its assortment of thrusters, gracefully maneuvered next to pier two. Even though it was too early for the shops to be open, Brick had spent the last half hour walking around the Aloha Tower Marketplace. He made a note to try to have lunch at Hooters, which was located at the end of the marketplace. Walking down the pier, pulling his wheeled suitcase with his go-bag thrown over his shoulder, Brick looked up and checked the accuracy of the almost ninety-year-old clock housed in the Aloha Tower. What amazed him was that the 1926 clock was still run by weights and a pendulum.

The dock line handlers were still in the process of doubling up the lines to the huge cleats on the pier while the security staff was getting the gangway ready. Because it was high tide, it was necessary to drag out the five-foot platform that was used to reduce the angle of the gangway.

As soon as the gangway was secured, Brick saw Raju Marwah walk briskly down to greet him.

"'Hurrah for the flag of the free! / May it wave as our standard forever / The gem of the land and the sea.' Don't you agree, Mr. Brick Morgan?"

"Aloha, my friend. How are the Gurkhas?"

"Ready to serve. Shall we locate our Ms. Fuentes?"

"You lead the way."

Brick started to lift his suitcase to make the assent up the gangway when Raju took it from his hand. "You are a guest of Nobility Cruise Line. I will do the heavy lifting. Your job is to solve the crime. 'Let eagle shriek from lofty peak / The never-ending watchword of our land.' Mr. Morgan, let Raju be your eagle on this adventure."

HIGH SEAS DARKNESS

The security detail was setting up the console that would check out the passengers as they disembarked from the ship. Passengers would have to insert their cabin cards into the slot in the console and wait for the click before being allowed down the gangway to enjoy their day in Honolulu.

Stepping onto the ship, Brick was greeted by Yvette. "Thank you, Raju. I'll take it from here."

Brick gave Yvette a formal handshake and whispered in her ear. "I think I heard three Sousa marching songs from the bottom of the gangway to the top."

"Only three? Let's get out of the traffic area."

They walked through a corridor on deck five. When they were away from the crowd lined up to leave the ship, Yvette gave Brick a hug and said, "Thanks for coming. I missed you. Let's get you to your cabin, and then I'd like you to meet our passenger. She's a little on edge. I hope you can convince her to stay on the ship for a few more days. We should check in with Captain Costanzo, too. We could catch some coffee and go to deck five to the Aurora Dining Room to review what we've discovered while you were in the air. The dining room is closed when we're in port."

As they headed to the Bootes deck on eleven, Brick could not help but notice how sharp Yvette looked in her white officer's uniform. Her white slacks seemed to be tailored, and the web belt with gold buckle was snug around her waist, accentuating her ample breasts. He was sure she caught him looking when she turned around at his cabin.

Yvette gave Brick his card key and said, "Hope this cabin meets with your satisfaction. If this is not what you want, we have an inside cabin just off I-95 next to the beef locker on deck four."

After throwing his bags on the bed, he reached inside his go-bag and retrieved his Glock 23, the Ruger SR22, extra magazines, and two boxes of ammo. He opened the cabin safe and locked away everything except the Ruger, which he inserted in a Gould and Goodrich 810 holster inside his waistband.

"Let's go meet Carolyn Luna," Brick said as he stepped out into the starboard corridor on deck eleven.

"She's on this deck, port side forward."

"Carolyn, this is Yvette," she said, knocking on Carolyn's cabin door.

Carolyn opened the door, and Yvette and Brick entered her sizable suite. "Carolyn, this is Investigator Brick Morgan. He flew all night to be here to help you."

"Miss Luna, I am so sorry to meet you under these terrible circumstances. I am here to help you. I am not an employee of the cruise line but a private investigator who has been hired to assist you. Before you decide whether to let me help you, I would like to explain my background. My judgment on something is only as good as the quantity and quality of my information; it is hard to make a decision without all the information. May I stay for a few more minutes?"

"Let's sit over there," Carolyn said, pointing to a round table with four chairs. She already seemed tired of this encounter.

"May I call you Carolyn?"

"Yes."

"Thank you. I'm an attorney who can practice law in New Jersey and Washington State. I spent four years with the Seattle Police Department conducting investigations. I then worked with the United States Justice Department with FBI agents on the East Coast. I went into private practice so I could provide help to victims of assaults and crimes on cruise and maritime ships. I'd like to ask you to give me a day or two to investigate this sexual assault that you endured. Will you let me help you?"

"Why can't I just fly home while you stay here and find the asshole who raped me?"

"Good question. There are a couple of reasons. The first is that today I might discover a clue or a piece of evidence that I would want to discuss with you. Second, we know you were drugged, and both Officer Fuentes and I are very experienced with the effects of date-rape drugs and know that it takes several days to get the drug out of your system. Every eight hours, the amount of drugs in your system falls by half. Between the second and third day, many victims start to remember faces and encounters that were blank to them after the attack."

"Okay, fine, Mr. Morgan. But as nice as this room is and as professional as Yvette has been, I just want to catch the bastard, castrate him, and fly home. Will you promise to keep me informed as you do your work? I get bored just eating room service and drinking the ship's wine, no matter how good it is."

"You have my promise. Give us twenty-four hours, okay?"

"Okay."

Brick and Yvette left Carolyn's cabin and headed to the bridge to meet with the captain of the *Matisse*.

"Captain Costanzo, Brick Morgan."

"Please! Call me Francesco. I remember you from the drug case with the crew members down in the laundry. How long will you be on my ship?"

"As long as you allow or until I help Chief Security Officer Fuentes solve the case."

"I hope you will join me for dinner one evening. As captain, I have the best wines. Maybe you can bring Officer Fuentes. She is so shy around me, but she has a great figure, if you know what I mean."

"Captain, I know exactly what you mean." Brick couldn't help but smile confidently at Yvette. She smirked back.

Chapter Thirteen

Raju, Yvette, and Brick found a table on the starboard side of the opulently appointed dining room. The room decor continued the celestial theme that was a signature of Nobility Cruise Line. They named their ships for famous artists, and many of the decks and rooms were named for cosmic or astronomical bodies, which were compatible with the cruise line's slogan, "Under the Stars."

"Can we start with the victimology?" Brick asked once they were all seated.

Raju opened a notebook and started speaking. "On the first day of the cruise, she spent thirty-one dollars, not counting the daily gratuity charge. She bought a book and had two drinks on deck six in the Luminosity Bar. On day two, she spent $175—one-hundred-dollar casino draw, sixty-dollar perfume purchase, and two drinks in the Luminosity. On day three, the day before the alleged rape, she spent ninety-eight dollars—eighty dollars for the spa and eighteen dollars at the Big Dipper Bar. Then on the day of the *alleged*—"

"Stop." Brick looked at Raju, exasperated. "This is twice that you've referred to the assault as alleged. Share with me your feelings about this case before we look at her activities on day four."

"Mr. Morgan, I think Ms. Fuentes is looking in the wrong direction. I think the passenger left the Big Dipper, picked up some blond guy, and took him to her room for consensual sex. She invented this rape thing so she could blackmail Nobility."

"How do you explain the drugs in her system?" Brick leaned back and folded his arms across his chest.

"Easy. She brought the drug onboard."

"Raju, if I thought she was faking the assault, you'd insist that the rape was done by the captain. This isn't about passenger Luna; it's about your anger for not being named chief security officer. Now do your job, and just tell us about day four," declared Yvette.

"Humpf. Well, on day four, she charged forty-eight dollars—thirty dollars for a wine-tasting class and then another nineteen dollars at the Dipper."

"Yvette, let's look at our list of suspects or people who had opportunity," suggested Brick.

"We currently have a list of eight, three crew members and five passengers. The first is the mystery blond guy who was spotted on the CCTV system hanging around the amidships elevator area on Cassiopeia. We have absolutely nothing on him. We asked the room steward and security to patrol the area in hopes that he reappears. We also have the London couple that had drinks at the Big Dipper when Carolyn was there on day four. We know their names and cabin number.

"Then there are the guys from Aquarius deck, cabin 418. They left the bar and spent two hours in the casino playing the poker machine. The bar-charge records show they were buying drinks in the Equinox Bar in the disco until 3:00 a.m. They're not high on my list because I feel she was given the rape drug between 10:00 and 11:00 p.m."

"How would you know when she took the drug?" asked Raju.

"We took three different urine samples, and the results were sent digitally to a friend of mine at the San Diego Police Department. It has software that tracks the residual sample specimen concentrations of Rohypnol. The degradation curve points to ingestion between 10:00 and 11:00 p.m." explained Yvette, trying not to lecture him.

"What about the bartender working the Big Dipper?" asked Brick.

"Nope, he has a solid alibi. Seems he spent the night in the crew bar. The bar's bartender remembers he was there, and also the charges for booze on his crew card confirmed that he was there. We also have Officer Cappelli, who said he talked to Sanan Jaidee—that's his name—between 11:30 p.m. and midnight that evening. The crew card for Jaidee also shows he bought a Jack Daniels at a quarter to one in the morning," explained Raju.

"The cabin steward is next," remarked Yvette.

Raju turned a page in his notebook. "His name is Caylo Flores. He has a great alibi. He was banging his girlfriend in her cabin on deck three most of the night. The girl that she shares the cabin with will back up the story. She said she walked in twice, and our steward was naked both times. Seems the cabin steward has a high sex drive. Tried to talk her into a threesome."

"Charming. If the passengers knew what happened below the waterline, they'd pay double to get cabins on deck three," added Yvette.

"That leaves us with another suspect, the bartender from the Luminosity on deck six," remarked Brick.

"No alibi. We have no activity on his card, and he says he went to bed after his shift. His roommate did not get off work till 1:00 a.m. Says he was there when he entered the cabin right after his shift change." Raju then added, "He had opportunity because no one can vouch for him between 10:00 p.m. and 1:00 a.m."

"Let's take a break. I could use some coffee." Brick got up from the table. "When we return, let's look at the physical evidence."

Yvette left to locate some real coffee while Raju went to the gangway area to ascertain the efficiency of the disembarkation process. Brick made the most of this short break to return to his cabin and hang his clothes in the closet. He still needed to follow up with Titus, but he hoped that what she found could wait until after the investigators reconvened.

"Okay, let's review the physical," said Brick as the three settled back in their seats in the Aurora Dining Room a few minutes later.

"The collections from the sexual-assault kit need to be analyzed on land. We sealed the swabs from the toilet and sink, and we have the toothbrush sealed also," said Yvette.

"Why did you take her toothbrush?" asked Raju.

"Let me answer that," said Brick. "Rape is a crime of anger. Many times, an assailant will spit on or hit his victim. We know of many cases where the criminal will hang around and do perverted things. I've had cases where the perp will piss on the victim's toothbrush or even shove it up his own ass as a continuation of his rage."

"That is sick," said Raju.

"Rape is sick," Brick replied.

"Brick, I found this piece of wrapper or foil on the cabin floor in Carolyn's room. My best guess is that it might be part of a wrapper from a condom."

"Good. We may want to come back to that in the future. What's the name of the bartender from Luminosity Bar?"

"Fakhruh. He's from Indonesia," said Raju.

"We should bring him into the security office and have a little talk. Yvette, while you and I conduct a little interrogation, Raju can go through his cabin," Brick stated.

"I agree. Raju, are you okay with that plan?"

"Sing out for liberty and light / Sing out for freedom and the right / Sing out for Union and its might."

"I assume that's a yes," Brick said as he got up from the table and started walking to the dining room door.

The security office had a small interview room situated in the corner of the larger office. Fakhruh was seated on one side of an old steel desk, Yvette was seated on the other side, and Brick stood next to Yvette. They had been interviewing, or interrogating (depending what side of the desk you were on), Fakhruh for about thirty minutes. Finally, Brick produced a picture of the suspect that appeared to show him on the Cassiopeia deck.

"Mr. Fakhruh, we have you nailed," Yvette said. "This picture was taken two nights ago when you said you were asleep in your cabin. Here is the deal. If you confess, we will remove you from the ship and send you home. If you do not confess we will arrest you and turn you over to the United States FBI."

"Fakhruh, it's your call!" Brick shouted as he towered over the bartender.

"Sir, please, I was asleep! I swear I did not hurt anyone!"

"Maybe you need more time to think clearly," said Yvette.

She and Brick left the room and slammed the door.

"Let's call Raju and see what he's found in his cabin," said Yvette.

"Nothing," announced Raju as he came into the office.

"Yvette, I don't think he did it," Brick said.

"I agree. Cut him loose."

Brick headed back into the interrogation room. "Fakhruh, we're going to cut you lose for now, but we want you to keep your ears open. Snoop around the crew bar and dining room. Somebody knows something, and we want to be the first to know. Are we clear?"

"Yes, clear, of course." Relieved, Fakhruh carefully slid by the big, abrasive American.

After he left, Yvette turned to Brick. "Where did you get that phony picture?"

"I ran to the purser's office, got his picture, and had the lady in Digital Experience do a little magic with Photoshop," answered Brick with a smile.

Yvette's cell phone rang. "Fuentes." She handed it over to Brick. "It's the purser's office. They want to talk to you."

Brick listened intently before thanking the crew member on the other end of the line. He handed the phone back to Yvette. "Chief Security Officer Fuentes, we're about to solve this case."

Chapter Fourteen

After convening with Yvette and Raju and updating Rob Spencer via conference call, Brick found a house phone just outside the double mahogany doors.

"Carolyn, this is Brick. May Ms. Fuentes and I stop by? I feel we have made some substantial progress on your assault."

"Fine. I could use some company besides these empty wine bottles."

As they walked down the hall on Bootes deck, Brick suggested to Yvette, "Let's invite Carolyn to lunch. She's probably getting a little cabin fever."

Carolyn appeared happy to see them. To their relief, she gave no indications that she was going to bolt for the mainland anytime soon.

"Brick and I are going to grab a fast lunch onshore at Hooters. Would you like to join us?" said Yvette.

"I think I'll pass, but thanks for asking. But if you're able to pick me up a bunch of buffalo wings, I'd be very appreciative. Hot ones, please."

"Consider it done," replied Brick.

While entering their cards in the disembarking console at the top of the gangway, they ran into Raju again.

"We'll be back in about an hour, Raju. I'd like to shut down the Big Dipper so I can examine that site for any clues," Brick said as he and Yvette headed down the gangway.

Walking past Irvine Park, they turned and ambled down Ala Moana Boulevard to the Hooters restaurant.

"We'll have an order of fifteen Hooters Nearly Famous Chicken Wings with blue cheese and celery. Also, can you make an order to go, please? We need a Hooters salad, twenty hot buffalo wings, blue cheese, and also ranch dressing," Brick told the provocatively dressed

Hooters girl. Yvette noticed where Brick's eyes fell on the waitress as she scampered away.

"Brick, would you be shocked if I told you I had a pair of those tangerine hot pants in my cabin?"

"Now *that* you're going to have to prove to me," replied Brick with a grin. Becoming serious, he said, "Here's what I'm thinking. I checked the records in the purser's office. This Sanan guy has never bought a drink in the crew bar after midnight during his whole contract on this ship. That's four months. And it gets better. Sanan's been on four ships, the *Monet*, *Goya*, *Renoir*, and now the *Matisse*. During his contracts with *Goya* and *Renoir*, there were also unsolved rapes. And the rape on the *Renoir* was determined to be a drug assault."

"So you think the drink he ordered at 12:45 a.m. was an attempt to establish an alibi?"

"Yes. Let's get back to the ship. I want to have a hard look inside the Big Dipper Bar," Brick said as he picked up the styrofoam container containing Carolyn's order.

Yvette dropped off the lunch to Carolyn, who was very happy to have any delicious deviations from the room service menu. Walking past the Galileo Pool, Brick noted three orange cones in front of the Dipper Bar and a sign that read, "Closed for repairs."

Brick walked back and forth, examining the exterior of the bar before he opened the hinged bar top and entered. He lifted each liquor bottle out of its well hole and looked for anything that might have fallen into it. He examined the back bar refrigerator and removed the various assortment of juices and mixes. The high-end liquors were arranged on shelves on the back bar wall, and a door led to a small supply room that held racks of clean glasses and an ample supply of bar towels. On a shelf were two bags containing two hundred palm tree stirrers. Next to the stirrers were six boxes of drinking straws, the kind used for tall cocktails and tropical drinks. The boxes were labeled

"D.S. 5506 Blu," "D.S. 5506 Red," and "D.S. 5506 Gre."

Moving the boxes to the counter, Brick reexamined the shelf and noted that the dust pattern indicated that the straw boxes had been recently moved. He opened the two blue boxes and looked inside. Then he opened the two red boxes and was greeted by surprise and renewed curiosity.

Just then, Yvette entered the supply room.

"Perfect timing. Take a look at this box of straws."

Looking inside, Yvette saw a small bundle of blank cabin cards secured with a rubber band. "Bingo," she said. "Now I know why Nobility pays you the big bucks."

"I want to grab the cutting board. If I were going to put a roofie in a drink, I wouldn't just drop the whole tablet in a glass. I'd put it on a cutting board and use a wooden muddle stick or something to crush the tablet."

"You're right," agreed Yvette. "I think it's time to have a look in Sanan's cabin." She dialed security to reach Raju. "Hey, Mr. John Philip Sousa, same drill as last time. I'll summon Jaidee to the security office, and you go through his cabin."

"Anything special I should be looking for?" asked Raju.

"If he had one roofie, he probably has more."

"Have him also look for any device that Jaidee could use with blank cabin cards. Some of these freaks like to keep souvenirs from their sick acts," added Brick.

Yvette called Sanan Jaidee's supervisor to request Sanan's presence while Brick set the plan. "Let's bring in our perp, and let him stew in the interview room. I need about thirty minutes to get ready. Raju can start with his cabin, and I'll join you in about half an hour."

When Brick returned to the security office, he was dressed in his tailored brown suit. His Glock was holstered outside of his pants and clearly visible to Sanan, who kept his eye trained on the American's big gun. Brick did not care for going the soft route with alleged rapists, so he decided to go full force from the outset.

"How long have you been a bartender on the *Matisse*?"

"What is this about? Who are you?"

"Dammit, Jaidee, don't screw with me!" yelled Brick, slamming his fist on the table.

Sanan jumped back in his chair and almost fell over. "Four months." He nervously looked first at Yvette and then at Brick.

"Have you ever seen this woman?" Yvette handed him a picture of Carolyn Luna.

"No. Is she a passenger?"

Before Yvette could respond, Raju called her on the department's two-way radio. Brick and Yvette locked eyes and stepped out of the room to hear what Raju had discovered.

"I went through his cabin for thirty minutes before I located the card magnetic strip reader. I also found condoms of the same brand as the scrap of wrapper you found in Luna's cabin."

"Good work. Spend another few minutes, and look for any tablets. See if he has any vitamin or aspirin bottles. I'm willing to bet they're not for headaches," said Yvette.

Returning to the interview room, Brick took the lead. "Mr. Jaidee, I want you to know, I think you are screwed. Now keep your mouth shut while I explain why your life is now over. If you interrupt me, I will wrap your face in duct tape. Are we clear?"

"Yes, sir—"

"I said, keep your damned mouth shut!"

On cue, Yvette intentionally stretched out the noise as she pulled a strip of duct tape. She looked coldly at Sanan as Brick continued.

"When you were on the *Goya*, you raped a woman. When you were on the *Renoir*, you raped a woman. We found drug residue on your bar cutting board in the Big Dipper. We know that after talking to Officer Cappelli, you left the bar for over an hour, returned, and tried setting up an alibi by ordering a Jack Daniels. We found your stash of blank key cards that you hid in the box of straws and your little decoder/encoder machine." Brick paused as if waiting for an explanation. "Okay. Now you can speak."

Sanan sat in silence. He leaned forward and stared at the top of the desk. His mouth felt very dry. Brick could not tell if Sanan shut down out of crippling fear or stupid defiance, but at this point, he didn't really care.

"We can do this one of two ways. Choice one: you confess, and we turn you over to the Honolulu Police. They will coordinate with the FBI and probably deport you back to Thailand. Choice two: you don't confess. We turn you over to the Honolulu Police, and again, they will speak with the FBI. Then the FBI will pack you up, drag you back to the mainland, and throw you in a prison with sex offenders and terrorists while you await trial. You'll probably spend two, maybe three, years being fucked in the ass by big black guys just like me until they find you guilty and send you back to prison where you'll get it daily from the really mean motherfuckers. And tomorrow, I'm going to fax this press release to the *Bangkok Post* and every paper in Thailand we can locate." Brick slid a sheet of writing toward Jaidee. The color drained from his face as he read.

> Press Release—FOR IMMEDIATE RELEASE
> Nobility Cruise Line turned Thailand citizen Sanan Jaidee over to authorities after he was arrested as sexual maniac onboard a cruise ship. Jaidee, accused of being a serial rapist, is currently being held without bail by the United States Federal Bureau of Investigation.

"Oh, one more thing, Sanan. We pulled your emergency contact info to get your mother's name and address, so she will get the first copy of this press release. Okay, so is it door number one, or is it door number two?"

Chapter Fifteen

"Rob, this is Yvette on the *Matisse*. If my math is correct, it must be about eleven in the evening."

"No, it's just one hour before midnight." He paused for her to respond to his little joke. The awkward silence refocused him on business. "Do you have any news?" he asked, getting out of bed.

"Good news. We have a signed confession from a ship's bartender, a crew member from Thailand. His name is Sanan Jaidee. He even admitted to sexual assaults on the *Goya* and the *Renoir*. We want to call Honolulu PD and get him off the ship before we leave tonight for Kauai."

"Yes, call Honolulu, and then first thing in the morning, I'll call the FBI office in Oahu. As usual, they'll be pissed, but I'll deal with that. What's the situation with the American woman?"

"Glad you asked. Brick did a solid job of keeping her calm. With that in mind, I think we should give him a shot at trying to get her to accept a settlement and sign a release."

"We have done that before, and Brick did a good job," acknowledged Rob.

"My gut feeling," Yvette said, "is that she'll be very persistent if we let her leave the ship and will lawyer up. She's an up and coming name in designer circles. This will spread fast."

"Okay, Brick knows the limits and processes. If he can get her to agree, we would, of course, have to run the numbers past legal and our liability insurance carrier. Go for it, but tell him not to give away the ranch this time."

"Will do, but a reasonable settlement will surely be better than a civil jury verdict of ten million. We're not going to duck culpability on this case. We have substantial exposure in this assault."

"Yvette, enough. Just get it done. I'm going back to bed to get at least a few hours of sleep before my dance with the FBI."

Raju called the Honolulu PD and then hauled Sanan down to deck two and oversaw him stuffing his personal items into a couple of beat-up boxes from food storage. When the gangway security called to say that the police had arrived, Raju used a zip tie to secure Sanan's hands behind his back and deliberately marched him through the crew's mess, down the hectic I-95, and then up the gangway. The walk was as much a demonstration of Raju's pride as it was Sanan's shame. Raju handed him over to the police and gave the lead cop an envelope with copies of the confession and an outline of the evidence. The original confession, sexual-assault kit evidence, the blank key cards, and the investigational report were being boxed up and would be FedExed to Nobility's corporate headquarters when the ship reached Hilo.

The next hour went fast. Brick and Yvette informed Captain Costanzo of the outcome of their investigation and then returned to the security office to organize the paperwork. Yvette made arrangements to meet Carolyn in Brick's suite shortly thereafter. Yvette explained that the attacker was no longer on the ship and was now in the custody of the Honolulu Police Department. She also told Carolyn that Brick's cabin was on the same deck as hers but on the port side.

On schedule, Carolyn Luna ventured outside her cabin for the first time in two days and walked the short distance to her meeting with Brick and Yvette. Yvette knew that Carolyn needed this step to really begin to tackle her trauma. Despite the pride in apprehending Sanan, seeing Carolyn standing tall at Brick's door made Yvette feel a greater sense of accomplishment.

"Carolyn, first let me thank you for staying on the ship while we conducted the investigation. I know it must have been hard, but again, thank you," said Yvette serving coffee she had ordered from room service. "Brick, why don't you bring Carolyn up to date on the details of her assailant?"

Brick had changed out of his suit and was now dressed in slacks and a blue polo shirt. As he started his delivery, he encouraged Carolyn to take notes. She reached into her purse, retrieved a pen and a couple of envelopes, and gave a slight nod to indicate she was ready.

"Your recollection that you purchased three cocktails at the Big Dipper Bar was the compass that pointed us toward the bartender. The ship's records indicated that you were charged for two drinks that night. That discrepancy made us wonder what the bartender did with your cruise card if he didn't enter your third Yellow Bird drink into the bar terminal. A search of the bar disclosed a bunch of blank cruise cards that he must have stolen. Even though he thought he'd set up an alibi, his patterns gave him away," recounted Brick.

"What do you mean by 'patterns'?" asked Carolyn.

"Patterns can be everything. The night he attacked you, he ran back to the crew bar on deck four and quickly bought a drink at 12:45 a.m. That was a pattern change. In the four months that he worked on the *Matisse*, he never once had a drink after midnight. That change in pattern alerted us to focus on him. He kept a hidden machine that copied your data from your cabin card to a blank card. He took your card to a supply room behind the bar to copy the data. That is how he was able to enter your cabin. And that was why he didn't ring up your third Yellow Bird."

"He's under lock and key in the custody of the Honolulu PD. And tomorrow the FBI will also interview him," interjected Yvette. She nodded for Brick to continue.

"Carolyn, you have several options now that the deviant has been arrested and removed from this ship. You do not have to listen to me, but both Yvette and I have substantial experience in these situations. With your permission, I would like to explain some of the options I feel you have. Is that okay?"

"Go ahead. I'm so happy that guy is off the ship. This has been an unbelievable nightmare, and I want it all over with," Carolyn said.

"Here's how I see it. Option one: you get off the ship, don't look back, fly home to California, and pick up your life and move forward with your career. Option two: you return to California, hire some big-name lawyer, and file a lawsuit against Nobility Cruise Line. Then there is option three: you let me work with Nobility on your behalf and negotiate a very large confidential settlement in exchange for your signed release.

"Before I explain the details of option three, though, allow me to share why I'm not a fan of option two—the hiring of a lawyer and a lawsuit. Carolyn, this crime took place in international waters. A citizen of Thailand perpetrated it. The *Matisse Under the Stars* is registered under the maritime laws of the Bahamas. Once Nobility knows that lawyers are involved, the dozens of attorneys in Florida will go on the defense and keep the litigation going for five to ten years. You would have to fly to Florida every couple of weeks for depositions and hearings. The prolonged litigation would take a huge toll on you mentally, physically, and financially."

Brick paused to allow Carolyn to assimilate his last point. He felt that prolonged litigation was a key point, and he wanted to make sure that she understood the downside of lawyering up. He knew all too well that some lawyers make survivors relive their traumatic experiences over and over again.

"The reason Yvette and I work with Nobility is so they do not hide from their responsibilities. They understand that Sanan Jaidee was their employee. My experience has been that in similar cases they've been very generous with their settlement offers. Carolyn, if you do not feel that their settlement offer is reasonable or fair, you can say no and hire an attorney." He paused. "You have had a very difficult week. Why don't you sleep on it, and we can discuss it further tomorrow when we are in Hilo?"

"Look, I just want this shit over. I've been screwed once this week, and I don't want to get fucked twice."

Brick wanted to know one more thing. "Let me ask you a question. Have either Officer Fuentes or I acted in any manner where you felt we did not have your best interests as our first priority?"

"Mr. Morgan, no! You two have been very professional. Compassionate, even!"

Yvette smiled. "We'll call you about ten tomorrow morning. Let me walk you back to your cabin."

After escorting Carolyn to her cabin, Yvette returned to Brick's suite.

"Captain Costanzo has been persistent about you and me having dinner with him tonight. Let's join him and drink his pricey Italian wine. I think we have a reason to celebrate." Brick walked over to his cabin phone to confirm with the ship's captain.

Chapter Sixteen

On June 28, 1974, the first employees of the Federal Bureau of Investigation moved into their new building. The planning and construction had been a prolonged ten-year project. Prior to this new building, the FBI was spread out in nine different locations. Zoning regulations required that three floors plus a huge parking garage be underground, and that the building be eight stories high on the Pennsylvania Avenue side and eleven stories on the E Street side.

Today, FBI Director Alexander Zittel's office was located on the seventh floor along with the offices of the deputy director and other senior executives. Director Zittel served as the eighteenth leader of the FBI, the first being Stanley Finch, who was director, or chief, from 1908 through 1912. The longest term of a director was forty-eight years, of which J. Edgar Hoover held the honor.

The twenty years spent at the National Security Agency provided Alexander "Ace" Zittel with a foundation of knowledge that made him exceptionally well suited for the FBI's refocused mission. During his first fifteen years with NSA, Ace specialized in cryptography and the development of standard encryption keys. His legacy was the creation of various backdoors that allowed the FBI to enter the most secure and encrypted sites.

Zittel's last five years with NSA were spent in charge of a very classified project called Operation Cobalt Shadow. This program aimed to thwart the use of online games and social media as a vehicle for terror groups and radical individuals to communicate. Zittel's forethought with this initiative marked him as a mover and shaker in the District of Columbia.

Director Zittel left his door open for Elizabeth Monroe to enter. Liz had been appointed deputy director six months after Zittel's appointment.

"Liz, come in, and shut my door, please."

"What's up, boss?" She was curious as to the director's request for a meeting on short notice.

"I just ended a secure conference call with the secretary of the Department of Homeland Security and the White House chief of staff. Halfway through the call, the president picked up his chief of staff's phone and emphasized that his chief's message was not to be diluted. POTUS said that his policy as explained by COS is firm. Then he handed the phone back to the chief of staff."

"Sounds like plausible deniability to me," Liz said.

"And weird. There was nothing new, nothing we didn't already know in the call. He reviewed POTUS's position that al-Qaeda has been wiped out and that we are not to classify any incidents as terrorism."

"Director, how do you feel about that call?" Liz carefully planned to tailor her reaction according to his.

"My position and the position of the secretary of the DHS are presidential appointments. We both serve at the pleasure of the president. Remember, Clinton removed Sessions in 1993. Based on that call, our marching orders are very clear. There is no more war on terror, al-Qaeda has been decimated, and if we are attacked, we will classify it as worksite violence."

"Just like Fort Hood," added Liz with a pointed touch of cynicism.

The infamous Fort Hood tragedy and fiasco took place several years earlier under a different administration. A radicalized army officer went on a shooting rampage, killing thirteen and wounding thirty. During this spree, he reportedly shouted, "Allahu Akbar," as he fired. This clear case of terrorism, perpetrated by a militant Islamist, was classified by the Department of Defense as workplace violence.

"Liz, your job is to make sure each field office understands this position. I do not want to read in the paper or see on TV that one of our special agents announced that an incident was an act of terrorism. Are we clear?"

"Do you really feel that this is the correct direction for the county?" asked Liz, baiting him somewhat.

"Dammit, were you not listening, Monroe? What I feel is not your concern. We will follow the president's lead. If you can't get the job done, please tell me, and I will find a deputy director who can!"

Liz closed her office door and reflected on the heated conversation with Ace. It was beyond her imagination how the director of the FBI had consumed the Kool-Aid of the naive president.

Liz had been with the Bureau for her whole post-college career. A large part of her FBI experience consisted of special assignments with Interpol. During those assignments, she worked hard to obtain her master's degree in organizational leadership. Prior to her appointment as deputy director, she spent three years as director of the intelligence division, where she developed the policies and capabilities of the FBI's mission to ensure national security. Her perspective on terrorists became increasingly inflexible to match her ambition.

During the first six months of her position, she developed a quick respect for the leadership of the director. But the last six months were different. The turning point was Zittel's directive to honor the Department of Defense's decision that Major Nidal Hasan, the Fort Hood terrorist, was not a terrorist but an upset employee. Then there was the attempt to disperse a bioagent at the Super Bowl. The powers-that-be instructed Zittel to declare that the three militant Islamists were just misguided youths who got carried away with an Internet game.

Picking up her phone, she dialed the executive assistant director of the FBI. "Herb, Liz here." For the next thirty minutes, she explained the ground rules that were now in place. Herb Wallace reacted with typical aplomb after listening to his boss.

"Deputy Director, you have gotta be goddamn shitting me! I have a bunch of special agents who are going to go fucking ballistic!"

Chapter Seventeen

The bridge on the *Matisse Under the Stars* was located forward on deck eleven. Captain Francesco Costanzo had just finished guiding the 135,000-ton ship out of the Honolulu Harbor and set the Northrup Grumman Sperry Marine Voyage Management System for Nawiliwili, Kauai. The 228-nautical-mile trip should take eleven hours at a speed of twenty-one knots.

"Captain leaving the bridge," announced Costanzo as he turned the management of the bridge over to the first navigation officer and the senior second officer. The captain opened the door to the navigation deck and walked into the plush area sometimes referred to as the "pre-bridge" and watched through the large glass windows as the two officers took command of the ship's functions. After a few minutes, the captain walked about twenty feet down a wide, wood-paneled hall and opened the door to his private quarters.

"Welcome, my friends. I hope the bar is open and stocked to your satisfaction," announced the outgoing Costanzo. "We will be having some great Italian wines at dinner, but feel free to kick-start your engine with a cocktail."

The captain's private quarters were similar to the larger suites on the ship but without all the polished marble and granite. His cabin included a large living room adjoined to a dining room with a long oval table that could seat eight, but tonight it was set for five. The quarters also featured a small kitchen that served more as a prep area than a kitchen suitable for preparing a multicourse meal. The kitchen area was equipped with several warming drawers and a GE Advantium oven. Off the living room was a door to the captain's bedroom. The one true luxury of the suite was its bathroom of considerable size.

"Mr. Morgan, I understand we have reason to celebrate this evening."

"Yes, sir. Officer Fuentes did a terrific job," replied Brick as the bartender poured him some Chivas Regal on the rocks.

"You are too modest. Come, join me for a tour of our bridge," requested Captain Costanzo.

As they walked through the entryway to the navigation deck, the captain pointed out many plaques and awards that the *Matisse* had earned. "This is a display of the original Tattinger champagne that christened the *Matisse* in 2009."

Opening a door in the windowed wall that separated the navigation deck from the bridge, the captain and Brick entered the large control center for the mega ship.

The captain continued. "When you measure the distance from the port wing to the starboard wing, you will find it is 172 feet." Walking to the starboard wing, the captain explained that, because the wings extended past the sides of the ship, you actually had a 360-degree view of the *Matisse*. Brick stood on a Plexiglas panel about three-by-five feet wide that looked down into the water.

"When we are docking, we can look down and confirm that the line handlers have singled or doubled up our lines," explained the captain. "We have six diesels that power the generators, giving the ship over eighty-six thousand kilowatts of electricity. That electricity turns the motors inside the three Azipods that each contains a motor and a four-blade propeller. Not long ago, ships used diesels to provide power through a transmission that was attached to a driveshaft, like a car. Most passengers think we have a big driveshaft running from the diesels to the propellers.

"Brick, you will see no charts on this bridge. The Electric Chart Display and Information System replaced the paper with digital displays. These two comfortable chairs are always occupied with two qualified officers when we are underway.

"Let's head back to my quarters and see how our chief of security is getting along."

Brick and Yvette sat on one side of the dining table across from Klaus Eberhardt, the ship's executive chef. The captain sat on one end of the table, and at the other end was the ship's senior medical director.

The captain's steward, Jorge, brought two different appetizers. The first was a platter of prawns wrapped in smoked paprika prosciutto. On another platter were ten button mushrooms stuffed with goat cheese and veal.

"Klaus selected the Tenuta le Velette Orvieto Classico Velico to complement our appetizers. Tell us why this wine is better than your German Liebfraumilch," joked the captain, holding up his glass of wine.

"It is not better, sir," replied Klaus. "But our captain said he wanted tonight to be Italian. Seriously, this white comes from the city of Orvieto in the province of Termi located in Southwest Umbria. But save room for a great Italian red later."

Jorge returned with the second course. He served everyone a dish of Gorgonzola and pasta with a Parmesan sauce. Halfway through the primo course, Jorge placed an enormous Bordeaux-type wine glass in front of each guest. Clearly, the whole meal meant to celebrate this selection.

"Herr Executive Chef, what surprise have you found in the wine cellar?" asked the captain.

"A true surprise. I selected a 2007 Gaja Barbaresco, Piedmont. See if you can identify the fragrant notes of raspberry. Enjoy!" proclaimed Klaus.

"To the success of our team of detectives. Cin cin!" said the captain.

The secondo, or second course, was brought out along with the contorno. Jorge presented a large platter filled with braciole surrounded by an assortment of mixed vegetables.

"Klaus, your Italian stuffed flank steak is superb!" announced the captain as he took another swallow of the Barbaresco.

"I got up this morning at 4:00 a.m. and stuffed and rolled it myself," the chef joked.

For the next hour, the captain and Medical Director Dr. Pedro Ramos shared sea stories, several of which could be the basis for at least a couple of great novels. All assembled loosened up comfortably as the third bottle of Barbaresco was opened.

Before long, Yvette's hand found Brick's right thigh. As she continued sliding her hand further and further up his leg, Brick was having difficulty concentrating on the table conversation. Taking another drink of his wine, he realized that Yvette's touch was having a dramatic effect, as he felt his package coming to life.

Soon, everyone was nearly finished with either a tiramisu or a glass of Cognac. Figuring it was a perfect time to excuse themselves, Brick thanked the captain and announced that he and Yvette had a busy day tomorrow finishing all the paperwork from the case.

Maneuvering from the officer's country to Brick's cabin took some skill, especially after the ample supply of wine. As Brick entered his card key in the lock, Yvette stopped him. "Excuse me, Passenger Morgan, but in the interest of your very personal safety, I think I should come in and perform a security sweep of your bedroom."

Chapter Eighteen

There are subtle noises that can be heard and felt as a big ship leaves the open ocean and slowly begins maneuvering to enter a port of call. Brick figured that the *Matisse* would require a couple of hours to work its way down the channel created by the Hule'ia Stream before arriving at Nawiliwili. Reaching across the bed, he carefully placed a large hand on one of Yvette's perfect 34C breasts. As he slowly started circling her areola and nipple, Yvette softly said, "Hey, big guy, didn't we just do this a few hours ago?"

"I thought it would be a good idea if we went for the trifecta."

"I like the idea, but if I don't get to the security office by seven, Raju will probably call Florida and tell them I fell overboard." As Yvette slid out of bed, she added, "That's why I think you should consider staying on the ship for the trip back to the States."

Brick was so taken by her naked body and natural beauty that he only heard part of her comment. "I'm sorry. What did you say about the trip to the States?"

She chuckled to herself at his obvious distraction. She repeated her idea, and Brick nodded with a grin.

"If you promise to conduct a security check in my room each night, I'll strongly consider the idea."

After Yvette dressed and returned to her cabin to get ready for the day, Brick also got dressed and then logged onto the ship's Internet that was supported by the Digital Experience department. Deck five was the location of the area dedicated to computer classes and a dozen computers for the usage of passengers. The Digital Experience also housed the hub for the ship's access to the Internet that allowed guests to cybersurf from their cabins.

Eleven e-mails entered his inbox, but the three from Titus piqued his curiosity. The first thing he checked was the time that each of her messages was sent. They each were separated by four hours, which was consistent with her system. Brick saved e-mails one and three and deleted number two. Titus's coded messages would be in e-mails one and three, while e-mail two always served as a decoy or red herring. He knew that the real message would be less than twelve words and spread between the two e-mails.

The code that Titus used was called "Prime Five," as she doubted that the traps used by NSA would flag the communication. Brick looked at the first e-mail and numbered each word until he reached thirty. He wrote down the prime numbers one, three, five, seven, eleven, and thirteen. He then circled the first, third, fifth, and seventh words, and so forth. Next, Brick numbered the words in the third e-mail. This time he circled every fifth word, stopping when he got to word twenty-five. Before combining the two e-mails, he reread the first e-mail to double-check his numbering.

"Blog me with your e-book possible best book list. Ship me some Hawaiian sugar cane. Take some pictures of your trip."

As he decoded Titus's e-mails, Brick saw that the third e-mail was just as benign.

"Do you plan any activity with music? New band Ashkarla has a song called 'Alamaa.' May go on party cruise this week. Going to target the good-looking captain."

Alternating between each e-mail, he wrote down the ten words he had circled to decode the actual message.

"Blog activity with Ashkarla e Alamaa. Possible cruise ship target."

The other part of the code was if Titus felt there might be any words that would trip the NSA traps or intercepts, she would move the first letter to the end of the word and add the letter *A*—standard pig Latin.

From every word ending in *A*, Brick dropped the *A* and moved the last letter to the front of the word. He made the changes and then read the fully decoded message.

"Blog activity with Lashkar e Aalam. Possible cruise ship target."

Standing up, Brick ran his hand through his short hair and thought about what he had just decoded. He had assigned Titus to monitor websites known to be sympathetic to Islamists. She had a software program that could translate Arabic to English. Not only would the MegaTrans online software translate individual words, it could also translate complete sentences. Titus even incorporated her own word-search program to search for the Arabic word أ. سـفينة سيا حية, which translates into the English words *cruise ship*.

It was time to clean up and make arrangements to meet with Yvette prior to the scheduled meeting with Carolyn Luna. But as he processed what he learned from Titus, Brick turned on his cabin's TV and carefully watched the bridge cam channel.

Earlier, Yvette contacted Robert Spencer to discuss the parameters for a possible settlement with passenger Luna. She and Brick discussed their approach and also reviewed the maximum amount that Rob thought he could get through the insurance carrier and headquarters' legal group.

On schedule, Yvette and Brick arrived at Carolyn's cabin.

"Good morning. We brought real coffee from deck five," Yvette announced as she set the cups on the round table in the suite.

After taking a drink of his coffee, Brick recognized this as the right time to make Carolyn an offer. He scooted his chair closer to the table and adjusted his glasses. "Carolyn, both Yvette and I are excited about what we are going to present."

"Well, now that I've got my head on straighter, I hope to hear something good."

"I think it's very good. Take this paper so you can take notes and jot down any questions you might think of. First, the cruise line wants to apologize and is extremely embarrassed about the harm that you sustained. Second, they want to refund all of your cruise costs and any charges on your account through yesterday and also give you a ten-thousand-dollar credit for a future Nobility cruise. Third, they want to compensate you for your pain and suffering in the amount of $200,000. And finally, they will, of course, provide you with a first-class plane ticket home if you do not wish to continue this cruise. This offer would be contingent on a confidentiality agreement and a release from future litigation. That's it. What are you thinking?"

"That's a lot to assimilate. It sounds pretty fair, I must admit. I'm not one to sue at the drop of a hat, but the asshole who raped me was an employee of this ship. What do you think would happen if I hired an attorney?"

As a contracted entity, Brick felt he possessed the freedom to be honest with her. "Here is my read on that option. Let's assume you could rush this along and, with the help of an attorney, get a verdict of settlement in five years. And let's assume that the verdict is for one million dollars. Because this would be an extremely expensive case to litigate, the law firm would take 40 percent. That would leave you with $600,000. The customary procedure would be to calculate the $600,000 as a future value of an annuity. The offer would pay you $30,000 a year for twenty years. Because you would not get your final payment for twenty years, the $600,000 payment is not really worth $600,000 in today's dollar. If we work with a rate of 4.5 percent to determine the present value, the offer equals $248,785 in today's dollar. What's interesting is that if you took the Nobility offer and invested it at 4.5 percent, in five years it would grow to be $249,000. Of course, there are federal income tax issues with all verdicts or settlements, but that's largely outside the scope of my expertise."

"So what you're saying is that after the law firm takes their cut, and when you bring an annuity type of settlement to present value, it might make sense to take the offer." Carolyn's brain assimilated Brick's figures quickly before she generated her response. "Alright. I'll accept what you've presented. But I want $250,000, not $200,000. Can you make that happen?"

Yvette jumped to assure her. "I think we can, and I think you're making a good decision. You do understand that the settlement will be confidential and that the paperwork will include penalties if you break the confidentiality clause?"

"Yes, I understand. What happens next?" Carolyn got up from the table to stretch, looking noticeably stronger than a few days ago.

Brick leaned back in his chair and explained the steps to her. "We'll go downstairs and submit your counteroffer. They'll check with their senior executives, lawyers, and liability insurance carrier. We should hear back in three or four hours. In the next ten days, they'll send your check and settlement paperwork with an attorney. They will then meet with you and a notary. If you want an attorney to review the paperwork, that wouldn't be considered a violation of the confidentiality agreement."

"Carolyn, it would be normal if you wondered in the next few days whether you made the correct decision," offered Yvette. "Let me share a story. When I was in San Diego, I observed a fellow police officer dealing with three years of litigation for a work-related injury. Those three years ate him alive. He was never the same. These international maritime litigations can go twice that long. Believe me, you are making the right choice."

"I feel that I am, too. I need to decide when to fly home."

"You just let us know, and we will have the purser's office make the arrangements," replied Yvette as she stood and picked up her cold coffee.

"Alright then. Let me know if Nobility agrees to the $250,000. Oh, and one more thing. Can I buy you both a drink tonight?"

"Absolutely, as long as it's not in the Big Dipper Bar and you're not buying Yellow Birds," said Yvette as she and Brick walked to the cabin door.

Chapter Nineteen

The line handlers first singled up the four lines that secured the ship to the dock at Nawiliwili, Kauai.

After a call from the bridge, the men on the pier released lines two and three from the dock's davits, and the maneuvering gang on the *Matisse* pulled the lines onboard. On command, they slackened line one as the first officer used a little push from the bow thrusters to nudge the bow of the 135,000-ton ship away from the pier. When the *Matisse's* bow was ten feet from the dock, the bridge ordered line one released, and line four slackened and then also released. When the second bridge officer, looking aft from his vantage point on the starboard wing, confirmed that line four was pulled onboard, he signaled, "Line clear," and the Azipods pushed the stern of the big ship away from the dock. The combination of bow thrusters and Azipods allowed the *Matisse* to move sideways in the water.

Over the years, cruise ships advanced from fixed propellers to the traditional Azimuth Propulsion System and then to the new Azipod system. With the Azimuth system, the motor is inside the ship with gears connecting the motor to the propellers. The Azipod advancement places the motor and propeller inside a pod located farther away from the ship's hull. Not only do these pods rotate 360 degrees, eliminating the need for a rudder, but their four-bladed propellers face forward. A cruise ship like the *Matisse* operated three Azipods, and fuel efficiency increased about 7 percent. All five ships of the Renoir class ships were equipped with the Azipod Propulsion System.

Captain Costanzo invited Brick to watch the disembarkation process. Brick found no opportunity to leave the ship during its stay in Wiliwili, the nickname for Nawiliwili, but watching these procedures kept him busy while Yvette took charge of contacting Nobility. Her communication with Rob Spencer went smoothly, and within ninety minutes, the counteroffer of $250,000 was accepted. Carolyn seemed thrilled and also relieved to get this chapter of her life over. Neither Brick nor Yvette thought she would have buyer's remorse.

That evening, the Luminosity Bar was about half full. Eight of the twelve bar stools were occupied, and four of those passengers were involved in tasting some of the many bourbons the bar stocked. The Luminosity Bar stood out as a high-end space with its black galaxy granite bar stretching a full twenty feet. The back bar shelves were stocked with a very extensive and diverse selection of liquors. Being in the Luminosity felt like being among the stars.

Several members of the ship's orchestra played the Luminosity that evening, forming a casual jazz ensemble. The combination of saxophone, keyboard, electric guitar, and drums was in the middle of the signature Duke Ellington song "Take the 'A' Train" when Brick arrived at the lounge. Written by Billy Strayhorn, the song's name comes from the instruction given to Strayhorn so he could locate Ellington's home in New York. The map, or directions, started with "Take the A train." For three decades, "Take the 'A' Train" was a major piece for the Duke Ellington Band. It also happened to be one of Brick's favorites.

Brick stopped by the bar and ordered a sixteen-year-old Black Maple Hill small-batch bourbon—no ice, neat—and then located a table in the vicinity of the jazz musicians. When the waiter arrived with his drink, Brick breathed a small sigh of relief. Whenever he ordered an expensive scotch or whiskey, he feared that the language issues aboard cruise ships might screw up his drink orders. "Neat" means a shot of liquor poured into a glass. "Up" or "straight up" means shake with ice and strain into a cocktail glass. Most English-speaking bartenders know that ordering good quality bourbon straight up probably means neat. But on a cruise ship, assumptions that a bartender will understand such requests can sometimes lead to disappointing experiences with exceptional liquors. Brick had learned this the hard way on his first few cruise gigs.

Brick first spotted Yvette, who was wearing her dress whites, and quickly noticed Carolyn following her. He stood up and pulled out a couple of chairs for the women, noticing that Carolyn was smartly dressed with a pair of creased blue slacks and an oatmeal-colored cable-knit sweater. As if on cue, the musicians started playing "Mercy, Mercy, Mercy" as they began their slow walk toward Brick.

"'Cannonball' Adderley," said Carolyn as she sat down and glanced at the drink menu. "Notice how the drummer uses a brush with his right hand on the cymbals and a stick on the snare. Just enough percussion to complement but not compete with the saxophone. He's good."

"What's going on here? We have a pretty little white girl giving a jazz lecture to the big black guy," laughed Brick as he flagged down a waiter.

Soon after the drinks arrived, the jazz quartet took a break. The conversation turned to Carolyn's business and the big project in Newport Beach that she had lined up upon her return.

"The way I understand it, this fifteen-thousand-square-foot house was owned by a Lakers' basketball player who got into drugs and then went through a divorce. It has a ten-seat home theater, a cigar room, and a huge library. The colors throughout the house are an abortion, though. An Anaheim attorney bought the house with the money he collected from his fee on that famous lawsuit against the amusement park where the roller coaster shot off the track with four passengers."

"I remember that accident. They calculated that the car left the track at seventy-five miles per hour. Another car was hanging by a thread for three hours before they could rescue its passengers," added Brick as he took another sip of his bourbon.

Carolyn, Yvette, and Brick enjoyed another round of drinks, and Carolyn ended up hearing some salty police stories from both Brick and Yvette. Yvette told the story of working the Gaslamp Quarter in downtown San Diego when she stopped a guy who was taking a piss on the street. After she had hooked him up (put him in handcuffs), she asked him to sit on the curb while she called in his name to check for outstanding warrants. The guy begged her to let him stand and not sit on the street. When she explained it was for his safety as well as her own, he continued to say that he could not sit down. "I said, 'You have to sit your butt down on the curb. It's procedure,' and then he starts to cry! So I ask him, 'What the hell's wrong with you?' Almost whimpering, he tells me that he just left a sex club, and that he still had an eight-inch dildo shoved up his ass."

"Oh my God! Seriously? What did you do?" Laughing, Carolyn was shaking her head and wiping tears from her eyes.

"I undid one hand from the cuffs and reattached it to the door handle of the cruiser and told him to use his free hand to drop his pants and pull out the goddamned dildo, which he did. Thank God I had a big enough evidence bag!"

Before the group called it a night, Carolyn said she was going to get off the ship the next day in Maui and catch a flight home. The goodbyes and good wishes lasted another ten minutes before Carolyn started to cry. "Guys, I will never forget how kind and caring you've been. Thank you again for your patience and sensitivity." She then stood up and gave both Brick and Yvette long hugs.

Yvette offered to escort Carolyn back to the cabin because she needed to stop by the office. Brick stayed to check out the piano player who was on the starboard side of deck six forward near the Comet Bar. Brick's mind was a thousand miles away as he sipped a snifter filled with Grand Marnier. The music of the piano player was far in the background as he reflected back on his first assignment with Nobility.

When he formed Morgan Maritime Investigations, he focused mainly on bringing some sanity and fairness to how cruise ships handled crimes. Back then, it was common practice that when a passenger was a victim of a cabin burglary or, worse, an assault, a cruise line would instantly go on the defensive and abandon the passenger. The cruise corporations wiped clean any available evidence and flew out a zillion lawyers who aggressively protected the interests of their employers first and foremost. They got away with this behavior for years. Their attitude about their passengers seemed to be a carryover of their treatment toward their crew members.

When Brick contacted Nobility, he argued that the methods of the past were not going to work in the future. He set them straight by warning cruise companies about the explosion of social media usage and that the growing scrutiny of congressional insight could both seriously harm their bottom lines if they did not reform. He proposed that his new firm, Morgan Maritime Investigations, would ultimately minimize the enormous liability they incurred with their embarrassingly adversarial approach to addressing passengers who were injured or victims of crimes while they were guests on cruise ships.

As the piano man played Abba's "Dancing Queen," Brick took another drink of his Grand Marnier. *Dammit,* he thought, *I really did a good job of helping Carolyn. If Nobility had played hardball with her, she could have made a YouTube video and created a publicity nightmare for Nobility. And who knows what a jury could have awarded?*

Yes, he was making a difference, and it was also a great payday. Now he needed to make a decision: Does he get off in Maui and find a flight home, or does he take a well-deserved vacation and ride the *Matisse* back to the States?

Chapter Twenty

There are always passengers who choose not to take the tender to shore and instead prefer to relax on a ship with only a third of the normal amount of voyagers. One of those passengers who elected to stay on the ship had a cabin on the Aquarius deck.

Just outside his cabin's bathroom was an open-shelf cabinet that contained a safe for use by visiting passengers. Yusuf waited for his officious room steward to leave before he walked across the cabin and entered the code for the safe. After hearing the click, he turned the knob and opened the safe. Instead of holding jewelry, cash, or a passport, his safe's only contents were three glass vials. Satisfied that all was in good order, Yusuf Al Omar closed the safe door and reentered the locking code.

International Maritime Organization's Life-Saving Appliance Code states that the maximum capacity of a lifeboat cannot exceed 150 passengers. Furthermore, the lifeboat's occupants must all be able to take their seats within ten minutes after an "abandon ship" signal is given. These same lifeboats also serve as the tenders that ferry passengers to shore at the ports of call that do not have piers that can accommodate cruise ships.

The purser's office made arrangements for Carolyn Luna to be on the first tender to Lahaina, Maui, and volunteered a representative from the purser's office to join her on her car ride from Lahaina to the Kahului Airport. Since Brick planned to go ashore anyway, he finagled a seat on the same tender and helped escort Carolyn. The first tender usually ferried the security team and their equipment so they could station themselves at the pier to help passengers when they wanted to return to the ship.

The still seas cooperated on that beautiful Maui morning, and the trip from the anchored *Matisse* to Lahaina took only fifteen minutes. After a few more hugs and tears, Brick saw Carolyn Luna drive away in a Maui Pleasant taxi. He watched the car shrink away and silently wished her well.

Brick arrived ashore with a plan of his own. He decided to check out some of the art galleries on Front Street as he moved toward his ultimate objective of having a relaxing lunch at Bubba Gump Shrimp Company. As much as he enjoyed fine dining seated across from Captain Costanzo, today he craved some Southern cuisine without any pretension.

Walking down the busy street, Brick easily located 889 Front Street. As he turned to walk into Bubba Gump's, he almost knocked down Antonio, the ship's chief engineer. Brick extended his hand.

"Officer Antonio, Brick Morgan."

The *Matisse*'s engineer turned when he heard his name and laughed. "Mr. Brick Morgan, everyone knows who you are. Down in the engine room you're called 'the big celebrity.'"

Brick, a little taken aback, walked up to the restaurant desk just off the sidewalk. "Antonio, I don't suppose you'd like to join me for lunch today? Southern food needs company."

"Only if you let me buy you a drink, Mr. Brick Morgan."

"Only if you call me Brick."

Brick found them a table with a view and ordered himself an Alabama Sunrise, the restaurant's version of a Bloody Mary. He looked out the floor-to-ceiling windows and watched the flotilla of tenders making their trips back and forth to the *Matisse*.

Brick never needed to look at the menu at Bubba Gump's. When the waiter arrived with their drinks, he ordered his usual. "I'll have the Best Ever Popcorn Shrimp and the Dixie Style Baby Back Ribs."

Antonio spent the better part of the lunch explaining the intricacies of the ship's engineering. He seemed especially proud of how they heated up the Bunker Green prior to injecting fuel into the diesels. Antonio virtually beamed when he explained that Bunker Green was the traditional Bunker C with glycerol mixed in to reduce sulfur emissions. Brick soaked up his words as he devoured his food.

"Mr. Brick, while we're docked here in Hilo, would you like a special private tour of the belowdecks engineering spaces?"

"That would be wonderful. With all the new security rules, I hope that won't get you in trouble with Captain Costanzo."

"Not a problem. Even though we stopped all tours after the 2001 terror attack, we chief engineers have some discretion. Besides, Mr. Brick is a celebrity! I will go on ahead and meet you when you get back onboard."

Before Brick returned to the ship, he stopped in a small craft store to look around. He was looking for something definitively Hawaiian when he discovered the koa products. Koa wood comes from the largest native forest tree. Its rich, reddish wood often becomes gorgeous handcrafted bowls. Sometimes it even becomes amazing acoustic guitars. Brick barely resisted purchasing a new instrument for himself when he found the right koa wood bowl for Titus. He figured she would somehow already know that in Hawaiian the word *koa* means "bold" or "brave." Those words resonated with him after he got back on the *Matisse*.

Back in his cabin, Brick looked again at the decoded message from Titus. "Blog activity with Lashkar e Aalam. Possible cruise ship target." Tomorrow he would use a computer in the Digital Experience and find a search engine that did not record a user's IP address and try to figure out who or what Lashkar-e-Aalam was.

A sudden vibration shuddered throughout the ship. Brick went out onto his balcony. The anchor and its chain were being pulled up from the seabed. A typical navy-style anchor has flukes to dig into the harbor's floor. The shank pivots between the flukes and is connected to an iron chain. Each chain link could weigh over two hundred pounds.

Even though the weight of the anchor is important, it is the extra chain dropped around the anchor that holds the ship in place. Because the *Matisse* was only in sixty feet of water, the noisy process of raising all the chain and the anchor only took about five minutes.

As Brick reentered his cabin, he heard a knock on the door. Opening it, he was greeted by a beautiful Filipino woman carrying a bottle of wine and a little overnight bag clad in a form-fitting dress rather than her dress whites. "It's a tradition to have a party when a ship pulls up its anchor and leaves the waters of Maui," explained Yvette as she put the wine on the round table and dropped her bag on the queen-size bed.

Brick jumped on the bed and flashed a big smile. "Who am I to go against the honored traditions of Maui? I certainly don't want to upset the Mahalo gods."

Yvette turned the TV to the bridge cam channel and took her bag into Brick's bathroom. Brick got up off the bed and opened the wine, a nice French Bordeaux. As he poured two glasses, Yvette returned from the bathroom dressed only in a pair of tangerine Hooters hot pants. "Come on, Mr. Investigator. Let's get in bed and watch the ship leave Maui waters."

Chapter Twenty-One

The starboard hallway of the Aquarius deck was absent of any ship passengers. Cabin steward Dakila Salazar pushed his heavy service cart back toward the linen room adjacent to the amidships passenger elevators. The linen room held the supply of bedding, pillows, towels, and, of course, toilet paper for the cabins on the Aquarius deck.

Deck twelve held 244 cabins, and Dakila was assigned nineteen of them. It took him ninety minutes to freshen up his assigned nineteen cabins on this deck alone. Ice service, towels-and-toilet-paper replenishment, turn down the bed and, the most important thing, chocolates on the pillows. *God help the world,* he thought, *if the cones do not get their fucking chocolate.* Salazar could not remember the origin of the word *cone,* which is slang for "passenger," but he did remember that the word *coning* meant having sex with a passenger.

He pushed his cart into its assigned space and gathered up the wet towels. After replenishing glasses, tissue, and towels, he left the linen room and headed down to the crew's bar. As he took the service elevator down to four, he reflected back to the day that his world changed.

Salazar was halfway through his first contract on the *Bernini Under the Stars*, the lead ship of the Bernini class. He had completed his shift and was looking at porn on his laptop in his cabin on deck three. He switched from a video of tits and asses to the AOL log-on. A news banner of breaking events took his breath. The cruise ship on which his brother Bayani worked had run aground and was sinking. On January 13, 2012, the *Costa Concordia* struggled to stay above water while it carried 3,206 passengers and a crew of 1,032. There were 296 Filipino crew members on the ship, and one of those was Bayani Salazar.

Dakila and Bayani had grown up in the city of Caloocan. North of Manila, Caloocan was the home of the Sogo Hotel, where they worked in housekeeping for a year and a half. Their experiences at the Sogo Hotel gave them the qualifications to secure employment with cruise lines. Despite their closeness, the Salazar brothers found themselves on different ships with different lines, though.

It took Dakila nearly three days to learn that his brother was not one of the thirty-two who died in the accident. Not that Dakila was naive, but after hearing what happened on the *Costa Concordia*, he completely lost faith in European officers and American cruise-line management. His brother told him that the *Costa* passengers each secured as much as eleven thousand euros in compensation, but management saw to it that crew members only garnered paid wages until the end of their contact year or a minimum of two months, plus up to 2,250 euros for property loss. Dakila did not advertise his new life philosophy, but he now lived by the motto "Life ain't fair. Better to be the screw than the screwed."

What Dakila wanted now was a couple of Heinekens. Then he would return to his cabin to pull up some porn on his computer—but not just any porn. He collected his own special porn.

The crew bar was very upbeat because the ship would be nearly empty of the cones tomorrow, as the *Matisse* would be docked in Hilo. With three Heinekens in hand, Salazar found a table of five Filipinos and pulled up a chair.

The secret formula, the unspoken agenda of some cruise lines, was to manipulate and exploit the crew members that came from thirty different countries. Most of the crew originated from Third World countries where litigation and labor laws remain largely nonexistent. A ship like the *Matisse* was not always a big, happy, integrated family. On the contrary, it could serve as a successful model of segregation. The cruise lines figured out how to keep peace and tranquility on their floating cities by separating the various cultural groups into different departments. Russians and Eastern Europeans staffed the casinos, Indians mostly composed the security team, and it was difficult to find a deck officer who was not Italian. A large percentage of cabin attendants come from the Philippines, and bartenders tended to be from Thailand or Indonesia.

After ordering his drinks, Dakila found a group of Filipinos sharing what they each knew about the Big Dipper bartender who was thrown off the ship. He took a long pull of his Heineken and added what he had heard. "That blond girl from Sweden who works in the purser's office said that the guy got caught drugging and raping a cone on deck ten. By now, he should be home having drinks with his friends."

"Dakila, I don't think so. I heard that a big black cop from America showed up on the ship and had him arrested," added a waiter from the Renoir Dining Room. The banter and speculation continued long enough for Dakila to finish his second beer. By that point, all of this scuttlebutt became too tedious for him.

"I am turning in," announced Dakila as he got up from the table and put the third beer in his pocket. He made the familiar journey down a steep stairway, or ladder, as he called it, to deck three and then walked aft for what seemed like twenty miles. Even buzzed, he navigated between the forklifts moving pallets of number ten cans of beets.

He looked back at the large cans of beets and wondered, *How can anyone eat that shit?* He tried a bunch on some lettuce once when he first started his contract and had pissed red for two days. He went to the ship's doctor, thinking he picked up some disease from screwing one of those available Ukrainian women, but the doctor told him that his red urine was caused by betanin, the pigment in beets. He diagnosed the condition as beeturia. Dakila schemed to get a day off by telling his department leader that he contracted the debilitating condition of beeturia. Nonplussed, they assigned him another two cabins to clean instead.

Using his crew card, Dakila opened and entered his little cabin deep in the bowels of the ship. Some crew members meant that literally, as the smell in this part of the *Matisse* struck them as that of the colon of a dead goat.

Reaching under his thin mattress, he fished out his laptop computer and powered it up while opening the Heineken. He opened video file 519, climbed into his bunk, and rested the computer on his lap. The wireless micro-spy camera transmitted 5.8 gigahertz color to the receiver he had taped to the back of the television in cabin 519. When Dakila placed the spy camera, he positioned it to capture all the activity from the cabin's desk to both of its beds. He fast-forwarded the video to get past the useless shots of the empty cabin. Thirty minutes of scanning was rewarded when one of the French girls returned to the cabin. When he cleaned their cabin on day three, he secretly installed the wireless camera. The receiver was the size of a pack of cigarettes, and the spy camera was as thick as a pencil and about two inches long. He could not see how any cone could find it.

Salazar watched as the girl walked out of view and returned carrying a pair of jeans and what looked like a sweater. The girl, who he suspected to be about thirty, took off her blouse and threw it on the bed. She then sat on the bed and pulled off her gray slacks. Wearing only a European thong and a bra, she walked up to the TV and turned it on. She returned to the side of the bed, pulled on a pair of impressively tight blue jeans, and walked out of camera view. With anticipation, he waited for her to walk back into view. His impending reward shriveled when she returned to grab an oversized sweater and again left the view of the hidden camera.

Frustrated, Dakila closed down that file and opened one of his favorites, a video he had captured on a previous cruise. He liked to refer to this video as his homerun. In it, a married German woman masturbated when her husband abandoned her for the casino. Dakila secretly filmed her on two different occasions, and it seemed that one video must have gone on for twenty minutes. When the video was over, he closed his laptop and shoved his right hand inside his pants. He figured that he had just enough time to jerk off before his roommate returned from his shift.

While Dakila ran his fingers up and down his shaft, he fantasized about the two French girls. With eight days left, he hoped he would get some naked shots of them as they walked around in cabin 519. If he was really lucky, they might turn out to be lesbians.

Chapter Twenty-Two

An early morning docking at Hilo required Yvette to join Raju in supervising the logistics of setting up the equipment for the disembarkation process. She slipped out of Brick's bed and was almost out the cabin door with her overnight bag before he realized she was making her escape.

Brick scooted up in the bed and adjusted the pillow behind his head. "Hey, hot stuff. You aren't doing a love-'em-and-leave-'em, are you?"

"Good morning, sleepyhead. Thanks for the party last night. You know I wouldn't leave if I didn't have to, but I need to run to my cabin and then get down to deck four. We'll be secured to the dock in thirty minutes, and the passengers will be lining up to do Hilo."

"I'll find you after I have my tour of engineering," replied Brick as he got out of bed and searched for his boxers. She gave him a quick peck and teased his left nipple before she sauntered out of his cabin. He did not see any reason to tell her why he was so eager to visit engineering. Titus's message was only speculative right now.

Engineering Officer Antonio was waiting for Brick at the coffee kiosk on deck five. "Mr. Celebrity, are you ready for Engine Room University?"

"Just Brick, please. Mr. Celebrity is my father," he joked. Antonio stared at him blankly, and Brick surmised that his gag did not translate well. As he secured himself a large cup of fresh-brewed, he asked Antonio if he wanted some coffee.

"Thank you," replied the belowdecks officer. "But I've been up for hours and am on my third cup. Did you bring your hiking shoes, Mr. Brick? We will descend deep below the waterline—where most fear to tread . . ." he teased.

But that joke he gets? thought Brick as he followed Antonio down the port side of deck five. They passed the Digital Experience and entered a door labeled "Restricted—Crew Only."

"We're going down three decks, two below the waterline, and we will start with the desalinization equipment." Stopping on a catwalk over an engineering space that can only be described as huge, Antonio looked back at Brick as he tried to take it all in. "Do you know how many bathrooms are on the *Matisse?*'

"No clue," Brick said.

"For the passengers and crew, 2,280. And eighty more for public areas. The question is where do we get the water to flush the toilets?" Officer Antonio walked over to a large piece of equipment and continued. "We operate three water systems onboard. The first is the water system for drinking, showers, cooking, and dish washing. Then we have a water system for the toilets, and finally, we maintain a water system for ship cleaning and laundry."

He took Brick over to several large tanks. "These tanks hold nearly six hundred thousand gallons of freshwater. The process of making water starts in the engine room. We receive the hot water that has been heated from cooling the cylinders of the diesels. This hot saltwater arrives from the engine room at a temperature of about ninety degrees Fahrenheit and enters the Hamworthy Serck Como's desalination multistage flash evaporators. This process can produce three hundred thousand gallons a day."

Brick walked over to one of the flash evaporators and touched the side. He expected it to feel more than just warm.

"We use a water jacket around the FE to keep it cool, and then the warm saltwater is also redirected into the unit. I have three guys we call "the chemists"; they spend their time running quality checks on the water. You can see that we keep this area as secure as the bridge. When we do threat assessments, the water system always comes up, and I for one don't need any surprises. Let's go down another set of stairs and look at engine room one."

"Antonio, I expected to hear lots of noise down by the engines. Are those the diesels?"

"Oh, well, these are my sixteen-cylinder Wärtsiläs. There are three twelve-cylinder Wärtsiläs in room two. Each diesel is coupled to a generator. Each of those engines is a two-stroke, sixteen-cylinder diesel. Each cylinder is 460 millimeters, or 18.1 inches in diameter, and the stroke is 580 millimeters, or 23.5 inches long. We need to receive one thousand kilowatts from each cylinder. That is 16,800 kilowatts per engine. These diesels are the best and were made in Vaasa, Finland. We keep factory representatives rotating on about half of our cruises at any given time. The main concern with any large diesel? Keeping a close eye on the wear of the cylinder's jacket. My crew does its best to maintain the standard wear loss at less than .03 millimeters per one thousand hours of runtime. The trip from San Francisco to the islands takes 120 hours of engine time. That adds up very quickly, so we're constantly observing jacket wear.

"Brick, if you look at the starboard side of the ship, you'll see some seams or weld stripes that outline a big rectangle on the interior of the ship."

Brink looked to starboard and saw a faint weld outline where Antonio pointed.

"We call that a soft patch. Every five to seven years, we need to replace one or more engines, so we cut open that section of the hull. We cut out thousands of feet of pipes and cables and remove and replace the engines. Then we weld the soft patch back in place, pump out the water from the dry dock, and go on our way. But let me ask you: do you smell any diesel exhaust fumes?"

"No," replied Brick "I'm also surprised at how clean everything is in the engineering space."

"Thank you for noticing. We assign six men to do nothing but clean engine rooms one and two. These Wärtsiläs are cleaner now than when they arrived from Finland. Our key word is *fire*. I want to see any leaks of oil or diesel before we discover them the hard way. That's why everything is spotless. One of the challenges, Brick, is to move the exhaust up through fifteen decks. If you look at the blueprints of this ship, you'll see a channel about two-thirds of the way aft that extends from two decks below the waterline all the way to the stack collector. That twenty-foot diameter tube, or channel, collects the various exhaust pipes from our six diesels and runs to the highest point on the ship—the funnel, or exhaust stack."

Brick locked up, trying to imagine how many feet that extended.

"We have one more stop. Follow me."

"Where are we going?"

The prideful engineer smirked as he pointed to another catwalk and set of stairs and said, "We're going to the coolest place on the ship. We're going past engine room two and into Azipod country."

After navigating more stairs and catwalks, they came upon another door labeled "Secure Area—Limited Access Only." The engineering officer pulled out a gold key card and opened the door to a room that looked like something built by NASA. This was the farthest space aft on the ship. Brick observed no less than ten flat-screen monitors and three high-tech workstations. Antonio continued with Engineering 101.

"Below us, you will find the three Azipods that drive the *Matisse* through the water. Each pod contains a large motor attached to a four-blade propeller. What's unique is that the propeller is located in the front of the pod, and because we steer by turning the pods, we do not need a rudder. To put the size of these pods in perspective, each propeller is sixteen feet in diameter. The motors are so large that a man can climb inside the motor rotors—though that would be a bad idea for him while we're at sea, obviously. These controls over here are a backup system to the bridge. If there was ever a fire, or say an RPG wipes out all the white shirts on the bridge, we can control the

Azipods with these little controls here."

Realizing how much information he had thrown at his guest, Antonio clarified. "Mr. Brick, here's our executive summary. The six diesel engines spin the generators that create the electricity that run through those cables to the motors in the pods that turn the propellers."

Brick's mind cataloged every potential security loophole, though he would admit that he found almost none.

"I have to finish some reports," Antonio said. "Do you think you can find your way back to deck five?" Before Brick could answer in the affirmative, the engineer added, "Just kidding. Let's retrace our steps."

Once they were back on deck five, Brick offered to buy Antonio another coffee, but the officer confessed the tour already made him late for a staff meeting.

Brick decided to take his coffee and pay a visit to the Digital Experience, where he could research the terrorist group Lashkar-e-Aalam. Tucked into a fairly private booth, he pulled up the browser to access Ixquick, which advertised itself as the world's most private search engine. Adjusting his glasses, he leaned forward and started his research, oblivious to the young man two booths away from Aquarius 509.

Yusuf smiled when he logged in to "baseballfan999" and saw that the draft message was gone. Quickly, he created another message that he did not intend to send and saved it as another draft.

"Leader, we sail in six hours. Package will then be delivered. Baraka Allah. Thank you for this opportunity to serve."

Chapter Twenty-Three

"Radio, conn. We have arrived at position Delta. Operational depth fifty-eight feet. Commence elint search."

"Conn, radio. Roger. Permission to raise BSD-2?"

"Radio, conn. Raise BSD," replied the deck officer. "Radio, have the chief report to the conn."

"Roger," acknowledged the second class ITS.

Captain Theron Tower sat observing the diving officer as he carefully maintained a depth of fifty-eight feet. The captain's seat was located in a spot in the control room that previously would have stored the large cylinder making up the bottom of the periscope. The *North Dakota* SSN-784 did not have a periscope; instead, the Virginia-class submarine contained two AN/BVS-1 photonic masts. Located outside the pressure hull, these masts eliminated the need for the large steel tubes that penetrated the hull in the older class subs.

The *North Dakota* had just completed the transit from New London, Connecticut, to the Strait of Gibraltar without incident. As usual, the Russians kept one of their improved Akula nuclear-powered attack submarines as well as a Vishnya-class intelligence collection ship stationed between Tangier and Gibraltar.

The superb passive sonar on the *North Dakota* was able to pick up and identify the Akula, even though the Russian sub secured its seven-blade propeller and activated the two OK-300 electric propulsors. The *Dakota*'s sonar station, located on the port side of the control room, could still track the Akula, though. The new BSY-2 wraparound antenna, past of the state-of-the-art passive sonar and the signature library, analyzed the unique sounds of the Akula's propulsor and identified the sub as the Gepard K-335.

Captain Tower proceeded as cautiously with this electronic

intelligence mission as he would on their next mission deep into the waters of Syria. Elint like this that could be secured from the waters off of Tunisia were of great interest to the NSA.

Even though Tunisia claimed territorial waters out to twelve nautical miles, Captain Tower maneuvered the SSN-784 to within five miles of the coast. The digital navigation charts indicated that the continental shelf of the African plate made for shallow water in the whole Gulf of Gabes, specifically no deeper than six hundred feet.

The sub's chief information systems technician left the radio room and approached the captain. "Chief, I'm going to try to stay on station for two hours, but this area is as busy as an Irish bar on Saint Patrick's Day. Sonar is tracking a dozen fishing boats in this area. Seems that sponges, tuna, and terrorism are big business here. Captain, the guys want to raise the AN/WLR-IH."

"Okay, but if we get company, I want to go with a clean sail. No need to have eight masts sticking up in the middle of the Tunisian and Libyan fishing fleets," replied the *Dakota*'s CO as he stood and approached the chart table.

"Thank you, sir," acknowledged the technician.

The sail of the Virginia-class submarine had room for eight different masts. The groups of masts were divided between the photonic masts, the HDR mast for satellite communications, and communications antennas contained in the OE-538. The remaining masts supported the BLQ-10 ESM system. What made the *North Dakota* such a valuable asset was its ability to quietly sneak into shallow water, raise one or two masts, and suck electronic information right out of the air.

NSA needed data on the terrorist groups that had set up shop in North Africa. This spot in the Gulf of Gabes was only six hundred miles from Algeria. NSA sources maintained that terrorist groups operating out of northern Mali were also moving in and out of Algeria. The sub's mast captured a full range of frequencies, but more importantly, it read GSM bands used by cell phones. There are fourteen different bands ranging from 380.2 megahertz, or MHz, to 1,929.8 MHz, but African cell phones usually operated in the nine- and eighteen-hundred MHz range.

The ship's intelligence officer on the *Dakota* entered the top-secret codes and readied the SSIXS for a burst-data transmission through the HRD antenna. SSIXS was the acronym for Submarine Satellite Information Exchange Sub-System, a part of the Navy High Ultra High Frequency Satellite Communication System. The two hours of data collected from the backyard of North Africa would be in the hands of the National Security Agency analysts in minutes.

The deck officer reviewed his watch orders and soon ordered the 377-foot, $2.4 billion submarine to return to safe waters. "Make depth one hundred feet, course 085, speed ten knots."

"Radio, lowering all masts." Three of the large flat-screen monitors still displayed video from the photonic mast, then only water was visible and the monitors went blank as the AN/BVS-1 was lowered into its housing in the middle of the *Dakota*'s sail.

As the nuclear attack submarine changed course and depth to sneak out of Tunisia's territorial waters, the executive officer of the boat entered the control room and approached the captain. "Theron, were the intel guys able to find any electrons?" asked the XO.

"They think they got a lot of local cellular plus a variety of data from the frequencies used by Tunisian military," answered the captain. "XO, you will get a kick out of this. Look at this chart of the coast of Tunisia and Libya. In 1969, my father was an E-5 quartermaster on an old diesel sub called the *Sea Owl*. It was SS405."

"Captain, I didn't know you were a second-generation bubblehead!"

"Yep, my dad said they were going through the Mediterranean in transit to Greece. It turned out that several months prior to their Mediterranean trip, a group of military officers staged a coup d'état against the king of Libya. The senior officer in charge of the coup was only twenty-seven, and he declared that the territorial waters would

HIGH SEAS DARKNESS

be two hundred miles. My dad, the acting navigator, told me that it was a real big deal to make sure they didn't test the Libyan's claim of those two hundred miles. You've got to remember, we were in the middle of the Cold War, and this was about a year after the *Scorpion* was lost. And that twenty-seven-year-old army officer? Muammar Gaddafi. Is that a cool story or what?"

"How long did your dad stay on the boats?"

Captain Tower walked over to a sonar waterfall. "I think a couple of years. Then he joined New York Life and spent a career in life insurance."

The *North Dakota* turned right and steered a new course of 110.

Only a thousand miles away, Zaeem Hasan Al-Ajmi sat down to meet with his chief chemist, Faroug Hasan Ahmed. "Faroug, in a few hours we will learn, if Allah wills, whether your poison will kill the infidels."

"Zaeem, it is not a poison. The test will involve a cytotoxin called abrin. I extracted the powder from the rosary pea. I pray that Yusuf will be careful with this test. Abrin is very dangerous. If he inhales any dust or swallows as much as a grain of salt, he will die. May Allah, peace be upon Him, reward our Yusuf for the good."

"Faroug, we will pray that he is successful and returns safely so we may do our small and humble part in carrying out our jihad to rid the world of Israel and the Western infidels."

"Zaeem, with all respect, cannot we help establish a worldwide Islamic order without all the killing?"

"Faroug, you are speaking the nonsense of your Shia wife. This would never happen if you had married an obedient Sunni woman. When you go home tonight, you must beat her as never before for feeding you, my chief chemist, these stupid thoughts."

"I am sorry, Zaeem. I seek Allah's forgiveness."

Chapter Twenty-Four

"This is Captain Costanzo," boomed the speakers throughout the *Matisse Under the Stars*. "I hope everyone enjoyed our day on Hawaii's Big Island. We have a surprise tonight. The weather is cooperating, so I am going to delay our transit to Ensenada for an hour so you can observe the beauty of the volcano Kilauea. Once the *Matisse* clears the breakwater of Hilo Bay, we will steer course 135 degrees until we are adjacent of Cape Kumukahi. We will then turn starboard and follow course 225 degrees along the southeast coast. Kilauea has an elevation of 4,190 feet above sea level, is the most active of all volcanoes, and has its own magma source. Hopefully, we will have a spectacular fireworks show. As a reminder, the *Matisse* will continue our practice of keeping the ship's lights at low intensity while near the coast in our effort to cooperate with the Hawaiian environmental efforts with regard to light pollution and the native bird population. Please enjoy the evening."

Closing and locking the door to cabin A-509, Yusuf reached under his bed, pulled out his suitcase, and placed it on the bed. He examined the zipper to ascertain if the small piece of tape was still in place. Satisfied that nobody had gone through his property, he unzipped the case and removed an MSA Safety Works toxic dust respirator. Yusuf hoped that the dust of the abrin powder was not smaller than .3 microns. The instructions for the mask indicated that particles of .2 microns or less would not be filtered.

Faroug had explained that abrin was many times more lethal than ricin. With the understanding that this was a test of both the toxin and the method of distribution, they agreed that Yusuf should dilute the potent toxin. The goal was to try to limit the deaths to fewer than twenty and sicken no more than a hundred so as to minimize the global reaction to the incident. It would be perfect if a violent strain of the Norovirus were blamed. With excitement, Yusuf mentally calculated the possibilities of a simultaneous attack on many ships, not with a diluted toxin but a disbursement of the pure powder.

Selecting a hooded sweatshirt with a zipper, Yusuf removed his American-style T-shirt and put on the hoodie. After entering the four numbers on the keypad to the cabin safe, the locking mechanism clicked open. He put on the respirator and a pair of rubber gloves and removed a flint-glass vial with a screw cap from the safe. He carefully carried the fourteen-milliliter vial into the bathroom and poured the full contents of the vial into a glass. Next, he added about a teaspoon of salt to the abrin and rolled a piece of toilet paper into a tight, long paper stick and used that to stir the mixture. When complete, he flushed the contaminated paper down the toilet. Using a copy of a Hilo excursion trip flyer, he fashioned a makeshift funnel and carefully poured the diluted abrin back into the glass vial.

Without removing his respirator, Yusuf turned on the water and let it run into the toxic glass while he ripped up the flyer and flushed it down the toilet. With equal care, he washed and removed the rubber gloves.

The Gallery Grill and Food Court was almost empty as many of the passengers were on the starboard side of the ship watching the glowing lava flow into the sea. Yusuf had read that Kilauea is the home of the Hawaiian goddess Pele. Maybe goddess Pele would bless his important work. With a ball cap tilted down and his hood up, he paused at the hand sanitizer and applied a single application of the gel. After being handed a plate, he entered the food court.

Yusuf sat his plate on the buffet plate rails and discreetly removed the vial from the front pocket of his sweatshirt, unscrewed the lid, and poured the yellow-brown powder onto his plate. Within five seconds, he had transformed himself into a weapon of mass destruction. With practice, Yusuf Al Omar had learned how to hold his breath for seventy seconds; he estimated that he had sixty seconds left.

Avoiding the closed-circuit cameras, he headed to the salad bar and located the Caesar salad dressing. Picking up the dressing ladle, he placed his plate over the bowl and sprinkled the toxin into the dressing. When he replaced the ladle, he nonchalantly stirred the deadly mixture into the bowl. Quickly, he placed some lettuce on his dusty plate and dumped an ample amount of Thousand Island dressing on top to cover any residual powder.

After setting down his plate, Yusuf walked about five feet away, looked at a plate of chocolate chip cookies, and took a deep breath. Returning to the stainless steel rails where he had left his plate, he picked it up from the bottom and left the buffet area. Yusuf found a table, set his plate down, and walked to the coffee, tea, and water center. While filling a glass of water, he allowed a generous amount of the water to spill over his hand that had handled the glass tube.

Yusuf did not return to the table. Instead, he left the food court, walked by the Galileo pool and Big Dipper Bar, and went directly into the deck fourteen lavatory. With a paper towel, he removed the empty vial from his hoodie and dumped it in the garbage. Five minutes later, he was still washing his hands. Satisfied that his hands were finally sterile, he then proceeded to rinse out his nose and wash his face in the sink.

Since the lavatory was empty, Yusuf chose a handicap stall and closed the door. From his back pocket, he pulled out a large plastic Ziploc bag that contained a black T-shirt that said "New York Yankees" across the front. Unzipping his sweatshirt, and using extreme caution, he removed it and placed it on the hook on the stall door. After putting on the T-shirt, he rolled up the sweatshirt and jammed it into the plastic bag. When he left the lavatory, he had disposed of the shirt and hat and had rewashed his hands.

While Yusuf was making his escape from deck fourteen, another passenger was dealing with his own issues. Kyle Throckmorton was a little pissed that because of the volcano sightseeing detour the casino would not open for another hour. It had been four days since the casino had been opened because the four islands that the ship visited were all inside the territorial waters of the United States. Kyle had seen his fill of volcanoes on the Discovery Channel, so he decided to hit the food court for some prime rib. After loading his plate with meat and a dose of straight horseradish, he figured that he needed to be healthy and have some rabbit food. Using tongs, he piled romaine leaves next to his prime rib and covered the romaine with a ladle of Caesar dressing.

Chapter Twenty-Five

The Nebulae Prime Steakhouse was a specialty restaurant on the ship by reservation only. As Yvette entered the Equinox Disco on deck six and walked down the beautiful brass spiral staircase to the Nebulae's entrance on deck five, she hoped to find Brick alone. Instead, she found his ear being talked off by the ship's art auctioneer, Rick Lansteiner, and his newest high-profile artist find, the world-famous Eastern European Antonina Kartashov. As much as Yvette appreciated that Rick's job was to wine and dine artists in addition to bringing in $150,000 in art sales each cruise, she found his aggressiveness more akin to a used car salesman. She marveled that Brick, however, found himself at ease with anyone from any deck on the ship.

Earlier, Rick had approached Yvette and explained that Antonina Kartashov had asked if Yvette and "that Morgan guy" would join them for dinner at the Nebulae.

"Rick, 'that Morgan guy' has a first name. It's Brick, and he owns Morgan Maritime Investigations."

"I know that. I was being funny. I've known Brick for two years."

When Yvette asked Brick, he agreed, saying he liked Rick and art, just not as much as he liked music.

The Nebulae was one of seven upscale venues that charged an additional seating fee of twenty-five dollars per person, which served as another revenue source.

The waiter, Sergio, first asked the ladies for their orders.

Antonina handed her menu to him. "I will have the small bacon-wrapped filet, asparagus, and house salad. No dressing, please."

"How would you like your filet?"

"Medium rare," replied Antonina with the sexiest of accents.

"Officer Fuentes, what would you like tonight?"

"Top sirloin, medium, sautéed mushrooms, and house salad with Thousand."

Sergio turned to Brick. "Mr. Detective, I am honored to serve you tonight."

"Sergio, Brick Morgan. Glad to meet you. I'll have the small filet, medium, the mushrooms, and a cup of soup, please."

"And Mr. Rick?"

"I will have the rib eye, medium, asparagus, and small Caesar. Please check back in a few minutes after I have had an opportunity to review the wine list."

Antonina had tea, so the two bottles of Château Lynch-Bages were more than enough for Rick, Brick, and Yvette. Throughout the meal, they talked about art and Antonina's life in the Ukraine and her immigration to France. But as the wine flowed, Antonina took the conversation in a different direction.

Clutching Brick's arm, she purred, "Mr. Morgan, you are quite the celebrity yourself, according to Rick."

Yvette bristled visibly. She knew Brick had no problem flirting, but she felt that she'd shared him enough this evening already.

"Only in small circles, I promise," Brick deflected.

"But you are the hero here, no? Come to help the lost crew with all these cruel and diabolical assaults? Certainly, you must have some salacious stories of your own."

"We're actually far from lost," Yvette said. "Mr. Morgan's here to aid us, but we are more than capable of handling the issue."

"You mean the rape, Yvette?" asked Rick.

"How did you hear about that? That's not common knowledge."

"Everything's common knowledge on a ship," Rick corrected her. "I may only be the art auctioneer, but everyone knows that Brick doesn't show up for dumb stuff like stewards swiping earrings. How hard is that?"

Yvette politely restrained herself. "Actually, Rick, we prefer to keep a lid on ongoing investigations unless they represent a clear and present danger to the ship."

"Of course, Yvette. No one's asking for names. But certainly Mr. Morgan could tease some sordid details . . . for me?" Antonina cooed, locking eyes with Yvette.

"Oh, it's nothing polite enough for dinner conversation. And really, I'm only here to help Yvette. If anyone's got stories, it's her. She's worked with the San Diego police for years."

"Ugh," Antonina said. "San Diego is just so . . . well, you know . . ."

Yvette had had enough. "I'm certain it's not as glitzy as the places you've been. Then again, I know a lot of 'working girls' in the Ukraine end up there. I wonder if you might remember them from your previous life?"

Brick and Rick grew uneasy. They didn't expect this kind of tension over their steaks. But Brick knew that Yvette could handle herself. Drug dealers or artists, it made no difference to her. She could stare down a statue.

After a chilly moment, Antonina laughed unexpectedly. "You certainly give as good as you get, Ms. Fuentes. Mr. Morgan had best keep his eye on you."

"Everyone should," Brick added. He winked at Yvette.

The meal then took a turn for the better. Afterward, Rick insisted that he pick up the check. Normally, Brick would never have allowed a crew member to pay for dinner, but the auctioneer was second only to the captain in compensation. And it only seemed fair that Rick take the extra step toward smoothing things over between all parties. The last thing anyone wanted was a disaster.

One deck above the Nebulae and closer to the bow was the ship's casino where Kyle Throckmorton was moving between three different dollar slot machines. For the first two hours, he warmed up on the quarter machines and was up about fifty dollars. He preferred a machine that did not penalize him if he did not play the maximum amount. He had just inserted a hundred-dollar bill in the slot and was waiting for the credits to show on the screen. Kyle's theory was that luck runs in streaks, so if he had a winning pull, he would then double his bet and hope to have two wins in a row.

Kyle stayed with his system and was thrilled when he had three wins in a row. His first bet was for a dollar, and that win resulted in twenty credits. The next bet he placed was for two dollars, and that win gave him one hundred dollars. He increased his bet to three dollars and won again, this time receiving sixty credits. Looking at the total credits, he noticed that he had won $220 dollars. He pushed his key card into the machine and selected the choice that downloaded the money from the machine's bank to his card.

Feeling like a big winner, Kyle decided to grab a mai tai from the casino bar and return to his cabin. As the bartender finished making the drink, Kyle said, "Skip the umbrella, please."

Walking out of the casino, he was struck by stomach cramps and an urgent need to find a restroom. *What did I just eat?* The king of the dollar slots barely made it into the bathroom stall before his bowels let loose. After washing his hands, he made a fast return to the toilet he had used five minutes before and vomited. "Fuck," he muttered, wondering if he could make it to his cabin.

When Kyle entered his cabin a few minutes later, he bolted to the bathroom and threw himself at the toilet.

Norovirus is the trend name of acute gastroenteritis and is the result of severe inflammation of the stomach and intestines. The most common symptoms are diarrhea, vomiting, nausea, and stomach pain. The most common symptoms of abrin poisoning, caused by the toxin penetrating the cells of the body and inhibiting cell protein synthesis, are diarrhea, vomiting, nausea, and stomach pain, which mimic those of Norovirus. If the dosage is concentrated enough, severe dehydration will result and blood pressure will plummet. After two or three days, the person's kidneys, spleen, and liver will stop working, and the patient will die.

The medical center on the *Matisse* was located in the center of the great ship on deck four. The *Matisse* was proud that two medical doctors and four registered nurses staffed the facility.

Nobility had made maritime medicine a priority and had dedicated considerable shipboard space and technology to provide the passengers and crew with the best medical care. The center had a lab and diagnostic area and equipment to perform blood analysis testing for liver and kidney function and heart enzyme levels. It had a two-bed intensive care unit, a seldom-used surgery unit, and a six-bed hospital ward. The center also had a pharmacy and two examination rooms.

The medical center was closed when the purser's office received an emergency call from Mrs. Throckmorton at 1:00 in the morning. Within five minutes, Nurse Mercado had arrived with a wheelchair at Kyle's cabin, and together with his wife, they rushed him down to deck four. When they arrived, Dr. Jose Resende had already turned on the lights and was waiting in examination room one.

Fifteen minutes later, Dr. Resende invited Mrs. Throckmorton into the exam room. "I want a complete blood testing, but this has all the signs of a Norovirus case. I must say that I am surprised at how fast it has progressed because the ship has been free of Noro on this trip. We have been waiting for the new and more persistent Australian strain called GII.4 to show up. I hope that this is not what your husband has. The good news is that the symptoms will be gone in two to three days. The most important and critical thing you can do is keep Mr. Throckmorton hydrated."

While wheeling Kyle back to his cabin, Nurse Mercado explained to Mrs. Throckmorton the quarantine protocol and the best type of liquid and food to speed recovery from the Norovirus.

Nurse Mercado returned the wheelchair to the medical center at 1:45 a.m. and found two more very sick passengers along with two lights flashing on the phone console. By 3:00 a.m., Dr. Pedro Ramos, the senior medical director, and the three other nurses had joined Dr. Resende.

At 3:45 a.m., Dr. Ramos made the dreaded call to the bridge. "Martin, this is Dr. Ramos. We have a near full center, and they are still calling and arriving. Looks like GII.4 Noro. I am declaring a code orange!"

Chapter Twenty-Six

"Rick, good morning. This is Brick."

"Hi, Brick. We had fun last night," replied the ship's auctioneer.

"Thank you for picking up that huge tab. That was very kind of you. Would it be possible for me to check out any originals you have of Antonina's art?"

"Let me know what works for you, and I will meet you on deck five."

"I'm going to hit the gym for about an hour and half. How about eleven?"

As Brick changed into a pair of shorts and a T-shirt, he considered the next four days at sea. He could not remember the last time he took a vacation. He was looking forward to sipping Grand Marnier on deck six while listening to jazz or piano music from the Great American Songbook.

The gym and fitness center was located next to the beauty salon on the forward part of deck fifteen. The aerobics center was a large room situated next to all of the free weights, resistance machines, elliptical machines, and exercise bikes. After an hour of working out, Brick took advantage of the empty aerobics room to focus on a series of solo judo drills. These could be performed on a mat without a partner and consisted of break falling, rolling, mat pulls, and reverse bicycles.

Brick had noticed the smell of chlorine when he walked from the Bootes deck up to the fitness center. He did not think much about it at the time, but now he noticed crew members using a stronger cleaning agent to re-clean handrails he thought he saw being cleaned earlier. Brick had been on so many ships that he was certain he was observing crew activity that would only occur if the ship were under code orange. He had to meet Rick at the art center, so he reminded himself to ask him if he had heard of any cases of the Norovirus.

The majority of the cruise lines use the same vessel-sanitation program, and the Nobility Cruise Line was no exception. When there have not been any Norovirus cases reported, the *Matisse* operated under code green. When four or more cases were diagnosed, the ship would set code orange.

Code orange involves several procedures and steps to sanitize the ship to stop the virus from spreading and causing a code red. If a crew member contracts Norovirus, he and his roommate are both quarantined for forty-eight hours. The food court buffets are covered with Saran Wrap, and the food is served by crew members. Sealed individual packets replace condiments, such as ketchup and mustard. Hundreds of crew members are called on to wipe down every surface that is touchable by passengers. Each member of the cleaning crew is assigned three buckets, each a different color. One bucket contains clean water, another is for dirty water, and the third contains a special cleaning solvent. During code orange, the concentration of chlorine is doubled.

In the unfortunate case where 2 percent of the ship's population contracts Norovirus, the ship will be required to set code red. The magic number for the *Matisse* would be eighty-eight. If eighty-eight out of the 4,400 members of the ship became sick with the Norovirus, CDC must be notified immediately and code red would be declared.

From the perspective of the crew, a declared code red would be a living hell. Not only would the crew be operating in sleep-deprivation mode, but also the crew's mess would be shut down except for bins of sticky rice and bread rolls. The crew would not be allowed to serve themselves, and the security team would be posted to make sure that tongs and protective gloves were the order of the day. The food court on deck fourteen would be secured, and passengers would only be allowed to eat in dining rooms. Cleaning crews would clean and re-clean every handrail, toilet, and faucet, and the fitness center and special outdoor buffets would all be closed. Strict quarantine rules would be enforced, and the crew would have to wear latex hand protection when in contact with a sick passenger.

In the event of a code red, the most important rule that must be followed is the completion of the AGE report. Under the vessel sanitation program, the ship must send to CDC an Acute Gastroenteritis Surveillance Log.

While Brick was meeting with Rick, the medical team on deck four was being swamped with more and more new cases of passengers who had become violently ill.

Dr. Ramos walked into the exam room where Dr. Resende was finishing another diagnosis. "Jose, we are at sixty-eight. I have never seen over fifty cases in the first twelve hours of an outbreak. We might be at 2 percent in an hour or two."

Dr. Resende looked up from his initial evaluation form. "We might as well move to Red and get ahead of the power curve."

"No, some bean counter in Florida would raise shit because we did not have eighty-eight cases."

Nurse Mercado rushed from the intensive care room, getting the attention of the senior medical director.

"Dr. Ramos, passenger Throckmorton is slipping. Looks to me like he is having both kidney and liver failure. I have the lab doing another test of enzymes." Just then the lab technician handed Dr. Ramos the results.

"Nurse, you are correct," said Dr. Ramos. "His liver is off the chart for SGOT, alk phos, and SGPT. Kidneys not much better. Microalbumin/creatinine ratio 116. The failure of his organs is unusual for acute dehydration of only twelve hours. My guess is that he had the Norovirus long before his wife called us. All we can do is keep him on IV drip and hope that his cells start absorbing the Lactated Ringers."

Dr. Ramos stuck his head in exam room two and waved for Dr. Resende to join him. "Jose, I am going to call the director of fleet medical for an update and then suggest that the captain announce code orange."

During the next several hours, only one more passenger was diagnosed with the Norovirus symptoms. Captain Costanzo made a ship-wide announcement, urging everyone to use all of the hand-sanitizer equipment and spend a minimum of thirty-two seconds washing his or her hands.

Dr. Ramos looked up at a clock mounted on a wall above a cabinet filled with medical supplies. In Throckmorton's file inside the box labeled "Time of Death," he wrote: 16:15.

Chapter Twenty-Seven

The sudden knock on his cabin door startled Yusuf. "Mr. Omar, is this a good time to refresh your room?"

Why does this guy hang around so much? Yusuf thought. *First he cleans the room in the morning, and then he refreshes it in the late afternoon, and now the jerk wants to turn down my bed and give me candy.*

"Yes, Dakila, come on in."

This might be a gift from Allah, Yusuf mused. *Maybe if I am nice to him, I can learn what is happening on the ship and the results of the abrin.*

"Dakila, I want to tell you how pleased I am with your hard work."

"Thank you, Mr. Omar," replied Dakila Salazar with a big smile.

"How long have you worked for Nobility Cruise?"

"This is my third cruise. My brother Bayani was on the Italian cruise ship *Costa Concordia* when it sank." Dakila turned down Yusuf's bed and picked up some dirty towels.

"Oh," replied Yusuf. "Is he okay?"

"Thank you, yes. Actually, I am trying to get him a job on the *Matisse*."

"I heard the captain speak to the ship this afternoon. Are there a lot of sick passengers?"

"Yes, sir. We are on code orange. I understand that over sixty passengers are sick and was told that one passenger died."

Yusuf decided he would push a bit more. "What do they think caused all the people to get sick?"

"Our deck supervisor said it was the Norovirus."

Yusuf was beside himself with excitement. He was anxious for the room steward to leave so he could inform Zaeem about the success of the test.

HIGH SEAS DARKNESS

As soon as Dakila left, Yusuf logged onto his Gmail account and drafted a message announcing the success of the abrin. He hoped that Zaeem would instruct Faroug Hasan Ahmed to manufacture enough of the toxin so he and four others could obliterate all the passengers on five of these floating cities-ships that are the symbol of American and Israeli decadence.

Walking over to the blue curtains that covered the sliding door to the balcony, Yusuf's mind recalled his childhood in Lebanon. After opening the curtains, he reached into the mini-refrigerator and chose a can of ginger ale. Unlocking the latch to the balcony door, he pulled the door open and walked out to his small terrace. Looking down, he noticed that only about 10 percent of the balconies were occupied. Yusuf appreciated the Aquarius deck because there were not any cabins above him.

As he gazed out at the blue ocean water, he could not help but reflect back to the beauty of Lake Qaraooun and the canals that provided water to his father's vineyard. Numerous representatives of the Hezbollah movement occupied the southern part of Lebanon, but his father had ignored Hezbollah's recruiting efforts and focused his energy on building a business that his family could be proud of for generations to come. There were a dozen quality wineries in Lebanon, and his father's was one of those. His father and brother planted the native grapes of Merweh and Obaideh for the local favorite wine called Arak. They also had planted their vineyard with the upscale Viognier grape. His father had told Yusuf that he felt he might be awarded a gold medal for their Viognier wine.

Taking another sip of his ginger ale, Yusuf remembered the day that everything changed. His father was excited about their plans to upgrade the irrigation drip system that moved water from the canal to each one of the vines. All that was needed were twenty regulator valves that were waiting at a farming store in the city of Zahle. His brother and father were traveling north on the Beirut-Damascus Highway when they observed a small convoy traveling south.

The Israeli military had been trying to remove the top leadership of Hezbollah and had credible intelligence that two of Hezbollah's highly valued militants were leaving Zahle and driving in a four-car convoy to the Baqaa Valley. Working with the support of the United States, a drone *Predator* was deployed and spent three hours circling and waiting for the convoy. The command center observed a convoy, just as predicted, heading south on the Beirut-Damascus Highway.

It took less than a minute for the command center to arm and release the GBU-12 Paveway II. Just as Yusuf's father's northbound truck passed the southbound convoy, the laser-guided bomb unleashed five hundred pounds of Tritonal, which is 80 percent TNT and 20 percent powdered aluminum. With the circular error probable (CEP) of 3.6 feet, all the cars of the southbound convoy and the truck occupied by Yusuf's father and brother were disintegrated in a fraction of a second.

Patiently, Yusuf surfed the Internet to find a group he could join that had values similar to his own. It took him three months to discover a group of militant Islamists that he felt would be a correct fit. A month later, he had developed a relationship with the group that was headed by Zaeem Hasan Al-Ajmi. The infidels would call the death of his family "collateral damage." So be it. The death of twenty thousand passengers would also be "collateral damage."

While studying at the University of Beirut, Yusuf had taken a political science course on the writings of Machiavelli. He remembered one phrase from Machiavelli's discourse, which Yusuf took the liberty of making a few changes. After his family's death, this had become his mantra:

> Where the very safety of the mission to destroy Israel depends on the resolution to be considered, no consideration of justice or injustice, humanity, or cruelty should be allowed to prevail, the only question should be what course will save the life and liberty of the Islam faith?

Yusuf left the balcony and closed both the glass doors and the curtain. He must now take time for his daily prayers and thank Allah, the sacred and the mighty, for the success of yesterday's test.

Many decks below, the medical team was pausing from nearly twenty hours of nonstop pandemonium. Dr. Ramos, Dr. Resende, and Nurse Mercado walked out of the clinic and headed up to the crew's deck to get some fresh air and clear their heads.

"We are at seventy-four and holding," said Nurse Mercado.

"What is unique about this outbreak is how fast it spread and how fast it tapered off," Dr. Ramos said. "The normal spread capacity among the passengers and crew usually does not slow down until after thirty-six hours. This strain stopped after about twenty hours."

"It makes you think that all seventy-four had been exposed early in the day while on shore in Hilo," added Dr. Resende.

"Let's try to get some sleep and study in depth the history of the infected tomorrow," suggested Dr. Ramos.

Before retiring to his cabin, Dr. Ramos informed the captain that the ship would not need to declare a code red but that they would stay with code orange until the next morning.

As he walked up to his cabin on deck eight, Dr. Ramos tried to make sense of this Norovirus strain. Tomorrow he would review the Kaplan criteria for confirmation of Norovirus. He was extremely tired, but he recalled that the Kaplan criteria called for a mean incubation period of twenty-four to forty-eight hours. This strain had an incubation period of twelve hours. "Strange," he said aloud as he entered his cabin.

Chapter Twenty-Eight

Deck fourteen was not just home to the Big Dipper Bar and the food court; it also bragged of having the best hamburgers on the high seas. Brick was just finishing his second burger when Yvette pulled up a chair. "Those things are going to kill you, Mr. Morgan."

"Young lady, I would like you to know that I was the first person in the fitness center this morning. And one other thing. The Latin word *incidere* means, "to cut." In English, that word translates to incisor, the first four teeth in the front of our mouth. The upper incisors are called the premaxilla, and the lower ones are the mandibles. The *Homo sapiens neanderthalenis* had incisors and canine teeth. Man has these teeth to cut and tear into the lions and the tigers that we catch. Man was created by God to eat meat, not rabbit food. Would you like some of my French fries?"

"Morgan, you are crazy, but I kind of like you," replied Yvette as she took one of his fries, dipped it in his ketchup, and suggestively pulled it into and out of her pursed lips.

"What is the latest on the ship's medical emergency?" inquired Brick as he fed Yvette another French fry the same way she had teased him a minute before.

"A couple of hours ago, I ran into Dr. Ramos while getting some coffee in the officers' mess. He said that the number of sick had stopped at seventy-four, but one of the first to be diagnosed had died. They are testing blood, stool, and vomit for any bacteria that could be the cause."Yvette saw the puzzled look on Brick's face. "You don't like my answer."

"No, it isn't that. I just assumed that they declared this issue a Norovirus episode."

"I asked the same question. Ramos said that there were a few aberrations with this encounter. He said the onset was too fast and about the time the outbreak should have been going up logarithmically, it just stopped."

Brick gave some thought to her answer and then asked her about her dinner plans. "How about you and I returning to the Nebulae Prime Steakhouse—just the two of us—for a nice romantic dinner?"

"I'll make the reservations," replied Yvette as she stole one more French fry. "I have to get back to work."

"Do me a favor. Would you snoop around with the medical people and try to get an update on the virus?"

"Will do. I'll make a reservation for about seven thirty."

Dr. Ramos was reviewing some of the lab reports from the analysis of samples from patients. "Jose, when you get a minute, I would like to compare notes on the Kaplan criteria."

Before 1982, the medical profession had difficulty distinguishing outbreaks that were due to Norovirus and those due to bacterial etiology. When the Kaplan criteria were established, the credibility of diagnoses rose to 90 percent. The four criteria are:

1. Illness duration of twelve to sixty hours;
2. Illness incubation period of twenty-four to forty-eight hours;
3. More than 50 percent of people with vomiting;
4. No bacterial agents found.

Actual testing for Norovirus is a specialized analysis and is only carried out in a special laboratory. The human Norovirus cannot be grown in a cell culture; however, the key to a diagnosis is to detect RNA or antigen. The test uses real-time reverse transcription-polymerase chain reaction, or (RT-qPCR) assays.

"Pedro, when you were practicing in Valencia, did the internists rely on Kaplan to firm up a gastroenteritis diagnosis?"

Dr. Ramos leaned back in his chair and closed his eyes for a long fifteen seconds. "No, we were pretty fast to diagnose any intestinal or stomach inflammation as just stomach flu. My brother, who still practices at HM Universitario Sanchinarro, told me they use Kaplan criteria. They have a big World Health Organization grant for the study of how a virus gets enclosed inside a coat of protein, so it is important for his hospital to differentiate between virus and bacterial agents where the DNA and RNA float freely in cytoplasm."

Dr. Ramos again closed his eyes but continued his discussion with Dr. Resende. "Jose, I read where 30 percent of outbreaks do not fit the Kaplan criteria. I used our Vision V 4000 microscope and found no signs of unusual bacteria in about ten stool samples. The duration criterion was closer to ten hours than the twelve to sixty hours. What doesn't fit," he opened his eyes to narrow slits, "is the incubation period. Kaplan calls for twenty-four to forty-eight hours, and our outbreak took off in twelve to eighteen hours and then just stopped."

Dr. Resende stood up and rubbed his chin. "I am comfortable writing this up as Norovirus, and with regards to Throckmorton, he died of acute dehydration. His condition might have been caused by a weakened immune system."

Dr. Ramos opened his eyes all the way and got up from his desk. "I agree. I will call the fleet medical director and bring him up to date and prepare the report for CDC."

Yvette returned to her desk in the security office and began reviewing her department's schedule for the next few days. She figured she would need another hour at her desk and then would make some inquiries in medical.

The phone rang. Yvette noticed it was hotel management. The crew's jobs are sometimes divided up between the engineering and security department, the food and beverage department, and the hotel department.

"Security office, Officer Fuentes."

"This is Mary Hernandez in housekeeping. Our cabin steward working on the Draco deck called and said one of her cabins has a bird living with the two guests assigned to that cabin."

Yvette wanted to laugh, but she was determined to act professional. "Did the steward think the bird flew in the cabin window or balcony door?"

"No, she thinks someone in the cabin snuck the bird onboard."

After getting the cabin number, Yvette thought this would be a great assignment for Raju.

"Raju, you are wanted on Draco."

The deputy security officer walked over to Yvette's desk, and she handed him a note with "D-543" written on it. Beneath it were two words: *Bird Lady*.

"Housekeeping thinks that D-543 is keeping a pet bird in their cabin," explained Yvette.

"I am on my way. Should I check out one of the Remington 870s?"

"I'll keep the shotguns locked up for now, but you might want to swing by the galley for some bird seed," fired back Yvette.

Raju headed to the office door and then stopped and turned back to Yvette. "I march to the cabin of birds / To save the guests of the great ships. / My love for my job is not only words, / I march forward with my wings and your beautiful lips."

With a big grin, Raju headed to cabin D-543, determined to save the lives of the passengers on the *Matisse Under the Stars*.

Chapter Twenty-Nine

Senator Michelle Murphy had crossed the Capitol and walked down to the basement of the Longworth Office Building, or as named by many, "The Trough." Senator Murphy had a meeting with the Speaker of the House and another high-level government official, and she had told Speaker Daniel that she would pick up some buffalo chicken wraps.

The Longworth House Office Building was completed in 1933 and was one of three buildings designed and built for the United States House of Representatives. The Longworth Building's architecture was designed as an example of Neoclassical Revival style as compared to the Cannon Building that has a style of theatrical Beaux-Arts. The LHOB has twelve committee rooms and a large assembly room that is now used by the Ways and Means Committee. Two hundred-plus congressional suites are located on the top three floors of the four-floor building. The largest and most famous suite is reserved for the Speaker of the House.

Speaker Martin Daniel was behind closed doors with a very important government dignitary when the Speaker's staff announced the arrival of Senator Murphy. Speaker Daniel pulled himself out of a large, gold upholstered wing chair and walked across the large private office and greeted the senator.

"I brought nourishment for our honored guest," said Senator Murphy.

"Thank you Michelle. I am honored to be in the company of the top leadership of both the House and Senate," the guest replied as he stood to shake hands with her.

Speaker Daniel walked over to a highly polished credenza and added additional coffee to his china cup. "Let me kick-start this discussion.

The president seems committed to advancing his agenda of embracing the Islamist movement. Let me clarify my last remark. First, we have the word *Islam,* and I think we are all comfortable with the meaning of that word. When I use the word *Islamists,* I am referring to those of the Muslim faith who are committed to spreading Islam and replacing governments and, in our case, replacing the constitution with Sharia law. These Islamists believe that society is best served and governed by Sharia law. When I use the words *militant Islamists,* I am referring to those who advocate the use of violence and force to establish Sharia."

"Speaker, I wish we could get more people in DC to agree to use those terms. It would make communication so much easier, but then we would be upsetting the PC police," the Speaker's guest added.

Martin continued. "I believe that POTUS does not advocate violence or is even in favor of Sharia law taking a hold in our country. But I think the problem is that the president does not have any idea how to deal with the jihadist movement and hopes that if he sends signals of a moderate approach to the terrorists, they will not attack the United States until his term is over."

Senator Murphy leaned forward and added her opinions as if they were clear facts. "Gentlemen, the major problem with his approach is that our security infrastructure continues to get weaker and weaker each day. His insistence that all terrorist acts be defined as anything other than a word that might offend the Muslim community is undermining our counterterrorism organizations."

Standing up, the Speaker's guest walked over to the credenza and popped open a Diet Pepsi. "That is why I came to Capitol Hill. We are having serious morale and attrition problems in our major departments. I know that a large number of analysts at the National Security Agency are leaving, and the FBI and CIA are all fighting a battle to deal with an epidemic of poor morale. I do not want to be an alarmist, but I think in the next twelve to eighteen months our ability to deal with future terrorism will be nonexistent. We might be able to keep our young talent for a few more years, but the core talent, those who have the most experience, are already taking early retirement and joining the private sector. Every time the administration denies there is still terrorism, our agencies receive a dozen resignations. The CIA and NSA have lost the most agents and analysts."

"Are we in agreement that we cannot just wait for the president's current term to end?" asked Speaker Daniel.

Both Senator Murphy and the visitor nodded in agreement. Then the visitor added his solution. "We are not going to change the philosophies or core values of this POTUS. He understands only social issues and his agenda of wealth redistribution. He is so far over his head with regard to foreign policy and the expansion of the al-Qaeda movement that he could not contribute to the solution even if he wanted to. We have to either start a movement toward impeachment or find a smoking gun that can act as a hammer to blackmail or strong-arm him into changing his direction and turning counterterrorism back to the agencies."

The meeting continued for another twenty minutes before the visitor was directed to a door that allowed this well-known official to leave the Longworth House Office Building discreetly.

Chapter Thirty

Sergio, the senior waiter, was anxiously waiting for the VIPs. He had reserved a nice table for two in one of the private corners of the steakhouse.

As Brick and Yvette entered the Nebulae Prime Steakhouse, they were flanked by the maître d' and Sergio. After an abundance of pomp and circumstance, they were finally seated.

"Mr. Morgan and Officer Fuentes, may I bring you something to drink this evening?"

Yvette was the first to reply. "Sergio, I will have a Yellow Bird." She quickly put her hand on his arm. "I am joking. How about a White Russian, please?"

"Does the Nebulae have any special bourbon?" asked Brick.

"The good bourbon is stocked in the Comet Lounge. I can run down to deck six if you like."

"No, no; that is not necessary. Bring me what you have here. No ice, please. Just pour some bourbon in a glass."

A few minutes later, Sergio arrived with the drinks and a plate of fried calamari. "My treat. I hope you like calamari."

"Wow," Brick said. "Thank you. It is one of my favorites."

"Sorry about the bourbon. I had some Maker's Mark. I did not have their good stuff, just the bottle called Maker's 46, so I poured you a double."

"Sergio, Maker's 46 is the real good stuff. This is perfect, thank you."

"Brick, this afternoon I assigned Raju to a very special assignment. He went to the Draco deck to investigate a stowaway," said Yvette.

"How can you have a stowaway on day twelve of a cruise?"

Yvette took a slow drink of her White Russian and let the suspense hang for a few seconds. "The stowaway is a bird. To be precise, a Bobwhite Quail. Raju said you can tell the Bobwhite Quail from the Mountain Quail because the Mountain Quail has two straight feathers that arch over its back."

Brick could not hold back his laughter. He picked up the menu and said, "Hey look. They have added quail to tonight's menu!"

"That is terrible, Mr. Morgan. Raju says the lady is very nice, and that she is some kind of quail expert. I have heard about her. She has even written a book about a pet California Valley Quail she had for fifteen years."

"Now are you going to tell me that the quail can read?"

"Dammit, Brick, this is serious. She is a little obsessed about her birds, but she is nice. We are going to let her keep the quail, but she has to contain it when either housekeeping or room service arrives."

They were still laughing about the Quail Lady when Sergio arrived to take their dinner order.

"Mr. Morgan, on your last visit to the Nebulae you ordered the small filet, medium, mushrooms, and soup."

"My goodness," said Brick. "Sergio, you are amazing. Tonight I will change to the rib eye. The rest of the order is just like last time."

"Officer Fuentes, the top sirloin, medium?"

"I would like the small filet, medium, sautéed mushrooms—"

"And house salad with Thousand," said Sergio.

As Brick picked up the wine menu, Yvette started explaining what she had learned from Senior Medical Director Dr. Pedro Ramos. Brick put down the menu and gave Yvette his full attention.

"The doctors said they were going to report to CDC that the outbreak was Norovirus. They have this system they use called the Kaplan criteria, and according to Dr. Ramos, this occurrence did not exactly fit."

"What do you mean, 'did not exactly fit'?"

"The number of passengers that got sick in the first few hours was very high, and the doctor said the virus did not spread to other passengers like in past cases. They ran a few tests to see if it could be a parasite or bacteria, but microscopic examination ruled out both. That is why they are sticking with Norovirus as the cause of one death and seventy-three sick passengers."

"How many crew members came down with the Norovirus?"

Initially dumbfounded by the question, Yvette answered, "I understand just one. A dishwasher on deck fourteen. Why?"

"I want to think about this for a few minutes," said Brick as he again picked up the wine list and ordered a bottle of 2003 Lynmar Quail Hill Vineyard. He then finished his bourbon.

When Sergio arrived with the wine, both Yvette and Brick broke into laughter.

"Morgan, you are out of control, but I love it."

As Brick finished his rib eye, he figured he should share with Yvette the information he had received from Titus.

"Yvette, what I am about to share with you is for your information only. For the last two years, I have been getting cyber-information from a techno-geek that I hired. She has skills and techniques that are way out there. I think it is better if I don't understand or ask too many questions. You know, plausible deniability.

"She has just reported back to me about an assignment I gave her two months ago. She was to monitor, infiltrate, and God only knows what else the blogs and websites that are popular with militant Islamists. Her report included some traffic from North Africa about a cruise ship as a target. The Internet post appears to come from a group called Army of the World. The Arab speak is Lashkar-e-Aalam."

"I've never heard of them. The news has a lot of coverage of al-Qaeda, but not this Lashkar group," Yvette said.

"My guess is that they are a splinter or break-off group from al-Qaeda. The threat may be bullshit, or it may be credible. My business needs to be ahead of the power curve with respect to any threats on cruise ships or any maritime vessel."

Taking a sip of her wine, Yvette tried processing what Brick had just told her. "You think there is more to the Norovirus than meets the eye?"

"Let's just say that my radar is sending me a series of yellow alerts. What do we know about the seventy-four sick passengers? Did they all go ashore, or did they all attend a show in the Nobility Entertainment Center? Maybe they all drank water from the Galileo pool on the Constellation deck."

Yvette took notes on a napkin before making a suggestion. "Let me start with ten passengers on the sick list, and if we need to expand to twenty or thirty, we can. Help me with a list of questions."

"Start with the day before they got sick and the day of the onset. I would start with meals, shore visits, and shore excursions. What activities did they participate in? You might ask when they first felt sick, what were they doing, and what were they doing before that."

Brick took Yvette's napkin and made a few notes for her. "Here is what is bugging me," he said. "Norovirus is spread by a pathogen. People get sick because a fungi, parasite, virus, or bacteria gets into their body. One person brings the Norovirus bug onboard, and then they touch a handrail or toilet and it moves to two other people. Those two people don't wash their hands, and they give it to four more people at the food court. After a couple of days, the virus is brought to the attention of the medical team, and they declare a code orange. Everyone cleans up the ship with chlorine, and in a day or two, it stops spreading. From what I understand, fifty or sixty people got sick within a few hours and within twenty-four hours the epidemic was over. Yvette, this stuff did not seem to spread from person to person."

"You know what is scary? I think both Doctors Ramos and Resende would probably agree with you, but the culture at Nobility is to just say it was Norovirus, get the passengers off the ship, and get ready for the next thirty-two hundred and the next sailing."

"Are you ready for something scarier?" Brick poured the last of the Quail Hill into Yvette's glass. "How hard would it be to fill an asthma aerosol container with *Clostridium botulinum* and hold the aerosol sprayer under a table and just push the button?"

"That possibility is both scary and upsetting," said Yvette with a grave look.

"We need to change the subject and have some fun. Let's hit the Comet Lounge and see what music group is playing."

Yvette pulled the entertainment schedule from her handbag. "You're in luck. There's a Led Zeppelin tribute band playing until midnight."

Brick put the charges for dinner on his cabin card, and they left the Nebulae. "Led Z will be terrific, but I was hoping it would be John Philip Souza so we could invite Raju," joked Brick as they headed to the staircase that would take them to deck six.

Chapter Thirty-One

Turning on channel twenty-eight, Brick tuned into the *Matisse*'s morning show that featured Reggie, the ship's cruise director/cheerleader. Room service had brought a large pot of coffee an hour earlier, but Brick chose to catch one more hour of sleep before kick-starting his day. Reggie was in the process of reviewing the entertainment and special events that were planned for the last day at sea before docking in Ensenada.

Cruise directors are some of the most valued employees of a cruise line. Their incomes can exceed $100,000 a year, placing them at an economic level with the ship's auctioneer and close to the income level of the captain. A good CD can dramatically impact the ability of the ship to meets its financial goals. Usually, the cruise director reports to the executive purser and is held responsible for the profit objectives at the casino, liquor and beverage sales, and shore excursions. Bonuses from each of those revenue drivers can add substantially to the CD's salary.

Pouring his first cup of coffee, Brick thought about last night's activity. Sergio provided outstanding service at the steakhouse, and the Zeppelin cover band was better than he expected. The guy playing bass announced to the large crowd in the Comet Lounge that *Vintage Rock Magazine* had discussed the possibilities of a Led Zeppelin reunion. At home, Brick had an original record of the Yardbirds from 1968 mounted on his wall. After signing a big record deal with a new label, the Yardbirds changed its name to Led Zeppelin.

Yvette had quietly returned to her cabin at two in the morning. As she was leaving, she gave Brick a little kiss and announced that she had surveys to fill out. He could not remember the last time he had partied with such a sex machine. Even though he was anxious to return home, he knew he was going to miss Yvette and her desire for uninhibited, wild sex.

Working on her third cup of coffee, Yvette had already finished ten interviews and decided to expand her survey to fifteen. She called Brick and said she would meet him in about ninety minutes. She was having mixed emotions from the trend she was observing from the interviews. A few of the passengers she had met with were still a little sick; however, they were still able to provide her with some good answers. She was excited that there was a trend, but she also was alarmed because it appeared that Brick's fears might be correct.

The Nobility Entertainment Center was located in the bow section of the ship. The two-story theater utilized both decks six and seven. Deck six enjoyed 550 plush seats while deck seven had 250 seats arranged in balcony fashion. Yvette had chosen the huge theater because she knew it was going to be empty for another hour.

The theater productions are one of the few attractions on a cruise ship that do not contribute to the bottom line. The cruise directors feel that the key to a high rebooking ratio correlates to the quality of the ship's productions. The ship's entertainers can each earn between $1,600 and $3,000 a month, depending on their experience level. Most dancers feel that $25,000 plus free room and board for ten-month's work is a great way to gain experience before the challenges of Broadway or Vegas.

Brick had picked up a couple of cups of coffee and was waiting near the theater door on deck six.

"Houston, I think we have a problem" was Yvette's greeting as she unlocked the door to the entertainment center. "Let's go all the way to the front. There's lots of legroom, and we can spread my surveys on the edge of the stage. Thank you for the coffee. My batteries were starting to run down."

"Before we dive into this problem, I want to thank you for a wonderful night last evening," said Brick as he put his arm around her in the privacy of the theater.

"Don't you mean the wonderful morning, Mr. Morgan?"

Looking at his watch, he replied, "You're right. And make sure I'm on your dance card for tonight, okay?"

Yvette arranged the fifteen surveys in three piles on the hard maple dance floor. There were twelve in the first pile, two in the second, and one in the last.

"Let me start with this last pile. This one sick passenger is still not at 100 percent and has no idea what he did or where he ate the day he got sick. This next stack of two questionnaires has one passenger spending the day in Hilo and the other staying on the ship, but both had their spouses bring dinner to their cabins from the food court. Now this big pile is interesting. Half went ashore on Hilo and half did not, but all twelve had dinner at the deck fourteen food court. Out of the twelve who remember eating at the buffet, nine said they were sure they had the Caesar salad."

"Shit, Yvette, you've hit a home run. Tell me what you're thinking." Brick sat down in one of the cushy seats and propped his feet on the stage edge.

Yvette gathered the papers from the stage and took a seat next to Brick. "I'm now 100 percent certain that something happened at the food court buffet that caused Throckmorton to die and seventy-three other passengers to become very sick and that a strain of Norovirus was not the cause."

Both Brick and Yvette heard a noise from the back of the theater.

" 'Other nations may deem their flag the best / And cheer them with fervid elation / But the flag of the North and South and West / Is the flag of flags, the flag of Freedom's nations.' Ladies and gentlemen, I have solved the mystery. I have five more questionnaires. These prove that the sicknesses were caused by the Norovirus." Raju walked down the aisle and handed the surveys to Yvette. "Every one of these sick passengers ate at the food court on deck fourteen."

For the next half hour, both Brick and Yvette tried explaining to Raju that the food court connection demonstrated it was *not* the Norovirus.

Raju shook his head. "I'll tell you what happened. The Throckmorton man went through the buffet and sneezed on the food. Everyone who then ate the food he contaminated eventually got sick. That is it. Clear as a bell."

"Raju, if Throckmorton was sick and he spread his germs at the food court, those people who caught his germs would not get sick for twelve to twenty-four hours. As it was, they all got sick within a six-hour period," explained Brick again.

"Nope. Norovirus!" Raju stomped by a couple of dancers entering the theater for a rehearsal.

Yvette said she would call Rob Spencer, and Brick decided he would visit Dr. Ramos.

The director of security for Nobility Cruise understood that long hours came with the territory of overseeing a fleet of floating cities. He had ships two time zones to his east and eight zones to his west. The call from the *Matisse* came in as he was cleaning up his desk after a twelve-hour day.

"Mr. Director, this is Fuentes on the *Matisse*."

"Yvette, I was expecting your call. Your buddy just sent me an e-mail."

"What buddy is that?"

"Raju, the marching-band guy. What's new on the *Matisse*?"

"I assume you were copied on our medical incident report. One fatality plus seventy-three very sick?"

"Yes, the medical team here thinks it was that new strain Noro that originated in Australia. The good news is that you guys got the ship disinfected super fast and avoided a code red."

"Rob, I don't think it was the Norovirus. Even Ramos and Resende waffled on the diagnosis and put down Noro because they did not have any other answers."

Yvette reviewed with Spencer her research, the results of her passenger questionnaires, and then finished with Brick's speculation that cruise ships were on the radar of radical Islamists.

"Yvette, look. This is a real hot potato, and if I were you, I'd think twice about betting your career on speculation. And by the way, Raju feels you are wrong and says he was able to prove that the Norovirus started in the food court. On a side note, according to Raju, you've moved into Morgan's suite and are in violation of the line's rules regarding sex with passengers."

"Look, Spencer, Morgan is not a fucking passenger. Second, on the last cruise, Captain Costanzo arranged to have his wife and four-year-old ride the *Matisse* from Hilo to San Francisco. On this trip, Costanzo had his Italian ship-squeeze get on the ship in Hilo, and as we speak, he is up in his cabin fucking the shit out of her. Goddammit, Rob, do you really want to go there?"

Chapter Thirty-Two

Zaeem walked across the large room in his home in the city of Gao, Mali, and greeted Yusuf with the traditional cheek-to-cheek kiss. He also gave his friend a big bear hug, as this was the first time Zaeem had seen him since he returned from the cruise ship. Yusuf reciprocated by kissing Zaeem's forehead.

"My friend, you must be tired. I have a special black tea to celebrate our victory. Here, Yusuf, your favorite—a Yemen black tea with just the right amount of cardamom and mint. Sit down, we have so much to talk about." Zaeem gestured to a large collection of colorful pillows that were positioned next to a low tea table.

Several cups of tea later, Yusuf had shared the success of the abrin toxin. He explained to Zaeem how he had carefully diluted the toxin so as to minimize the number that would die or get sick.

"My objective, Zaeem, was to prove that we could poison the food of the infidels yet not alert the world to our grand plan. Leader, we now have the knowledge and toxin to move ahead with our magnificent event with the blessing of Allah, the one and only god."

Zaeem rose from his favorite floor pillows and walked to the room's side door. Speaking to a guard, he requested the presence of Faroug Ahmed. "Yusuf, I want you to share this victory with our chemist."

Zaeem, Yusuf, and Faroug discussed the amount of abrin they would need to cripple the cruise line and maximize the deaths. Yusuf enlightened Faroug on his global vision of terror.

"Faroug, we are going to attack five ships at the same time. If you can produce enough abrin, I want to not only poison the food but also pollute the pools and pour the toxin on the supply of cabin towels."

"It might be possible to make 150 grams in two weeks. That would be thirty grams per ship. Yusuf, you had six grams for the test," explained Faroug. "I have a shipment of *Abrus precatorius* coming in from Indonesia, but I will need more."

"You are speaking of the rosary pea, correct?" inquired Yusuf.

"Yes. I want another two kilos."

"Faroug, you get started," Zaeem said. "I will get your peas." He then stood. He had felt Faroug's lack of focus in manufacturing the poison. "Faroug, I am still concerned about your commitment to me and Lashkar-e-Aalam."

Faroug looked startled. "Leader, you know of my loyalty to you and our jihad. I just wish we could establish the world caliphate without so much killing."

"Faroug, the problem with you and your wife is that you have not felt the personal pain from the Zionists and their Western allies." Before continuing, Zaeem reflected back to his own personal journey.

Zaeem Hasan Al-Ajmi was born in Egypt in 1966. By the time he was twenty-two, he was aggressively critical of the Mubarak government. Zaeem had hoped that with the 1981 assassination of Anwar al-Sadat, proper reforms would be established in his country. Under Mubarak's iron fist, Zaeem had become an Islamic fugitive. In 1989, he fled with many others and joined with Hadee al-Masai. Zaeem's skill in explosives was useful in training terrorists in Somalia and Sudan. He and Hadee al-Masai were involved in the battles against the Americans in Mogadishu. The team of Hadee and Zaeem then focused on putting together the 1998 coordinated bombings of the United States embassies in Kenya and Tanzania. During the next ten years, Zaeem, his wife, and their two daughters lived in southeastern Iran under the protection of the Revolutionary Guard.

"Faroug, when you feel the pain every morning and every night, you do not lose your focus. When my father-in-law was ill, I made arrangements for my daughters and my wife to travel back to their home village in Egypt to care for him. They were with my father-in-law for three days. The Mossad—I know it was the Mossad—located them and placed two bullets in the heads of my wife and then each of my daughters."

Zaeem picked up a cup of tea and hurled it against a far wall.

"My friend, do you know what I mean by living with pain? Do you not understand why we must do our small and humble part to rid the world of these evil aggressors? The very people who want to destroy our Muslim faith!"

After Faroug had left the room, Zaeem and Yusuf continued planning the attack. They agreed that Muhammad Bin Attash, Zahir Ahmed Hahid, and Mullah Saleh Rahim would be chosen to attack three of the ships. Zaeem recommended that an old friend named Muhamed Bashir could be recruited for the final cruise ship. After selecting a tentative date, they discussed the pros and cons of attacking Nobility Cruise Line again or selecting another line.

"If we stay with Nobility, I feel there are two advantages. First, attacking five ships from the same cruise line would certainly cause the company to declare bankruptcy and most likely go out of business. Secondly, training the others would be easier because of my familiarity with their ships. I want the team to fit in with the passengers and be comfortable with the layout of their ship," said Yusuf.

Zaeem agreed and added, "I am concerned about Faroug. I want you to watch him. Spend time in his laboratory, and pay attention to where he stores the finished product. I will also have Jari Atwa keep Faroug under close watch." Zaeem felt that between Atwa, his chief of security, and Yusuf, Faroug could be controlled. "Yusuf, you have done good work. You must stay with me for lunch. We will have *ful medames* and pita. After we eat, we will have some women."

"Zaeem, we will celebrate!"

Chapter Thirty-Three

Driving south on Ruston Way, Brick looked to his left as he passed by the Harbor Lights restaurant. It appeared there were three large cargo ships anchored in Commencement Bay as they waited for docking space at the busy Port of Tacoma. The large shipping line, Marine Pacific-Zone Shipping, had asked Morgan Maritime Investigations for a proposal to improve its security systems and procedures. Brick noticed that one of the anchored container ships carried the MPZ logo. Brick estimated that 70 percent of his firm's revenues came from the cruise industry; the other 30 percent was attributed to marine shipping.

His Audi made the transition from Ruston Way to Schuster Parkway and onto Pacific Avenue. Brick was getting back to his routine after arriving by plane three days before. When the *Matisse* docked at Ensenada, he booked a flight to San Francisco and then a quick connection to Seattle's Sea-Tac Airport. This week, Brick planned to connect with an old FBI friend and also get over to see Titus. Hopefully, she would have more cyber intel on Lashkar. But first, Brick had an important dinner meeting. Or was it a dinner date?

Brick dropped off his car using valet parking and headed to the Pacific Avenue entrance of the El Gaucho restaurant. After checking in with the hostess, he glanced down the wide staircase and to see if his guest, Heather Hunter, had already been seated.

"I hope you have not been waiting long, Mr. Morgan."

"Double H, long time, no see. As usual, you look fantastic, my dear."

The hostess escorted Brick and Heather down the staircase and over to a large table set for two.

When Brick was in his last year at the Justice Department, he had returned to the Pacific Northwest to participate in an alumni-directed fundraiser for the University of Puget Sound. At a pre-function, he had met Heather, the chief operating officer of Puget Sound Molecular Diagnostics. Ever since that chance meeting, she and Brick had been good friends. Heather had received her master's degree in molecular diagnostic science from the prestigious University of North Carolina School of Medicine, part of the Research Triangle Park, a research area between Chapel Hill, Durham, and Raleigh. In addition to her responsibilities at PSMD, she also taught a biochemistry class at the University of Puget Sound.

"Mr. Charming, what is it you desire tonight? My body or my brains?"

"Heather, why do they need to be mutually exclusive? But before we discuss our love life, I'd like to tap part of your 160 IQ for a while."

"Morgan, dammit, it's 170. Now that is going to cost you an expensive bottle of wine."

"Sir, your 2009 Long Shadows Pirouette," announced the waiter as he displayed the bottle of red wine blend.

Brick held the Bordeaux glass by the stem and swirled the ruby-colored wine for about ten seconds. After an aroma check, he tasted the upscale cuvee. "Great! Pour away."

"The vineyard says this wine has a pH of 3.67. What does that mean, Miss Hunter?"

Heather did a little hair flip and tucked the right side of her shoulder-length brunette hair behind her ear. She took a noticeably slow sip of her wine while looking deep into Brick's brown eyes. "A pH of 3.67 means that if we each drink a bottle, we can go to my Olalla beach house and run naked on the beach."

Heather listened intensely as Brick explained the details of the supposed Norovirus diagnosis on the cruise ship. He had brought notes that summarized as much of the facts as he could assemble. In addition to the history of incubation and duration times, he also shared with Heather his concern of possible terrorism.

"My God, Morgan, you're messing around in the big leagues."

"Yes, I know. What I'm interested in is what's available to test for whatever happened to the passengers."

They placed their order and decided to split the filet so as to leave room for the El Gaucho baked chocolate soufflé.

"Brick, let's look at your cruise-ship incident. People got sick because a pathogen entered their bodies. We break down the discovery and identifications of threatening agents into two groups: environmental samples and clinical samples. Poison in an envelope or in a container is called an environmental sample, and a sample of vomit or urine is a clinical sample. The laboratory industry has developed a national network called the Laboratory Response Network, of which there are 150. They are grouped into levels one, two, or three, depending on the sophistication of the tests. The most exacting analysis would take place in Atlanta at the nation's Centers for Disease Control and Prevention. How are we doing?"

"Fine. Good stuff. Keep going!"

Heather took another sip of her wine and continued. "There are certain agents that are favorites with terrorists. We call those 'terrorist agents.' We usually start with those when diagnosing a threat. Botulism is a condition caused by the botulin toxin, and it is produced by the bacteria *Clostridium botulinum*. Most bacteria can be seen with a good clinical microscope. You said that the ship's medical center looked at several clinical samples and ruled out a bacterium as the suspect pathogen. The same would be the case for a fungi or a parasite. That leaves us with toxins. A toxin is a poisonous substance from metabolic workings of a living organism.

"The next item in the arsenal of terrorists is ricin. Ricin comes from the castor bean. The poison is extracted from the beans by simple chromatography. Once the ricin enters the body, it interferes with the ability of the body's cells to produce proteins. After the victim gets sick, the next stage is organ failure and then death."

"Heather, I was told that the one fatality had organ failure. His liver and kidneys took a nosedive. The ship's MDs believed that the organ failure was caused by dehydration."

Heather considered Brick's input. "The test for environmental ricin is called time-resolved fluorescence immunoassay. We use an antibody that binds to ricin, and when exposed to fluorescence, it will light up. The CDC people have developed a procedure for measuring ricinine, which is a urine marker after ricin exposure."

Brick had heard enough. He knew he needed to determine what steps to take next. "If the ship sent clinical samples to their home office in Florida, could those be forwarded to Atlanta for testing?"

"An old sample could still provide data, but urine will grow bacteria unless the sample was frozen. I would try to follow up with your cruise line and see if they will cooperate. If you can get them to conduct further testing, you might also see if they will test for abrin and anthrax."

"I've read about anthrax—bad spores or something—but what the hell is abrin?"

"Abrin is similar to ricin, but instead of coming from castor beans, abrin comes from a red, berry-looking thing called a rosary pea. Brick, you have just passed pathogen testing with flying colors."

Heather and Brick had dated for several months the previous year, but both of their travel commitments broke the momentum of any burgeoning relationship. Heather looked deep into Brick's eyes as she let her mind wander *This guy is one of Tacoma's most eligible bachelors. Don't let him escape, girl!*.

"The next time we meet, I will teach you about prion propagation and misfolded proteins, but that is going to cost you much more than an expensive dinner—if you know what I mean." Heather smiled and winked.

Chapter Thirty-Four

The number of decks located under the waterline is limited to the draft of the cruise ship. The *Matisse* measured her draft as the distance from the waterline to the lowest part of the bottom of the ship. Because the *Matisse* did not have a rudder, her lowest point was measured from the bottom of the Azipods to the surface of the water.

The crew members' world took place on decks two, three, and four. The ABC television series *Love Boat*, which debuted in 1977 and continued until 1986, gave much of the world its first glimpse of the romance, adventure, and fun associated with cruising.

Today, more than sixteen million passengers step foot on their choice of ships with the expectation of great food, relaxation, and entertainment. In addition, others are attracted to the casino, cocktail lounges, and potential for their share of sex. What is not known to those sixteen million passengers is that the real party—the booze, fun, and sex—takes place on decks two, three, and four. On the *Matisse*, while families are relaxing around the Galileo Pool and the Big Dipper Bar, over a thousand crew members have turned on the party lights below the waterline. The three most important possessions or events for the crew are the distribution of their share of the tips, the cheap alcohol in the crew bar, and their private supply of condoms and birth control pills.

The aft section of the *Matisse Under the Stars* made up the majority of the engineering spaces. The aft four hundred feet of the ship involved the merging of decks one, two, and three into large spaces that contained the large engine rooms and space for the storage of diesel, water, and oil. On deck four, the only area accessible to passengers was the medical center. The remainder of deck four held the facilities for crew support.

HIGH SEAS DARKNESS

There were four dining rooms that serve the food needs of the crew—the officers' mess, the staff mess, and two other dining rooms. The *Matisse* had one crew mess that specialized in an Asian menu and another mess that was more European or traditional. A frustration of the majority of the crew was the lack of meal variation. Tuesday was kung pao chicken night, and that never changed.

Moving from the crew's plain dining rooms decorated in linoleum, fluorescent lighting, and stainless-steel serving cabinets, Dakila Salazar walked through the door that accessed the recreation area and the crews' Internet space. The Nobility Cruise Line allowed the crew to log onto the Internet at 40 percent of the cost of the passengers. Dakila did not see his friend Marcario Navarro, so he continued walking and entered the crew's bar.

The music system played some Jamaican reggae that Dakila assumed was a Bob Marley song although they all sounded the same to him. He recognized a Jamaican guy in the corner as a cook. He was standing at a bistro table and slapping the tabletop like it was a big bongo drum. Three beautiful Ukraine waitresses from the Renoir Dining Room were dancing suggestively to the Jamaican's table drumming. Dakila ordered two Heineken beers and found a table near one of the few portholes on deck four. Decks two and three were below the waterline and therefore did not have any portholes or windows.

Damn that last cruise, thought Dakila, *I came up empty on any great naked videos from my spy camera.* The French girls in cabin 519 provided a few shots of them in bras, but his hopes of a lesbian scissor act never materialized. This trip had potential, though, and one of his cabins on the Aquarius deck had three college-aged American girls. *Three drunken tramps*, he hoped to himself.

While Dakila waited for Marcario, Raju entered the bar and promptly turned down the music. Whether because of his position or his manner, other crew members tended to avoid any confrontation with Raju. The Jamaican stopped drumming, and the Ukraine girls stopped dancing and went to the bar to buy more wine. Though the crew mixed regularly at the bar, some divisions persisted, mostly along their most comfortable language.

Raju turned on the karaoke machine and announced that it was time for the First Night at Sea Karaoke Contest. To kick-start the singing, Raju entered his selection into the RSQ 787 HD. The one terabyte of memory contained all of his Sinatra songs plus room for another 199,000 karaoke songs, some as obscure as the best from the band Purple Cinnamon. A few seconds later, Raju settled into the song "Strangers in the Night." Even though Frank Sinatra reportedly did not like the song, his improvised "doo-be-doo-be-doo" remains a classic in music spontaneity.

Walking past Dakila and glancing at Raju on the karaoke stage, Yvette approached the bar and ordered a Meyers rum and orange juice. Locating a table near the karaoke corner, she sat down and waved to Raju to join her when he was finished.

"What is the problem, ma'am?" asked Raju as he sat down and put two Stella Artois Belgium lagers on the table next to Yvette's rum and orange.

"We need to talk. I'm getting pissed about all of the e-mails you're sending Rob Spencer. You continue to undermine my leadership in the security department. What is your motivation, Raju?"

"Ms. Fuentes, you do not understand the life philosophy of the Gurkha. The code of life and principles are what we live by, even long after we leave the Fourth Rifle Regiment."

"What's there about your code of life that causes you to undermine my department?" Yvette pulled up her chair and rested her chin on her palm.

"We Gurkhas are committed to upholding the traditions of the Gurkha knife and honor our commanders with integrity, loyalty, and the cheerful obedience of orders. My command was the government of India. Before our independence in 1947, our command was the

British. Today, my command is Nobility Cruise Line. Nobility has honored me by offering me its trust through my employment contract. This is my seventh contract with the cruise line, and I feel blessed."

"That's all well and good," said Yvette. "But I'm still not sure you understand. I want this to be clear. Raju, you are *not* a Gurkha anymore. You aren't shooting people. Your job now is mostly making sure that little old ladies don't break their hips after buying ugly, overpriced jewelry in Mexico."

"There is far more at stake than that, Ms. Fuentes."

He always saw her jaw tighten a bit each time he called her "Ms." She did not particularly like "ma'am," but to her "Ms." had a juvenile quality to it.

"Raju, you know what your problem is? You don't have faith in the leadership of our company. Maybe Nobility wanted to break with the old way and start being transparent about passengers' issues. Here's an expression for you this time. It goes like this: 'Small problems never go away; they just get bigger.' Nobility hired me because the line wants to stop the small problems; it wants to be different from the other cruise lines. Corporate told me they were looking ahead several years. Nobility saw big changes coming in our industry.

"If the tragedy of the *Costa Concordia* was not enough, there was the fiasco with the *Carnival Triumph*. There is more pending legislation proposed in Washington, DC, than at any other time in our cruise industry. The brass—or in your language, the command—feels that our industry competitors are going to get caught sitting on their hands." Lowering her voice, Yvette spoke slowly. "Raju, did you know all that information?"

Setting his beer down, Raju looked away, avoiding eye contact with Yvette. "No, I admit I did not understand all of that."

Assuming they were finished, Yvette got up to leave.

"Ms. Fuentes, what difference does it make if the cause of the sickness was the Norovirus or some crazy food poisoning? We need to protect our company. If we were to claim that some mysterious poison or a terrorist caused the seventy-four people to get sick, we would have panic, and Nobility Cruise Line would be hurt. It is my loyalty to my command that requires me to counter or renounce your efforts if I feel our ship or cruise line would be hurt."

"I understand where you're coming from, but I think there are many flaws with your thinking."

"Wait. I have not explained the traditions of the Gurkha knife. I am sure you have seen our knife with its special large blade. Not only is it our traditional weapon, but also it is a symbol of our Gurkha life codes. The blade has a unique notch to catch the blood before it reaches the handle and also to remind us to never use the blade of the kukri against the cow. We must wear our kukri during our wedding ceremony. You see, these are the traditions and honor that guide my decisions."

"Raju, let's go back to the time you were assigned to the Gurkha Rifle Regiment. Did you obey the orders that were issued to you by your commanding officer?"

"Yes, of course, and my regiment was the Fourth Rifle."

Yvette continued her rebuttal. "What would you do if your commanding officer gave you an order but you thought it might not be aligned with the desires of the Indian government?"

"In the field of combat, you do not think about the government. You follow the orders of your commanding officer."

"Why?"

"The government is too far away. You must trust your local command, Ms. Fuentes."

"*Chief* Fuentes," she corrected. "All right, since this is how you want to see it, I am going to put this in your terms. I am speaking to you as your department commander, *Deputy* Security Officer. When you're on this ship, I need you to work *with* me, not against me! You are not in combat in with me. I am your commander." Seeing an opening, she pressed him on his pride. "Raju, wouldn't you like to get back to doing something serious and really making a difference? That's why I am here; that's what I aim to do. Can you do that? Because if you can't, man up and tell me right now. Can you?"

"Yes, ma'am. *Kafar huna bhanda marnu ramro*. Better to die than live like a—"

"Coward," said Yvette pointedly.

Raju's eyes shifted from her triumphant gaze. Nodding, he got up from the table and headed over to the karaoke station.

Satisfied but still perturbed, Yvette carried the remainder of her drink back to her cabin. The bar was beginning to fill up. She did not notice the table of Filipino stewards whispering together in the back of the room.

Dakila had finally met up with Marcario, who was assigned to housekeeping on the Cassiopeia deck. He was on his third contract and all of his time was as a room steward on the *Matisse*.

"Dakila, are you going to participate in the foosball tournament this week?" In addition to his cabin steward responsibilities, Marcario was also on the crew's welfare committee. The *Matisse* made an effort to provide entertainment to the one thousand crew members, and the crew welfare committee coordinated activities for crew recreation and entertainment.

"That is not my thing," answered Dakila. "But I might show up and root for the Filipino team."

"You need to spend more time being social and less time watching your porn," replied Marcario.

"You just wait. I am assembling a collection that will make even you beg me for a look."

Chapter Thirty-Five

The monitor in Brick's fitness center showed a UPS truck driving onto his circular driveway. Pulling off his earbuds, Brick stepped from the treadmill and arrived at the door just as the UPS driver was about to ring the bell. The shipment from San Francisco required a signature because the box contained guns and ammo. Because Brick had left the *Matisse* in Ensenada, trying to fly home with his go-bag would have been an international nightmare. It was not long ago that a former Marine dared to declare an old shotgun at the Mexican border and ended up rotting in a Mexican jail for six months. It was easier to have Yvette hang on to the weapons and ship them once the *Matisse* pulled into San Francisco.

Brick had given a lot of thought about the incident on the *Matisse* and what he had learned in the past few days. Later in the afternoon, he was scheduled to meet with Titus, but first he needed to call an old friend. During his four years with Interpol, Brick had the opportunity to work with many associates from other agencies who were also assigned to Interpol. One of those coworkers was an FBI agent who had become a good friend. An earlier text message had coordinated the time that Brick could call Washington, DC.

Kryss Mitchell chuckled when he received Brick's text message. He remembered the crazy times the two of them had together while working the Interpol beat. Kryss and Brick had shared an office. Brick concentrated on developing intelligence about criminals who were likely to repeat crimes in other countries, and Kryss managed the Interpol notice system. Interpol uses seven colored notices in communicating with its member countries. For example, they use the orange notice to inform the international police community about disguised weapons and parcel bombs. A red notice works similarly to an international arrest warrant, with the understanding that Interpol does not itself have arrest powers in sovereign member states.

"I want you to know that I canceled a golf game this afternoon with the director so I would be available to take a call from the famous Brick Morgan," joked Kryss when he answered the scheduled call. For the next ten minutes, they traded stories as they played catch-up over the past twelve months. Then Kryss confided in Brick about his frustration with the FBI's current director and the FBI's soft approach to counterterrorism.

"Brick, I promised my partner, Nathan King, that I would try to stay off the director's radar and just wait out this foolishness. Hey, you remember that FBI gal who was hot for your bod?"

"Well, I don't know. There were so many back then," teased Brick.

"Right. How about the sharp IT genius we worked with for a year?"

"Oh, of course. You're talking about Lovely Liz."

"I should have known given that you never forget a pretty face or a hot ass. Did you know that she shot up to the top in the Bureau and is now the deputy director? We had a meeting last week where she ranted the administration's position of not jumping to conclusions that terrorism is terrorism. What's funny is that she has trouble looking me in the eye. She remembers that you and I were friends, and I think she assumes I know all about the wild sex the two of you had when we were all with Interpol," said Kryss.

"Whoa, we might've had a few drinks together, but wild sex might be a bit of an exaggeration."

"Brick, someday you'll come clean and let the whole world know the truth about the FBI's deputy director. Okay, how can humble Kryss help the legendary Morgan?"

"Fasten your seat belt, old friend. I'm going to take you on a Hawaiian cruise." Brick provided him with the details of the outbreak on the *Matisse* and his reasons for not buying into the Norovirus diagnosis. When Brick shared his intel from the militant Islamist cyber world, Kryss interrupted his presentation.

"Nathan and I get an extensive daily update of intercepts from the Bureau, NSA, and CIA every morning. I've never even heard of Lashkar-e-Aalam."

"Kryss, this tech gal may be more than a little quirky, but she's damned good. I'll see her this afternoon and will try to get verification of her info. The problem is her Internet discussions are way above my pay grade. My question is whether the FBI can push Nobility to forward their clinical samples to CDC in Atlanta. If we can prove those passengers didn't have Norovirus but actually had been poisoned by a pathogen like ricin or anthrax, we'll have a game changer."

"Okay. Let me rattle some cages at my end, and if you learn anything more from the cyber girl, call me back. Otherwise, give me a couple of days to dig around."

After opening his UPS delivery and locking away his guns and ammo, Brick prepared for his meeting with Titus.

Brick drove down Alameda Avenue parallel to the Fircrest Golf Course for half a mile. He turned left on Spring Street and parked before reaching Buena Vista Avenue. Before getting out of his car, he sent Titus a text announcing that he was one minute away. One of her idiosyncrasies was her obsession with stealth secrecy.

Walking down Buena Vista for half a block brought Brick to the nondescript one-story, moderately sized home. Probably built in the early fifties, Titus's house blended into the quiet residential neighborhood. As soon as he walked up the eight concrete steps and reached for the front door, Titus pulled open the door and stepped aside, allowing Brick to enter. He should not have been surprised—no one gets the drop on Titus.

Titus was twenty-eight when she made two life-changing decisions. The first was to resign from Boeing where she had spent five years, the last three of which honed her skills as a computer security and information protection specialist. During her five years at the "Flying B," Titus was like an intellectual magnet. Not only did she attend every possible IT seminar, but also her security clearance gave her access to Boeing's vast computer science library. During those five years, she was like a kid in a candy store and greedily consumed every bit and byte she could.

The other decision she made was to go underground and change her name to one word. When she attended Tacoma's University of Puget Sound, she ran into several international students who used mononymous names. She learned that some government agencies would process a single name if you put "NFN" ("no first name") in that field. Titus learned that Cher was a legal mononymous and a legal resident of California.

As a tall blonde at five foot ten, Titus always drew a double take from both men and women. Her hair was pulled back in a ponytail with one-half to three-quarter inch of grow-out from her long-overdue highlight touch-up.

Brick had barely entered the house when Titus quickly shut the door and then studied a CCTV monitor to insure he was not followed. Satisfied that neither Chinese spies nor rogue Soviet zombies were coming up the driveway, she walked over to a mahogany pole coat rack and removed her expensive Turkish bathrobe and hung it on an empty hook. Turning to Brick completely naked, she said, "Grab a chair, big guy. We've got work to do."

Brick had waited about sixty days before following up with Titus after their chance meeting at the Tacoma jazz joint Jazzbones two years earlier. She had insisted they meet at her Fircrest home. With what had been her usual modus operandi, Titus greeted him wearing a bathrobe. For over an hour, they exchanged information about each other's businesses, and Brick had forgotten that this brilliant cyber scientist was still wearing a bathrobe. She then said, "Mr. Morgan, there's something you need to know about me." Brick assumed she was going to tell him she was a wanted felon or maybe an escaped inmate from the Western State Psychiatric Hospital in Steilacoom. He held his breath; he really wanted to put this girl on his team, as she seemed to be above genius level. Listening, he hoped for the best.

"When I work on the computer, I don't wear any clothes. It helps me concentrate. The truth is, I *never* wear clothes. They're so conformist and bourgeois, don't you think?"

It took Brick several meetings to get over the shock of having Titus drop her robe and sit at her computer completely naked. Now when Brick meets with her, he never forgets that this beautiful thirty-two-year-old woman is nude, but he has learned to focus on their projects as much as a normal man can.

Brick pulled a chair next to Titus as her fingers starting doing their magic on the keyboard. "This is how I found the information on Lashkar-e-Aalam. On monitor one, you can see the door to a popular blogosphere, www.al-bab.com. The bad guys choose some obscure topic and set up their blogging inside a harmless topic. I combed through dozens of tedious blogs and found some comments that didn't really fit the normal troll-talk for the subject. I was using Purple Iris software to search fifty blogs at the same time. I got a hit on a blog for Arab stamp collectors. The actual name was 'Saudi Stamps and Postal History.' Most of the comment strings were in English and were offers to sell and trade a block of 1925 Saudi Arabian stamps. Then in the middle of a string of comments appeared one that seemed to be recruiting for the Army of the World."

Two hours later, Brick had almost forgotten that he was looking over a great set of tits while he watched Titus key in more commands. She explained to him that there were over fifty thousand Arab blogs and some were very radical. She demonstrated how she translated an English word like *bomb, poison,* or *cruise ship* and then entered that Arab Naskh script into her search software and let it look through fifty blogs at a time.

"Brick, here are three short conversations I feel fit the parameters we set up. The first one is my discovery of terrorism on a cruise ship and the link Lashkar-e-Aalam. This next blog I found was from an anti-Israel cluster, and it says that the package delivered successfully and will need soldiers for the final phase. That posting used the name Lashkar-e-Aalam. The final post was found on an Arab blog called 'Anti-Infidel Living Room.' What I found was a post trying to recruit committed men for a mission in Northern Mali, and again the name Lashkar."

"What's next?" asked Brick as he caught himself staring at the very sexy butt of his naked cyber girl.

"I'll continue searching with Purple Iris and will also attempt to install some malware in the computers attached to a few e-mails I've gathered."

"How do you place malware on someone's computer without getting caught?" Brick asked as he stood up.

"Oh, I have my ways. Those are my top-secret tools I discovered when working with Boeing. But I'll share one little secret. I place a deceptively simple fake virus on a network or stand-alone box. Then I send a disguised antivirus fixer that looks just like a Microsoft product. Once that's opened, bingo! My little snooper malware is installed and combines with the virus to start snooping for passwords and targeted e-mails. Malware stands for malicious software. And my malware is very, very good. Almost undetectable."

Titus stood up and stretched her yoga-toned torso. "It's time for my workout. Why don't you stick around so we can workout together?"

Brick looked at Titus as she stood with her hands on her hips. With all the self-discipline he had, he said, "Titus, I want a raincheck—and I'm serious. But I need to get home and reconnect with the FBI."

"Okay, big guy. But don't forget—I do not exist."

Chapter Thirty-Six

Ace Zittel, the director of the FBI, closed the right rear door of his limo and tapped twice on the glass window. That was his code releasing his security detail.

Walking toward the white canopy that covered the walkway to the West Wing of the White House, Ace reminded himself of the importance of being in the correct mental state for his meeting with the president. Ace committed himself religiously to two main priorities in remaining a successful director of the Federal Bureau of Investigation. The first was to keep the one half of the Bureau that did not like him away from the other half of the Bureau that had not yet made up their minds. The second priority was to try to understand what the hell the president of the United States wanted the FBI to do.

Placing his briefcase on the table, he looked down to ensure that his black Gucci loafers did not have a smudge. Wearing loafers, even if they were expensive, was a little act of defiance or independence as black wingtips was the correct shoe. Ace was a little anal when it came to his dress. He always wore two plains and a pattern. If he was wearing a striped or patterned shirt, he always had a solid jacket and tie. If he wore a patterned tie, the shirt and jacket were a solid color.

"Mr. Director, your case is fine. You don't have any cigars, do you?"

"Gave them up this morning, my friend. You have a great day," Ace replied to the Secret Service agent. This was an ongoing joke between them, as cigars were on the list of items that could not be brought into the White House. The further irony was that Zittel sometimes gave prohibited Cubans to this agent to get inside information about some of the less-classified White House comings and goings.

The director had the utmost confidence in his ability to carry out the mission of the FBI. Between him and Elizabeth Monroe, the deputy director, he knew that their leadership abilities were superior to any department, agency, or, for that matter, even the office of the POTUS. It was a game as far as Ace was concerned: support the president with his initiatives so as to keep off the enemy list and then focus on the real mission of the Bureau.

"Director Zittel, good morning. Mr. Bodner said for you to meet him in his office. Secretary Johnston has not yet arrived." The chief of staff's office was just past the West Wing office of the vice president, located in the corner. Vic Bodner had been the president's chief of staff for the last two years. Secretary of Homeland Security Maxine Johnston would be the only other person invited to this special meeting. The chief of staff said that POTUS was on an international call, and as soon as the secretary of Homeland Security arrived, he would see if the president was clear.

The Senate confirmed Maxine Johnston three months prior to Director Zittel's confirmation as FBI director. Her confirmation went smoothly compared to most confirmations because she had served in the Senate and was on the Committee for Homeland Security and Government Affairs for many years. Ace did not really care for Johnston, but he was careful to keep her blissfully ignorant of know how he felt. She reminded him of a cross between an NBA center and a pit bull, but what really pissed him off was that she was a one-way communicator. She always wanted the latest intel but was not forthcoming about sharing info with the Bureau.

When Secretary Johnston arrived, the chief of staff walked down the hall to the Oval Office.

Both Johnston and Zittel were surprised when the president himself stuck his head in the chief of staff's office and said, "Maxine and Ace, thank you for being flexible with your schedules." As they walked down the hallway from the COS's office to the Oval Office, they passed the Roosevelt Room on the left and the President's Dining Room on the right.

Director Zittel had never been totally comfortable in the company of the president. Zittel liked to joke that the president's low, baritone voice did not fit his five-foot-four frame. A successful four-year southern state governorship was his launching pad for the nation's highest office. The director wondered what POTUS did all day now that Congress had suspended the majority of the provisions of the prior administration's health care bill.

Maxine sat on one sofa with COS Bodner. Director Zittel sat on the other sofa while the president scooted one of the two blue-and-gold-striped armchairs a little closer to the coffee table.

POTUS held a cream-colored file folder with a bright red stripe that ran diagonally around the front and the back. Ace knew the folder contained extremely classified material.

The president opened the folder and began the briefing. "Today's agenda will deal with Operation Bridgewalk. Vic and I have firmed up a plan to deal with the ongoing threat of radical Islamists.

"Maxine and Ace, you both know that despite our best efforts, and the lives of too many Americans, the splinter cells of the original al-Qaeda are popping up so fast we can't destroy them." The president offered coffee from a tray that had arrived. "What's ironic is that we gave al-Qaeda and Osama their roots when we supported them in 1988 and 1989 in their Afghanistan fight against the Soviets. The drone initiative is limited due to the public pressure as a result of collateral damage."

Vic Bodner jumped in. "People forget that during World War II, Curtis LeMay used special incendiary bombs against the Japanese. Operation Meetinghouse took place in March of 1945, and as a result of the B-29 bombings, one hundred thousand Japanese men, women, and children died. If the president authorizes a drone strike against terror leadership and a civilian is killed, you have a group that wants to convene a war crime tribunal."

The president placed his coffee cup back on the table. "You both have reported that we have terrorist sleeper cells already established in our country. The demographics in Europe are frightening. Germany is going to lose a third of its population in thirty years and an alarming number of Italians have chosen not to have children. Muslim immigrants will overrun Europe in a few generations. The only hope we have is through Operation Bridgewalk. Europe has exacerbated its problem because of its failure to assimilate its Muslim immigrants. We need an assertive program to embrace our nation's Muslim community. We need to be sensitive to its commitment to daily prayers. We need to establish public footbaths and areas for prayer. Once the Muslim community starts to trust our sincerity, and our general population feels less threatened, we can then hope to break down its cultural walls. The ultimate objective is to assimilate them into our society, just as the Italians and Norwegians assimilated when they arrived in America. When they become part of our cultural fabric, they will be motivated to stand up against the radical members of their community."

Chief of Staff Bodner again added his thoughts. "Director Zittel, the Bureau is the key to Operation Bridgewalk. Every time we have an arrest that's labeled an act of terrorism by militant Islamists, we go backward. The general population becomes scared of the American Muslims, and members of the Islam faith feel ostracized from American society and retreat back behind their Muslim cultural walls."

"Mr. President, what I'm hearing is that you want the Bureau to classify any act of terrorism committed at home by Islamists as something other than al-Qaeda-generated Islamic terrorism."

"Ace, we know this is going to be challenged because your special agents are going to push back. Maxine, where does Homeland stand?"

The meeting continued for another five minutes when Bodner reminded the president that he had three children in the Roosevelt Room who were winners of the National Spelling Bee. As Secretary Johnston and Ace walked out of the Oval Office, Ace looked back and said, "Vic, make sure the president knows how to spell 'potato.'"

Everyone laughed as Maxine and Ace walked down the hallway and headed to the West Wing lobby.

While driving out the east appointment gate, Director Zittel dialed his deputy director. "Liz, I'm leaving the Puzzle Palace. Meet me in my office in about fifteen minutes. And one more thing. Break out the fifty-year-old single malt. We're going to need it."

Chapter Thirty-Seven

"Maali, why are you so arrogant, irrational, and selfish? Zaeem says you are filling my mind with Western poison. He instructed me to beat you with sticks and force you to sleep outside with the dogs!" screamed Faroug Hasan Ahmed.

Faroug's wife stood her ground. "Zaeem and others who think like him are the problem in today's modern world. Zaeem throws gravel and rocks in the gears of progress for our Muslim brothers and sisters."

"Your words have no truthfulness. You only speak slander!" yelled Faroug.

"Faroug, I will make you a deal. Give me an hour. Let me show you the Holy Quran and explain why I feel the way I do. If after hearing my commentary and the interpretation of my beliefs you still do not agree, you can beat me, and then I will leave. Will you listen to me?"

"Maali, I have promised my loyalty to Zaeem, but I have also promised my loyalty and love to my wife. I will listen."

After serving tea and placing her Quran on the table, Maali began her presentation. Faroug listened patiently as his wife spoke about the American war on terrorism, the global jihad, and the challenges of Israel's presence in their lands.

"Faroug, you have to understand the motives of those who follow a moderate approach to solving the challenges facing our Muslim culture versus those who are dedicated to a radical approach. Do you really think the future of our culture and religion is a world society where men have an unlimited number of wives? A society where the wives are kept in a tent all day long and at night used for sex and then beaten like dogs? Where females can't drive and must be covered head to toe in canvas when outside the house? People die every day because a bunch of dirty old men want to return to that perverted, backward lifestyle. Do the millions of Muslims throughout the world really believe that the lifestyle of the Afghani Taliban will be accepted in Jakarta, Kuala Lumpur, or New York City?"

She picked up her Quran. "Faroug, the killing of the infidels serves no purpose. How does killing innocent children bring the world closer to a world that respects our faith? Listen to the Holy Quran 2:83: 'Speak good words to all people.'

"What is wrong with a world where the Jews can go to their temple, Mormons to their temple, and Muslims to their mosque? After our prayers, we can all attend a soccer game or join each other at the opera." Reading again, Maali said, "'Whatever good they (people of other religions) have to do, they will not be denied it (by Allah), and Allah knows who the righteous are. Quran 3:115.'"

Pulling Faroug up, she looked him in the eye. "Where in our Holy Quran does it say we must have a jihad where we use poison to kill thousands of men, women, and children who someday may choose our Islam faith that is based on peace and forgiveness?"

Faroug and Maali continued sharing their interpretations of their faith and their concerns his allegiances created. They even spoke about the possibility of a world not filled with hate and persecution.

Time had escaped Faroug, and he was surprised that he needed to be back at the Lashkar compound in the next hour. As he made his way through the secluded entrance, his wife's words echoed within him.

Zaeem rose from his seat and greeted Faroug as he walked from the laboratory to Zaeem's living room. "Faroug, I understand that we now have enough abrin to achieve our goals. You have done a wonderful job."

Faroug smiled and stepped back as he discreetly reached into his pocket and gripped the handle of his *janbya*. He had given the situation a lot of thought. *There is only one way to stop this madness and demonstrate to Maali my commitment to peacefully spreading the word of Islam.* That Arab dagger would soon be plunged into the belly of Zaeem Hasan Al-Ajmi.

But first, Faroug wanted to tell Zaeem what he had done.

Defiantly, he confessed, "Leader, I have just left the laboratory where I have destroyed our supply of the abrin." Faroug then pulled the *janbya* from his pocket and lunged toward Zaeem's stomach.

When Jari Atwa, who was hiding behind a curtain, saw Faroug remove the *janbya* from his pocket, he increased the pressure on the trigger of his AK-47. Even though Atwa pulled the trigger for less than a second, nine 123-grain bullets first entered Faroug's abdominal cavity and, because of the recoil, climbed his body until the last of the nine bullets entered his neck.

"Zaeem, are you all right? Are you all right?" screamed Atwa.

Zaeem felt his stomach and arms before answering. "Jari, I am fine. Baraka Allah." Zaeem continued thanking his security man and proclaimed, "Jari, we are blessed. That traitor could have killed us. He said he sabotaged the chemical. We will be set back months, if not an entire year."

"We are truly blessed then," said Atwa. "I have the abrin. I secured it safely in our shed."

"But how? That dog said he threw it out?"

Atwa placed his rifle on a desk and motioned for Zaeem to join him on a group of floor pillows. "For the last week, I have been watching and monitoring Faroug's activities while he was in the laboratory. I even put on protective clothing and joined him when he produced the final batch from the rosary peas. When he left the lab, I returned and found a glass container that was exactly like the bottle he was using. I made a mixture of flour and just enough dry mustard to look exactly like the powder poison. Faroug threw away the bottle of flour and mustard."

Later that night, Jari Atwa and Zaeem dragged the bullet-ridden corpse of Faroug outside and dumped the scientist into the back of an old pickup truck that Zaeem used for picking up supplies.

The smell of the decaying body heralded the next morning when Yusuf arrived at the compound. He and Jari drove Faroug's body north toward the regional area of Kidal. After only forty-five minutes of driving, they spotted a uranium mine that had been abandoned for fifteen years.

"Yusuf, grab that piece of canvas and spread it on the dirt. We can dump Faroug on the canvas and then drag him over to that pile of dirt and rocks." Using shovels they had brought along, Yusuf and Jari dug a shallow grave and rolled Faroug face down into his new home. The piles of rocks nearby made it easy to cover the body. Jari stabbed at the rock pile, and a large section sloughed off and fell across the gravesite.

Yusuf threw the shovels in the truck bed and commented to Jari, "It will be a hundred years before anyone stumbles across that body."

Jari looked back at the pile of rocks. Despite Faroug's betrayal, we gave him a burial within twenty-four hours as directed by Islamic law, he thought. "Without a body, his wife will not be able to cause any trouble."

"Maybe Zaeem will tell her that her husband ran away with an American student to photograph the sites in Algeria," joked Yusuf.

An hour later, they pulled the pickup next to the main house and noticed that several older cars had arrived while they were gone. "Yusuf, it looks like your team has arrived, so maybe now we can go ahead with your grand plan," remarked Jari as he slammed the truck door.

Muhamed Bashir, Muhammad Bin Attash, Zahir Ahmed Hahid, and Mullah Saleh Rahim all stood as Jari and Yusuf entered the room. After the customary hugs and kisses, Zaeem served tea and passed around a large bowl of regional fruit. Zaeem then asked everyone to sit before making some opening remarks.

"By the grace of Allah, glorified and exalted be He, we are now ready to strike a devastating blow to the American devil and move closer to our goal of eradicating Israel from our sacred lands. We will soon attack five of those American ships and kill ten thousand infidels. We will cripple their cruise and travel industry for years. Yusuf has returned from a successful mission, and therefore, it is important that you learn from him. Three thousand died on September 2001, and if you apply Yusuf's wisdom, we will kill three times that amount."

Yusuf spent four hours handing out safety masks and gloves and explaining the dangers of touching or inhaling the abrin before he handed out the assignments. "Bashir, you will travel to Florida, and your ship is the *Rembrandt Under the Stars*. You will be on an eastern Caribbean cruise. Hahid, you will also fly to Florida, and your ship is the *Goya*. Your cruise will take you to the southern Caribbean. Attash and Rahim, you will join me and travel to California. I will return to the *Matisse*. Attash, your ship is the *Cézanne,* and Rahim, you get the *Lautrec*.

"Friends, this has been a special day. We are blessed. When I sprinkled the abrin while on the *Matisse*, I only poisoned the salad dressing. You will have four times the quantity I had, and you will spread the abrin directly on the salads, fruits, and potatoes. The fat Americans always eat their potatoes, so make sure you poison the infidel's mashed potatoes."

Chapter Thirty-Eight

Brick turned on his GRE PSR-400 police scanner and set the volume to six. Immediately, the triple-trunking scanner started to broadcast Tacoma Police Department dispatches. The scanner was the third leg in Brick's home security system. If an intruder could get past his door and window security alarm, he would need to bypass the ten CCTV cameras. If those systems did not deter the bad guys, they would walk into a house filled with the sounds of a TV cop drama from the seventies.

Picking up a plastic container, Brick set the home alarm code and headed to the garage. His Savanna Beige Pearl Audi A8 looked stunning parked on a spotless, painted garage floor. After placing the empty container in the trunk, Brick slipped into the velvet beige seat and backed out of the garage. Titus said she had hit the mother lode, but it would cost him a Frisko Freeze double cheeseburger. She also wanted a large fry, and he had to make sure he got tartar sauce, not ketchup. Brick had no objection to the fast-food run, as he had eaten Frisko Freeze burgers all throughout his tenures at Wilson High School and the University of Puget Sound. The founder, Perry Smith, would have been proud that his little red-and-white, flat-roofed building on a small triangular lot had become a Tacoma landmark. Southern California had In-N-Out Burger, but Tacoma had Frisko Freeze.

Carrying his white bag of burgers back to the Audi, Brick opened the truck and placed them inside the plastic container. The Frisko burgers might be the best hamburgers in town, but their traditional chopped onions would play havoc with the interior of Brick's new Audi.

Driving west on Division Street, he made the merge to Sixth Avenue and continued past the revitalized Sixth Avenue District.

Traffic forced Brick to slow down just as he was parallel to Jazzbones, where he had first met Titus.

As he entered Fircrest, he reduced his speed to the city's ridiculously provincial limit of twenty-five miles per hour. He passed the Fircrest Golf Course, continued on to Electron Way, turned left, and parked on Buena Vista Avenue about five houses from Titus's house. After making a cryptic call to alert her, Brick fetched the burgers and made his way up Buena Vista Avenue. *Dammit,* he thought. He was sure he could smell those onions inside his car.

Titus opened the door about a third and stepped back out of sight. As Brick entered her home, she reached out and relieved him of the bag of burgers. "Follow me. I'm craving French fries and tartar sauce. You did remember the tartar sauce, right?"

"Yes, Titus. Double cheese, large fry, tartar sauce. Any visits from federal agents while I was traveling?"

"No, still keeping a low profile. I don't think I'm on their radar yet. Let's eat. Then I have some hot damn shit to show you!"

Titus took off her robe, placed it on a wall hook, and motioned for Brick to take a seat at the small kitchen table. Naked, she walked over to a cabinet and removed two dinner plates and two salad plates. Opening the Frisko Freeze bag, she placed a double cheese on Brick's dinner plate and poured half of the fries on his salad plate. Brick was certain that her breast had brushed against his cheek as she was fiddling with the tartar sauce.

After devouring several fries, Titus started explaining the progress she had made. "Several years ago, a worm named Stuxnet was used against the Iranian computers that were controlling the uranium enrichment centrifuges. At that time, it was the most advanced malware created. There's been chatter among hackers of an even more sophisticated worm. The code name for this malware is Flame. Now let me jump ahead. I was able to get a bite on my little 'oops, you have a virus' trick. I hunted down a Gmail account with an ID of baseballfan999.

He or she was going to a lot of effort to hide the IP address. I knew he was a good target because he was using Tor."

"What is Tor?" asked Brick.

"Tor is a software that allows the user to become anonymous. It scrambles your IP address. It's the next generation of techniques to hide your identity. We used to use proxy computers, but Tor software is much better. Let me continue. Baseballfan999 clicked on my bait and—zoom! I was able to place my spyware on his computer. I was then able to read a few of his e-mails, which I have over at the computer station. While snooping with my spyware that had infected his unblocked browser, I made another discovery."

Titus stuck her index finger into the plastic cup containing the tartar sauce. Lifting her breast, she spread the tartar sauce around her nipple. Looking up and meeting Brick's eyes, she said, "Did you want some more tartar sauce? Or are you a ketchup man?"

Brick smiled. "Neither. But I am a tit man, and you're fucking killing me, girl. Now tell me what you found before we get into trouble."

"Okay, okay, but someday we need to let Brick's dick come out and play. I discovered that I was not the only visitor to baseballfan999. I found a line of code: Worm.Win32.Flame. The hottest and newest malware had already existed on baseballfan999's computer. Somebody placed Flame on the computer and covered his tracks with Tor software. It was a six-megabyte DLL file called mssecmgr.ocx"

"Titus, you're losing me."

"Somebody else is tracking baseballfan999, and because of the advanced malware and deception, I think it is either the Chinese or our agencies. Maybe CIA, NSA, or FBI. The good news is I used a proxy computer in Germany I had hijacked and also ran my tracks through Tor. The competition will know that I was there but will not be able to find me."

They walked into the front room and sat down at Titus's array of computers and monitors. "The baseball guy doesn't send that many e-mails, but he seems to be using the draft mail trick. He, or somebody with his username and password, creates a message and, instead of sending the e-mail, leaves it in the draft folder. This is the stuff I was able to grab before they deleted the drafts: Lashkar-e-Aalam, cruise ship, disguised as Norovirus, test successful, rosary peas cocktail.

"I worked on each of these names and phrases to determine if they had any special meaning. I was not finding anything with the phrase 'rosary peas cocktail,' and then I found a poem by a Joseph Heithaus. It's a sonnet about poisonous plants. I researched rosary pea and discovered that it is a poisonous plant and is listed in the top ten most dangerous. The rosary pea, or *Abrus precatorius*, consists of red seeds. In some countries, they make rosary prayer beads from these red seeds. If the coating of the rosary pea is broken, it will release a poison, a very dangerous poison, called abrin."

Chapter Thirty-Nine

After returning home from his meeting with Titus, Brick fired off an e-mail to Special Agent Mitchell. They agreed that Kryss would call Brick at eight in the following morning.

The news was not good.

"What do you mean the CDC lost the bio samples from the cruise line?" asked Brick, exasperated.

"I even called your buddy, Robert Spencer, and he confirmed that Nobility shipped the medical samples to Atlanta. Then I got a call from my boss, the assistant director of our national security branch, Herb Wallace. He goes ballistic and wants to know why I'm working on a case that's not in our division's active case registry."

"Kryss, I appreciate that you went out on a limb for me, but I have uncovered intel that makes me think there is a real threat against United States' assets."

"I did learn that we have on our radar a small spin-off from al-Qaeda that is operating from Mali. They call themselves Lashkar-e-Aalam. They stole a large quantity of arms from Muammar Gadhafi's armory, sold them, and now are sitting on millions of US dollars. The CIA ground assets are minimal in that area, so that's all I have."

"I want one shot at the National Security Branch guy . . . yeah, Herb Wallace. Kryss, you get me in front of him. If he blows me off, I'll catch the next flight back to the West Coast. Don't make me call Lovely Liz. Will you give it a try?"

"You do not want to call Elizabeth. She's not the same split-tail you were banging while assigned to Interpol. Let me give Wallace a call. I'll get back to you."

Brick was surprised when Mitchell called back within an hour informing him that the meeting was on. The only condition was that the three of them would meet away from FBI headquarters and Wallace would be without portfolio. Brick knew the game. "Without portfolio" meant that the assistant director would meet but on the condition that it was unofficial. If the shit hit the fan, Herb Wallace would swear that the meeting never took place. Plausible deniability.

The following day, Brick's Town Car pulled up to 1401 Pennsylvania Avenue NW, the Willard Washington DC, a grand institution that has hosted the world's most influential people. As he walked toward the entrance, Brick reflected back to August 28, 1963, when Reverend Martin Luther King Jr. was a Willard hotel guest, during which he finished his "I Have a Dream" speech.

The Willard was full of history. Folklore has it that President Ulysses S. Grant would walk from the White House down Pennsylvania Avenue and enjoy a cigar and brandy in the Willard lobby. Those looking for political favors would hang around the lobby of the Willard and try to buy the president drinks in exchange for self-serving decisions. Many attribute these actions to the origin of the terms *lobbying* and *lobbyist*. Regardless of evidence tracing the words' coining years before, Willard guests still share this colorful story. Today some senators and such still meet up there to watch *Jeopardy!* in the lounge.

Brick checked in and made his way to his Willard King room. He had reserved a meeting room on the second floor and also requested a coffee service. Regardless of the outcome of the meeting, Brick was determined to swing by the famous Round Robin bar for a traditional mint julep.

At three o'clock, Brick's cell phone rang, and Kryss announced that he and Herb were in the lobby. They agreed to meet in the Chase Room on the second floor.

"Herb, I would like you to meet Brick Morgan," said Special Agent Mitchell as Brick extended his hand to the assistant director of national security.

"Mr. Wallace, very nice to meet you, and let me thank you in advance for taking the time to listen to my story."

After they filled Willard china cups with coffee, they selected seats around the conference table. Herb was the first to speak. "Brick, it is my understanding from Kryss that this meeting is dark. It is not on my calendar or my schedule."

"Mr. Wallace, that is my understanding."

"Please call me Herb. I studied your biography, and I must say I am impressed. I just wish you had chosen the FBI instead of the Justice Department six years ago." Herb's flattery made Brick uncomfortable. He felt that Herb was trying to ingratiate too quickly. "I cleared my afternoon, so why don't you take it from the top?"

Brick first reviewed the death of Throckmorton and the illnesses of the other seventy-three passengers. "I reviewed the outbreak with several medical professionals, and they all agreed that they had never run into a Noro case that had this manifestation."

Next, Brick showed Kryss and Herb copies of the hacked intel from the blogs and the e-mails of baseballfan999. Then for another fifteen minutes, Brick provided them with an education of poisonous plants. Herb and Kryss were very familiar with ricin as a cytotoxin and its relatively easy manufacture from castor beans, but they were not familiar with rosary peas or abrin.

Brick brought his presentation to a close. "Gentlemen, it's my opinion that a terrorist group called Lashkar-e-Aalam plans to poison passengers on cruise ships by exposing passengers to fatal doses of abrin."

Herb stole a glance at Kryss and took a slow drink of his now cold coffee. "Brick, thank you, and I must say that you present a most compelling case. If I may respond. First, our counterterrorism group has Lashkar-e-Aalam on the grid. If memory serves me correctly, it stands for 'Army of the World.'

"Second, let me comment about your cyber source. I assume you are not the master hacker. He or she has done a better job than our billions of dollars in analysts and equipment. Third, I will not promise you anything, but I will try to run this info up the Bureau flagpole. I will be candid, though—and I only share this with you because of your reputation for being a stand-up guy who also has good judgment. During the last few months, Kryss, his partner, Nathan, and our whole counterterrorism division have been getting a lot of pushback from the seventh floor. The director is not real excited to recognize new terror threats. However, I am going to fill out an FD 302. That is FBI lingo for documenting an investigative interview. It was not my initial plan, but that will make this meeting on the record."

The three men left the meeting room and walked to the bank of elevators. As Kryss and Herb got on the elevator to take them to the lobby, Herb handed Brick a note. "You might want to call this number."

Glancing at the phone number, Brick took the next elevator back to his room.

Throwing both his suit coat and briefcase on the bed, he grabbed his cell phone and plopped down in one of the two wingback chairs near the room's coffee table. As he dialed the number, Brick noted that the area code was a local DC number.

"Hey, big guy. I have an unmarked sedan on the Fourteenth Street side of the Willard. You'll have your sexy ass in that car in ten minutes or you'll be arrested for interfering with a terrorist investigation. See you soon, love."

In the car, Brick asked, "Where are we going, Special Agent?"

"Miss Monroe—or should I say the deputy director?—has an apartment at 1301 Thomas Circle. The actual address is 1301 M Street, about three minutes from here."

Brick entered the luxurious apartment building and was greeted by a highly polished marble floor inlaid with light oak. The security desk informed Brick that Miss Monroe's apartment was on the sixth floor, number 603. Noticing an unusual number of CCTV cameras in the lobby, Brick was not surprised when Elizabeth Monroe opened her door before he had a chance to ring the doorbell.

The deputy director of the Federal Bureau of Investigation handed Brick a crystal bucket glass filled with an amber liquid. She then planted a kiss on his lips and held it just long enough for her tongue to ever so slightly penetrate his lips.

"Big guy, I hope you've missed me as much as I've missed you. I have been saving this bottle of Pappy Van Winkle fifteen-year-old bourbon for the time you would return to DC."

Together they walked through the foyer and entered the spacious and meticulously decorated living room. Brick was taken in by the rich appointments and the nine-foot ceilings. Liz poured a couple of ounces of the bourbon in her glass, walked over to Brick, and tapped her glass on his. Stepping back, she gave Brick a suggestive lookover and then reached over and gave his ass a little squeeze.

"Sit down, old friend. Shame on you for trying to sneak into the District of Crime without calling me first."

"Liz, you look terrific, and congratulations on your appointment to deputy director. Director Zittel must be congratulated for recognizing your talent."

For the next couple of hours, Brick and Liz reminisced about the good old days at Interpol and shared war stories of Brick's escapades and Liz's FBI experiences. Liz then brought up the issue of Lashkar-e-Aalam. Brick felt she had already been briefed on the details of the case, so he just emphasized the e-mail from baseballfan999 that used the phrase "rosary peas cocktail."

"Brick, I wouldn't be so naive as to suggest that you drop your interest in this case. On the contrary, you've provided the Bureau with intel we didn't have. But be careful, and also tell 'Spindleratchet' that we appreciate him or her, but he or she is fucking around with some very dangerous men."

Brick did not have any idea what Liz was talking about with her reference to Spindleratchet, but he kept his curiosity to himself.

"Here's the deal. Zittel is between a rock and a hard place. The president is out in left field. He thinks that if he kisses every Muslim, terrorism will fade away like a black-and-white television. If the director doesn't suppress these cases of terrorism, he is sure that some liberal wacko will replace him. Ace is willing to play the game for a few more years until this lunacy is over in an effort to save the FBI."

"What will happen if we have another September 2001? How will you guys hide or suppress that kind of act?"

"We can't, but we'll try and follow the orders of POTUS, and if we can reclassify a domestic attack as just worksite violence, we will."

"Just like the Fort Hood attack, right?"

"You got it. It's a tough position to be in, but we have a president who has his head up his ass with respect to the reality of Muslim Islamists."

Liz brought out the bottle of Pappy Van Winkle and refreshed both of their glasses. They spent another hour reviewing the different careers of the Interpol team they had worked with so many years ago.

The ringing of Liz's house phone interrupted their stories and laughter. Liz picked up the line. "Monroe." She paused and passed the phone his way. "It's for you. Take it in the den. Line one."

Brick walked to the den and picked up the phone.

"Mr. Morgan, this is Martin Daniel, Speaker of the House of Representatives. I hope I have not called at a bad time."

Brick's slight intoxication instantly disappeared. "Mr. Speaker, how may I help you?"

"Mr. Morgan, I am your number-one fan. You are pissing off a lot of people, and that includes the secretary of Homeland Security. I like that. We need you to be tenacious. One more thing: weakness and ambivalence lead to war. Stay the course, and good luck."

Brick slowly replaced the phone and pondered the dramatic message for a minute. "Liz, how much bourbon do you have left?"

Chapter Forty

Ensenada, Mexico, was the designated port of call as the international stop for the *Matisse Under the Stars*. The Passenger Vessel Service Act of 1886 directs that a foreign-flagged vessel cannot depart a US port and disembark passengers at the same or another US port without a visit to a foreign port. When Nobility Cruise Line departs Seattle for an Alaska cruise, it must visit the foreign ports of Vancouver of Victoria, Canada, before it can return to Seattle. Anytime a passenger leaves the ship prior to the required visit to the foreign port, the ship imposes a fine of $300 per passenger. Mexican and Caribbean cruises never have a problem with the Passenger Services Act, but cruises to Hawaii often arrange a stop at either a Mexican or a Canadian port.

The crew of the *Matisse* looked forward to the five-hour stop at Ensenada because a large percentage of the cones would get off the ship, making their day easier. The Hispanic members of the ship's crew always felt comfortable with the Ensenada stop, and those who could get a few hours off the ship used the port visit to stock up on a few necessities. For cabin steward Carlos Fernandez, it was a time to buy half a dozen Cuban cigars. He would skip the tourist shops on the pier and take the free shuttle bus into town, as he knew which store carried the three-pack of Montecristo #2 Cubans for four hundred pesos. The Montecristo #2 was a torpedo cigar with a ring gauge of fifty-two and could be sold to the rich Americans for twenty-five to thirty dollars each. His investment of thirty-two dollars for three cigars would fetch between seventy-five and ninety US dollars, or a profit of fifty dollars.

The Ensenada stop would also be a final opportunity for Dakila Salazar to capture naked videos of passengers assigned to his nineteen cabins on the Aquarius deck. On this trip, he tried to position his camera so he could watch the passengers open their cabin safes in the hopes of stealing some cash. His micro-spy camera captured the contents of the safes but was never able to get a clear picture of their combinations.

Dakila felt that cabin A-497 might hold promise for some sex shots. Mickey and Kathy Riddle were celebrating their fifth wedding anniversary, and Mrs. Riddle, who seemed to be about thirty years old, had a great figure. Dakila fantasized about her lying naked on the cabin's queen-size bed. He wanted so much to see her big tits. Knowing that the Riddles were dressed in swimsuits and headed to deck fourteen for some Mexican sun, Dakila used the time to reposition the camera so he could focus the lens on their bed.

At 8:30 p.m., Captain Costanzo sounded the ship's horn for a solid five seconds, signaling that the ship was leaving port. Now that the gangway detail was secured, Yvette and Raju met to review security threat assessments and other security department housekeeping items.

Yvette shared with Raju an unsubstantiated rumor of a dancer from the production show who was supplementing her salary by turning tricks. Dancers, who typically sign a six-month contract, are encouraged to mingle more with the passengers than the average crew member. A dancer who prostituted him- or herself twice a month could pocket an extra $300 to $400 a month, a huge bonus for a dancer from the Ukraine earning $25,000 a year. "Raju, what concerns me is the possibility that she's being set up by another dancer who wants her spot in the show. What concerns do you have?"

"My concern is always with the Mexicans who leave the ship in Ensenada. The temptation to smuggle drugs is just too great. I want to hire a drug dog to catch the bad guys who are sneaking cocaine onboard."

Yvette nodded. "Fort Lauderdale just busted a group who were paid $2,000 to smuggle cocaine onboard their ship in Grand Turk and then paid another $1,000 to sneak the coke off the ship when it returned to Fort Lauderdale."

"That is my point. What would it cost to contract for a sniffer dog?"

"We might be able to get some financial help from DEA," answered Yvette.

"There is a Mexican cabin attendant on Draco deck who has a habit of buying Cubans every time he gets off at Ensenada, yet he is a nonsmoker. It is not a big threat to the cruise line, but if he is selling them onboard, the idea could spread to other members of the crew."

"I agree. Keep your eye on him." Yvette folded up her notebook, signaling that their meeting was over.

Dakila pushed his housekeeping service cart down the starboard side of the Aquarius deck and stopped outside the door of cabin A-497 "Housekeeping," he announced before inserting his card into the door of Mr. and Mrs. Riddle's cabin.

He pushed the rubber wedge under the door and scooped up the cabin's dirty towels. As he picked another set of clean towels from his cart, he looked up and down the hallway. Dakila quickly set the towels on the bed and retrieved both the micro-camera and the receiver that was taped behind the TV. Wrapping both items in a towel, he then hid them in his cart. Dakila rushed through the last two cabins, stowed his cart, and hurried to his cabin on deck three.

Pushing the "save" video option on the download moved the 8.2 gigabytes of data to his laptop. Dakila figured he had about 103 minutes of video from cabin A-497. After thirty minutes of fast scanning through video shots of Mickey Riddle walking back and forth between the bed and the balcony, Dakila observed Mrs. Riddle, still wearing her two-piece swimsuit, cross in front of the camera and appear to close the curtains. She was out of the line of focus, but the room grew darker before she unhooked her swimsuit top and laid face down on the bed.

Dakila's patience was rewarded with a quite a show for the next forty minutes. He watched intently as Mickey Riddle rubbed some kind of liquid or lotion on his wife's back. Dakila could not believe his luck. Most of the time, the back of Mr. Riddle obscured the action, but then he would move, giving Dakila the perfect view. He witnessed a sensuous scene of Mr. Riddle pulling down Mrs. Riddle's swimsuit bottom and applying an ample quantity of lotion to her beautiful ass. He also watched Mr. Riddle's fingers explore between her ass cheeks. Dakila was beside himself when Kathy Riddle rolled over and her husband spent at least fifteen minutes gently caressing her breasts.

Dakila labeled the file 497, closed the computer, and left his cabin in pursuit of his friend Marcario.

Yvette was relaxing by herself in the crew's bar when the Filipino cabin attendant walked by and discreetly slipped a note in her hand. After he walked out the door, Yvette carefully opened the note and read the sentence written in Tagalog. *"Tumawag sa akin sa lalong madaling panahon,"* which meant "call me soon." The note had his name and cabin number at the bottom.

Marcario Navarro felt nervousness in his stomach unlike anything he had experienced before. He felt pulled in two different directions. Dakila was a fellow Filipino, even though Marcario was from Manila and Dakila was from the city of Caloocan. Marcario felt there was the possibility of career advancement in his future. His leadership on the *Matisse's* crew welfare committee had caught the eye of a few of the officers and division heads. So he made the decision to put his job before his friendship with Dakila.

Officer Fuentes suggested that they meet on deck fifteen near the *Matisse* golf links. They both agreed it would be private and highly unlikely that there would be other crew members hanging around.

"Officer Fuentes, I am afraid. I do not want to lose my job."

"Marcario, have you broken any of the cruise line's rules?"

"No, but—"

"Then you have nothing to worry about. Now tell me what is bothering you."

Marcario started by explaining that he was a cabin steward on the Cassiopeia deck, port side aft. Yvette was not ready for the bomb he dropped on her.

"My friend showed me a video on his laptop. Ma'am, it was a sex video. One taken with a secret camera he had hidden in a passenger's room. He had several videos. I think he has been putting cameras in passengers' rooms for most of the time he has been on the *Matisse*."

Yvette felt like she was on an elevator and the cables had broken. Her legs actually felt weak. "Do you think that he's shared these sex videos with any other members of the crew?'

"No, ma'am. Dakila is kind of a loner. I am one of his only friends. Officer Fuentes, do you think I will lose my job?"

"Let me ask you a serious question before I answer yours."

"Sure," replied Marcario nervously.

"Are you in any of the sex videos on Dakila's computer?"

"No, I would never—"

"Then I was just kidding. Your job is safe."

Chapter Forty-One

"Angie, call Herb Wallace and tell him I will be in his office in five minutes," said Director Zittel as he grabbed his suit jacket.

"Sir, are you sure you don't want him to come to your office?"

"Thanks, but no. I need a little exercise. The five floors will be good for me."

Ace walked briskly down the stairs until he arrived at the second floor. Several steps behind him was a member of his security detail. Even though the FBI building operated under the classification of a level-A security building, the director still had his own team for personal protection.

"Herb, grab your carry. We're going for a walk," announced the director as he stuck his head in Herb's office.

In addition to his reputation for Gucci loafers and "AAZ" monogram shirts, Ace maintained a reputation for having meetings while he walked around the FBI headquarters. There were those in the Bureau who felt he took pleasure in out-walking the younger special agents. One new FBI agent returned from a walking meeting declaring that the director was a member of the Fast Walkers of America club.

Ace and Herb walked out of the building and turned onto Pennsylvania Avenue. "Herb, we have a situation that just broke in Montana. Initial reports are that a couple of guys drove a van of explosives to the Yellowtail Dam and lit it off. Looks like they made more noise than damage, but the press is in full-court terrorism mode. We have a few agents on the scene from Billings, Montana, and Casper, Wyoming, but I want a couple of your guys to get out there and take the lead."

Herb, doing his best to keep up with the director, asked, "Do we have any reports of damage to the dam?"

"I have the deputy director coordinating the damage assessment, but I understand they are maximizing water release from the Bighorn Lake to reduce stress on the dam until they can complete their inspection. The van did explode, and at least two occupants are dead. Herb, this may or may not be a terrorist attack. It may have ties to radical Islamists, but I want to smother the rumors until we know the facts. The president is just about to convene a big Muslim outreach, and another backlash against Muslims would be devastating to the president's initiative. Get your best counterterrorism guys out there and have them do whatever is needed to keep this a low-profile event."

"Are you shitting me?" asked Kryss when Nathan told him they needed to be in Montana yesterday via the FBI's Gulfstream V. Use of the Bureau jet was only authorized for counterterrorism emergencies or for speeches by the director.

"We're to head up the Critical Incident Response Group for this dam explosion undertaking," added Nathan.

Their Washington, DC, cab passed through the two gates at Andrews AFB before depositing Kryss and Nathan at the foot of the jet's door steps. Standing near the nose of the jet was an FBI courier who handed Kryss a five-inch-thick packet that contained the latest incident damage assessments, along with reports from the special agents that were already on the ground.

The G-V at 488 knots would travel the seventeen hundred miles in a little over three hours. This gave the two special agents plenty of time to review the material they were provided.

"Looks like Bomb School 101," Nathan commented as he read from the files. "Rental van was filled with ammonium nitrate, powdered aluminum, oil, and a bunch of five-gallon propane tanks. They used a couple of semiauto pistols to shoot up the empty guard shack and then crashed through the chain link fence. They used a Remington 870 to put some twelve gauges into the propane tanks and threw in a flare. The guys don't think it was suicide, but two bodies were blown about fifty feet from what was left of the van."

Kryss went ballistic when he read the suggested media talking points. "Do you believe this bullshit? Listen to this crap. They want us to imply that this may be an act of civil disobedience caused by old wounds from the Crow Nation."

Nathan looked up, puzzled. "Explain, please."

"Here's what they have provided. Now understand that this is all bullshit. Some dude by the name of Robert Yellowtail was leader of the Crow Indian tribe in the forties. He was against the dam project. When he didn't get his way, there was a big disagreement about whether to sell the land or lease it. This issue divided the tribe into the Mountain Crows and the River Crows. We're supposed to convince the media that this explosion was caused by some old Mountain Crows who're still pissed about that deal."

Nathan shook his head, incredulous. "How are we going to explain that two dead Crow Indians just arrived in the United States from Yemen and had copies of the Quran in their jackets?"

Chapter Forty-Two

"Dakila Salazar, ship security. Open your door!" Raju stood in the hallway on deck three, waiting for Salazar to open his door, which he did thirty seconds later about six inches. "Dakila, you know who I am, right? Let me in."

Opening the door, Salazar stepped aside and allowed Raju to enter the small cabin.

"Get dressed. We have a meeting in the security office." At 1:30 a.m., Raju was in no mood to listen to any crap. "Get your ass in gear or I will drag you to the office half-dressed."

Once Raju had deposited Salazar at the security office, he returned to deck three to conduct a search of Dakila's cabin.

Yvette told Dakila to sit down at the metal desk in the interview room, walked over to her desk, and radioed another member of the security team to join her at the office.

"You are Dakila Salazar, correct?"

"Why am I here? You have no right to wake me up in the middle of the night!" protested the cabin attendant.

Yvette jumped up, hurled her chair against the wall, and then leaned against the desk until her face was three inches from Salazar's. *How would Brick take it from here?* she thought. "What did you not understand? Are you Dakila Salazar?"

"Yes, but I want my supervisor here!"

"Have it your way. Maybe some time in the brig will help you decide if you want to cooperate!" Yvette grabbed the crew member, placed him in handcuffs, and threw him into the brig.

Most cruise ships have a little jail, or brig, used predominantly for drunk or unruly passengers. The brig on the *Matisse* was actually a twenty-five-square-foot room with little beyond a rubber mat on the floor. The room contained no chair or toilet. A secure wire cage enclosed the only light in the room, and there was a small mesh window in the door through which very little was visible. Outside the door was a whiteboard with a magic marker tied to a string. Hoping that he could see her, Yvette wrote the time and Salazar's name on the whiteboard and then signed it "Fuentes." Without looking back in the prisoner's direction, she left the security office and returned to her cabin for a little sleep.

A couple of hours later, Raju piled Dakila's laptop, micro-camera, and video receiver on Yvette's desk. Looking at his watch, he made a note on the brig's whiteboard and entered the time: 4:00 a.m. He then unlocked the door to Dakila's cell and entered carrying several items.

"Wake up. Here is some water, a granola bar, a plastic bag, and an adult diaper. Put your clothes in this bag, and put on the diaper. I understand that you have decided to live in here for a while. You may be here a long time, and I'm sorry, but there is no toilet." Raju left Salazar rubbing his eyes, wondering what had just happened.

Fresh from four hours of sleep and a large cup of coffee, Yvette returned to the security office. She had another member of her security detail fetch Dakila from the brig. Wearing only his diaper, he was seated again at the desk in the interview room.

"Would you like me to remove your handcuffs?" asked Yvette.

"Yes, please," replied Dakila in a voice much more humble then when he first arrived several hours earlier.

Yvette returned to her desk, picked up the camera equipment, and dropped the items in front of Dakila. "Explain!"

"I am sorry. I was just trying to have a little fun. Nobody got hurt. I only did it a few times," he replied, avoiding eye contact with Yvette.

"Dakila, we have already looked at some of your computer's video files. I would say your psychosexual disorder has been going on for a long time. So here is what we are going to do. I am going to return your clothes. Then you are going to write down every time you made a video of passengers on the *Matisse*. I want the date, cabin number, and location of the video file. I'll be back in an hour with a cruise schedule to aid your memory with the dates."

The Constellation deck was almost empty when Yvette walked to the Gallery Grill and Food Court. A bagel and cream cheese plus another cup of coffee would have to do for today's breakfast.

Yvette pondered the timing of informing the captain and Rob Spencer in Florida about Salazar. Taking a final drink of her coffee, she decided to get Dakila's confession in hand before she started the corporate meltdown.

When Yvette returned to her office, she was surprised to see Raju already at his desk. "How is our cinematographer doing?"

"You are not going to be happy." Raju pointed to the blank pages in front of Dakila.

"Mr. Salazar, do we need to return to the brig?"

"No, ma'am. But I would like to discuss a deal."

"A deal? What do you think we're playing? *Let's Make a Deal?*" Yvette sat down across from Dakila.

"I did not just video naked passengers," said Dakila in a voice so low that Yvette almost could not hear him.

"Explain."

Dakila spoke with new self-confidence. "You remember the last cruise, not this one, but the cruise before this one? The one when we had a code orange because seventy-four passengers got sick?"

Having a strange feeling that it was going to be a long day, Yvette replied, "Yes, I remember. What about that cruise?"

"The cones that got sick did not have Noro. They were poisoned by a passenger."

For the next thirty minutes, Yvette and Dakila battled back and forth. Dakila wanted a deal, and Yvette wanted specifics and proof that Dakila had real information about a mysterious man he claimed had poisoned the passengers.

"Director Spencer, I know this is a hot potato. Even without his claim of information about a passenger-initiated poisoning, we still have the issue of a dozen cases of breach of privacy. Rob, you might want to check with legal, but it seems to me that regardless of all the disclaimers on our passenger contract, there's still no clause where our guests gave up their rights and expectations of privacy in their cabin beds."

Rob took a few minutes to reply. "Yvette, this is a real mess. We have a dozen or more passengers who could hang Nobility out to dry. But I just don't know if we need Morgan Maritime Investigations on this case right n—"

"Rob, there are two reasons why we do. First, I feel that Raju and I aren't going to crack this guy. We've been through his computer, and there are a lot of gaps. Salazar knows we're Nobility, and he thinks he can wait us out. Morgan's an outsider. He has the ability to motivate these jerks to cooperate. If we turn him over to San Francisco PD or the FBI, we'll never be able to do damage control with the injured passengers. The second reason has to do with that phony Norovirus diagnosis. This gives us a chance to finally get answers. If this plays out the wrong way, Nobility will have a PR problem of such epic shit that it'll be a case study at the Harvard Business School for decades. If Brick can get to the bottom of this poisoning situation, we can turn the sex tapes crime into a victory and save the Nobility brand."

"Fuentes, fuck. You sound like a goddamned lawyer. Okay! I'll call Morgan. And dammit, you and Morgan stay out of the hot tub!"

Chapter Forty-Three

There was a good chance that Yusuf Al Omar would be dead in a week. As much as he was a true believer and follower of his faith, Yusuf was never motivated by the promise of a paradise where the rivers flowed of wine and seventy-two virgins waited for him. He had a mission to do, and he was well aware of the danger of a single grain of abrin.

Yusuf closed and locked the door to his room at the Mark Hopkins Hotel located atop Beacon Hill in San Francisco. Tomorrow he would board the cruise ship *Matisse*, but today he would organize and hide the equipment needed to execute his plan. He placed the Smith and Wesson M&P9 on the desk and removed the magazine and set it aside. Pulling back the stainless steel slide gave him access to the sear deactivation lever. After flipping the breakdown lever, he was able to remove the slide. Reaching inside, he removed the spring rod and then was able to take out the barrel.

Yusuf chose the M&P9 because the frame was made of Zytel polymer and would not be picked up by the cruise ship's luggage X-ray machines. The slide assembly was inserted in the bottom of an old Dell laptop computer that had some parts removed to accommodate the largest metal part of the 9mm gun. A leg of his small camera tripod concealed the tiny barrel. Even though the magazine held seventeen 9mm bullets, Yusuf only brought ten. The ten Federal 115-grain bullets escaped detection as he had inserted them in four cigars that he had placed inside stainless steel cigar tubes.

Satisfied that he could smuggle the pistol onboard, Yusuf then concerned himself with his new identity. Members of Lashkar-e-Aalam had learned the ease of obtaining an American passport. Forged documents, submitted at passport application centers located at US Postal Service locations, had the best chance of being processed. Yusuf looked at three different sets of identities and chose a passport for Fredrick Batista. Born in Miami, Florida, to a Lebanese mother and Cuban father, Fred Batista attended the Drexel University and was an assistant manager at Home Depot. Yusuf memorized the address and phone number of the Home Depot on Roosevelt Boulevard in Pennsylvania.

Yusuf, or Fredrick, was ready to board the *Matisse*. The eighty grams of abrin was inserted into a sealed plastic test tube that had been inserted into a slightly larger plastic tube. Once placed inside a bottle of mouthwash, the plastic tubes would not be identified by TSA or the cruise line security as prohibited items.

Identical preparations were taking place in Los Angeles and Fort Lauderdale. Muhamed Bashir selected a different hotel than Zahir Ahmed Hahid, even though they were both boarding ships at Fort Lauderdale. Muhammad Bin Attash and Mullah Saleh Rahim had arrived in southern California and were anticipating boarding their ships at the Port of Los Angeles World Cruise Center in San Pedro. Attash would embark on a seven-day Mexican Riviera cruise on the *Cézanne*. The Nobility *Lautrec* would be the staging platform for Rahim.

Communication was going to be a critical component to the success of their mission. Yusuf was adamant that the attacks be coordinated. He explained to the other terrorists that once the abrin was disseminated and passengers began to die, they could expect a fleet-wide lockdown on all of the ships belonging to the Nobility Cruise Line. The Gmail account of baseballfan999 would be the primary system of distribution of information. The Scrabble HD game application had also been installed on each of their laptops where the chat feature would be used if online conversations were needed. Yusuf was confident that his tricks using Gmail and game applications would keep him a couple of steps ahead of the NSA.

The cat-and-mouse game between national threats and the United States spy agencies had been going on for decades. The ability of the FBI and now the NSA to monitor communications between those terrorists who were committed toward worldwide jihad was the most important element to winning the war. In 1994, Congress passed the Communications Assistance for Law Enforcement Act, commonly known as CALEA. This act required Internet providers and phone companies to cooperate with the installation of surveillance equipment that would provide real-time spying on all broadband Internet, voice, and voiceover traffic.

The expansion of traffic spying paralleled two separate data science developments. The first was the new cottage industry that provided the covert equipment and software to intercept all of the data transmitted and received through both wire and air. The second development was the enormous investment the CIA, FBI, and NSA have made in their ability to manage extremely large amounts of communication data they can access every day.

A large quantity of mass-intercept black boxes had been installed inside the Internet hubs of all of the countries' telecommunication companies. These mirror-ports or mirror-rooms are located in secret rooms actually inside the phone companies' hubs or data vaults.

Special software is used to sift through the data and intercept pen registry trap data. The capture of "who you call" information is called pen registry, and "trap" refers to who calls you. A leader in traffic analytics software is the Boeing-owned company called Narus. The Narus system has a sophisticated architecture that allows for the flow of data to pass through its system and provides customers with real-time forensic intelligence and also processes the data for detective and targeted storage.

The FBI created the Digital Collection Systems Network and first commissioned the Carnivore data software. The FBI upgraded its capabilities when it adopted Narus products and developed the NSA's super-secret spy center in Bluffdale, Utah. Code-named "Stellar Wind," the Bluffdale investment is another step for the NSA to analyze and manage the seven hundred petabytes of daily Internet traffic.

The most covert development in the capture, analysis, and storage

HIGH SEAS DARKNESS

of Internet traffic is project Black Owl. Even with the huge budgets of the US agencies involved in international and domestic spying, the advancements of technology and social network communications outpaced the government's ability to stay ahead of the terrorists. The solution was the creation of Black Owl.

Black Owl is nothing more than the CIA, FBI, NSA, and Homeland Security's move toward outsourcing data science to a shadow corporation. In 2013, an unknown company leased an unspecified amount of space in the Cheyenne Mountain complex. Once used by NORAD as the center for command and control of air defense, the underground center has been on standby since 2008. The corporate ownership of Black Owl is buried so deep in layers and layers of LLCs and exotic trusts that a thousand forensic CPAs could never figure out who owned the most powerful private company in the world.

The dirty secret is that Black Owl is actually owned by the United States of America. In addition to the hundreds of black boxes that are installed at every telecom company intersection, Black Owl supplements its intel gathering with mobile sniffers. These mobile sniffer devices, or MSDs, are the most aggressive challenge to America's Fourth Amendment rights. Black Owl contracted companies for the installation of thousands of sniffers on commercial trucks that service the homes of America. When national delivery trucks drive to the homes of Americans to deliver packages, a small, wide-spectrum frequency analyzer looks through the walls of every home and records cell calls, computer key strokes, and even any data being saved on thumb drives. A Black Owl proposal to funnel billions of dollars to the cash-strapped USPS would add tens of thousands of MSDs to the streets of America.

After creating a draft e-mail on his baseballfan999 Gmail account detailing a timeline for the attack, Fredrick Batista grabbed his new passport and took the elevator up to the Top of the Mark for what might be his last dinner—or at least his last dinner on dry land.

Chapter Forty-Four

Rob Spencer had asked Brick if he could get down to San Francisco again and meet up with the *Matisse*. Spencer explained that Yvette was holding a pervert who claimed he knew who had poisoned the passengers on the Hawaiian cruise that went to code orange. Brick confirmed with Rob that he would be in San Francisco by evening.

The Seattle to San Francisco Alaska Air schedule was fluid enough that Brick was able to set up a meeting with Titus before he drove to the Sea-Tac Airport. Titus had called, saying that she had discovered more Internet traffic that she felt Brick needed to see before he left town.

Titus had removed her bathrobe and was bringing up a digital file labeled "Red Ocean."

"Before we get to work on your agenda, I want to ask you what you know about 'Spindleratchet,'" said Brick.

Titus slammed her hands down on the keyboard and spun around in her chair. Crossing her arms across her chest, she yelled, "This is fucking bullshit!"

"Titus, calm down. When I was in DC, the Feds told me to be careful. Then the agent said, and I quote, 'Tell Spindleratchet that he or she needs to be very cautious. The international cyber-world can be dangerous.' I didn't take it as a threat, more of a warning."

"Morgan, I only use that name when I'm probing in the deep and dark world of the terrorist's blogospheres. I use the handle 'Spindleratchet' when I enter a multiauthor blog and try to swim upstream. I never use it when hacking or surfing other sites, just for hacking the Middle Eastern blogs. Remember when I found that malware after I probed the computer of baseballfan999?"

"Do you think the FBI is also watching these Lashkar-e-Aalam guys?"

"Yes, and I also think the Feds know who I am. There is only one way that the blue suits could know my blog ID."

"If the FBI or NSA are inside their computers, they sure don't act like it." Brick continued. "I get the feeling that they believe what I told them, but it seems they hoped I would just go away. Look, I need to get to the airport and catch up with the *Matisse* again. They have a crew member they're holding who claims to have information on that cruise where I had suspected terrorism." Brick finished updating the naked Titus and listened as she reviewed her latest material she had gleaned from her cyber explorations.

"I found a couple of e-mails sent from baseball's computer. He used another name, but it still originated from his machine. He was trying to locate a large quantity of peas—rosary peas. He needed them to be available in northern Africa. Ricin has been a weapon of choice for terrorists for a long time. It doesn't require an Einstein to make the deadly powder from castor beans. The same goes for the rosary peas. Ten pounds of peas will result in enough abrin to kill hundreds of people."

Titus told Brick that she had a strong feeling she would soon discover some additional leads on baseball's plans. "I'm very concerned that the government has me in its sights. You might think I'm paranoid, but I think I'm just cautious. What is a fact is that the FBI knows I am digging into what it feels is its backyard. We need to stay in touch when you're on the ship, but we cannot let the government listen in. I want to go to a one-pad code book."

"Titus, I can deal with your aversion to clothes, but codes get too complicated, and the NSA has big computers to crack any code."

"This will be simple, Brick, I promise. A one-pad code can't be broken. I'll give you five code keys. We only use a key once, and then we both destroy it. Each of your key sheets is identical to my sheets. All we need to do is clarify which key we're using, as they're all numbered from one through five. Each key contains over five hundred words, and each word has its own number. Let me show you." She handed him a sheet that read:

Key#1:
904 abort / 254 access / 378 answer / 802 abrin / 519 attack / 060 ask
759 alarm / 489 above / 993 airplane / 834 atomic / 639 AM / 780 atrium
154 bag / 509 bullet / 680 bomb / 399 build / 255 boy / 496 bureau / 555 boat

"If I wanted to send you a message that said, 'Atomic bomb above boat,' I'd send 834, 680, 489, 555."

Titus gave Brick his five key code sheets and explained that if e-mail wasn't operating, they could still use a cell phone and just read the numbers. She repeated that if they only used a code key once, it wasn't possible to break it. "And there's just one more thing."

"Go for it, but I need to get going if I'm going to make my flight." Brick put his sheets into a small folder.

"I'm being watched. Someone is hanging around my house. I have a bunch of cameras, and even though no one is showing up on the digital memory, I see shadows and the motion feature keeps going off. It's like someone is avoiding the field of view but is close enough to the camera that he or she is activating the motion sensor."

Brick thought for a few minutes. He felt responsible for any situation Titus was in because he had hired her to snoop around in some dangerous places.

"Why don't you set up shop at my house until I get back?"

"Thank you. That's very kind, but I can take care of myself. I just wanted you to be aware. Anyway, I'm very good with my Remington 870."

HIGH SEAS DARKNESS

As soon as Brick walked out the front door, Titus locked the dead bolt and set the alarm system. She then walked into the kitchen and removed the shotgun from the narrow broom closet by the back door. Returning to the front room, Titus leaned the Remington against the other computer chair and returned to her cyber-searches.

Chapter Forty-Five

"Morgan, Brick Morgan, Flight 338 to Oakland," Brick said as he handed the Alaska Airlines ticket agent a copy of his six-letter confirmation code and his driver's license.

"How many bags are you checking?"

"Two, and one bag contains a locked gun case."

"Here is your boarding pass, but you will have to check your bags over there at that special handling table."

Even though Brick was licensed by the state of Washington as an armed private investigator, he still was not eligible under Title 49 to carry a firearm in an airplane cabin. To qualify as a law enforcement officer, or LEO, an individual had to be employed by a government agency and have a letter of authorization from his or her department. If a gun case was lockable and was a hard case, it could be transported in luggage, so Brick had packed his weapons in an ADG Sports Two Pistol Range Case.

"Which bag contains the gun?" asked the TSA agent. Brick pointed out the bag, and the agent opened the luggage, took a quick look, and then sent both bags down the luggage conveyer belt.

Armed with his first-class boarding pass, Brick moved to the front of the TSA line and cleared the TSA station in less than five minutes. Slipping back into his shoes, he was soon on his way to Sea-Tac's N gates.

The digital display at gate eight indicated that Brick had a solid forty minutes before it was time to board his plane for Oakland, California. A little downtime was a welcomed luxury, of which he planned to take full advantage. Scrolling through his contact list, he selected the name of Stephen Marchione. Marchione Guitars have designed and built some of the finest guitars for many of the world's best-known guitarists. Since 2000, the primary guitar of Mark Whitfield had been the Stephen Marchione sixteen-inch Archtop. Mark had sent an e-mail to Brick, indicating that he had made arrangements for Stephen to ship him a custom Whitfield Archtop. It was Brick's plan to have Mark sign the guitar and then display it in his den. After speaking to Stephen and making shipping arrangements, Brick made a mental note to set up a scheduled endorsement on his homeowner's policy for the new $20,000 guitar.

Prior to boarding, Brick stopped off at the Hudson News shop and picked up a copy of the *New England Journal of Medicine*. Brick traveled at least sixty times a year, counting the return segments, and he tried to use each flight segment to learn a new subject. He calculated that in just three years he would gain knowledge of another two hundred subjects. This flight, his project would be a long article titled, "Stem Cell and Bone Marrow Transplantation."

"Mr. Morgan, can I get you another cognac?" asked the flight attendant.

"Yes, please, and can you give me a heads-up when we are about ten minutes from final approach?"

"Of course. May I ask you a question? Do you have a morning TV show—you know, as a news man or weather reporter?" The flight attendant picked up his empty glass.

"No, but thank you. I'm asked that a lot. Actually, I'm something of a consultant for the cruise industry." Brick smiled and returned to his magazine.

Two hours later, Brick handed three two-dollar bills to the six-figure-a-year doorman at the Mark Hopkins Hotel. One of the great debates of San Francisco was about the annual compensation of the famous doormen at the Mark. Dressed in their tailored uniforms with the big red cuffs, these smiling traditions on Nob Hill are a guest's first taste of the elegance of the Mark Hopkins.

Brick was anxious to check into his room and head to the Top of the Mark for a basket of breads with salami, cappa prosciutto, Muscovy duck breast, and liver terrine—and a drink, of course.

Placing his suitcase on the bed, Brick removed a clean polo shirt and put his travel bag of toiletries in the bathroom. Making a note of his room number, he grabbed his room card and headed to the elevator. Pushing the button for the nineteenth floor, he was looking forward to a Top of the Mark signature martini. The combination of the hotel being on the top of Nob Hill and the restaurant being located on the nineteenth floor made for a spectacular view. Brick would have preferred to be in the company of a gorgeous woman, but not lacking self-confidence, he was determined to enjoy the evening skyline of San Francisco.

Four ounces of Jack Daniels, one ounce of crème de cacao, and a half-ounce of lemon juice, shake with ice, and pour straight-up, thought Brick, as he took a second sip of his Golden Gate martini and looked around the room and checked out the other guests who were enjoying the historic atmosphere. Nothing out of the ordinary, observed Brick as he viewed tables of families, business meetings, and one table of three tall, good-looking women who could have been models.

Then he noticed a young man in a T-shirt drinking a beer by himself. What attracted Brick's attention was he was so underdressed for this upscale venue. Brick figured the guy to be about twenty-five and most likely from the Middle East. Brick's concentration was broken when the waitress brought him another Golden Gate.

"Sir, that table of three women wants to buy you a drink," said the waitress after placing the drink next to his original martini.

"Wow! Please thank them for me. That was very kind." Brick turned toward their table, flashed a smile, and mouthed, "Thank you."

For the next thirty minutes, he alternated between thinking about tomorrow's assignment, enjoying the lights of the city, and sipping his cocktail. Glancing at the table of women, he noticed that one of the ladies had gotten up and was walking in his direction. Without hesitation, she pulled out a chair at Brick's table and sat down.

"You're Brick Morgan, aren't you?"

"Well, yes. But you have me at a slight disadvantage, one I don't mind," he answered with a mischievous smile.

"My name is Rachel, Rachel Broussard. Until a few weeks ago, I was a dancer with Carnival Cruise Line. I was on one of their ships last year when you came onboard to investigate a sexual assault."

"And you and some of your dance team had drinks with me at the disco, right?" interjected Brick.

"You remembered." Rachel continued, explaining that the three of them were traveling together. "The three of us left Carnival and have just signed a contract with the Nobility Cruise Line. We're going to start our new dancing assignment tomorrow on the *Matisse*."

An hour later, the four of them agreed that they needed some sleep before they all embarked on the *Matisse Under the Stars*. After flipping a twenty on the table to cover tips, Brick got up from the table and walked across the dining room toward the door. His peripheral vision noticed that the Middle Eastern beer drinker turned away as he walked past his table, avoiding eye contact.

Yusuf was mentally reviewing his new identity. Fredrick Batista would be expected to drink beer and look at the American women. However, the more he watched the women, the more committed he became in succeeding in striking a blow against the West. *America's attempt at nation building and spreading democracy is just a disguise to corrupt our culture by brainwashing our obedient women,* he thought.

Watching the half-naked women flirt with the tall American man brought to the surface Yusuf's hatred for America's permissive society. The attempt to spread human rights to Muslim women was only a means to outlaw the hijab and undress the Islam women. The thought of Americans watching a Muslim woman and lusting over her bare arms and legs was disgusting to Yusuf, and his blood boiled. *Let the Americans have their erotic fantasies and mental masturbations in their own country, but not in our holy land.*

Chapter Forty-Six

Yvette had spent most of the night searching Dakila's computer for any clues that would substantiate his claim. If he were bluffing, how would he know that she and Brick did not believe that Norovirus was the cause of the code orange? She had no answers, and now Dakila's laptop was providing no further explanations.

Located on deck four, between the medical center and the engineering space, Yvette's department occupied over eight hundred square feet. A large percentage of the security department's space was used for storage of guns and antipiracy weapons. In addition to the Long Range Acoustic Device, the *Matisse* also carried a supply of Modular Crowd Control Munitions and several TBL-37, less-than-lethal ordinance platforms. If the fire hoses and slippery goo did not stop a group of pirates, a couple of shots of six hundred rubber balls should slow them down. As a last resort, the ship had six Heckler & Koch HK 416 assault rifles located in the captain's quarters and another six locked up in the security department. Raju once told Yvette that all of the weapons were a big waste of money; he and his big Gurkha knife could stop any threat.

Alone in the security department, Yvette walked over to the bulkhead that displayed the work schedule for her department. Her thoughts were interrupted when the main door to the department slung open.

"San Francisco brings the *Matisse* back home / all the cones will now be free to roam. / Yet the deputy director is pledged to serve / and any criminal will be his to observe. / Do your eyes weep for the lack of sleep?"

"Okay, Raju. Yes, I have been here most of the night. I still can't find anything on Dakila's computer."

"I went through his cabin again and even looked in his toothpaste and soap for a hidden thumb drive. We'll have the gangway secured in about ten minutes Do you want me to meet Morgan, or do you want to go?"

"I want to give this computer another try. Knowing Morgan, he's probably already on the pier. Would you get him onboard and aim him in this direction?" Yvette returned to the laptop.

Brick watched as the longshoremen doubled up the four lines and secured the *Matisse* to pier Thirty-Five South. As he waited for the hydraulic door on deck four to open, he watched the dozens and dozens of forklifts that stood ready for the next eight hours of pandemonium and chaos. Over six thousand suitcases would be off-loaded, along with thirty-two hundred passengers. Several hours later, another six thousand suitcases would be loaded onboard, and thirty-two hundred new passengers would be issued cruise cards, photographed, and boarded. Another dozen forklifts would off-load tons of garbage and then load the *Matisse* with twenty-eight thousand pounds of beef, nine thousand pounds of fish, and forty-five thousand eggs.

"Mr. Morgan, welcome home!" shouted Raju from the top of the gangway.

A crew member escorted Brick up the gangway that still lacked the side rails. The main passenger gangway would be attached to deck six and would not be operative for another half an hour. Raju stayed on the pier to supervise the security logistics but had a security guard escort Brick to the security department.

"Officer Fuentes, doesn't a guy even get a chance to put his luggage in his cabin?"

"Brick, thank God you're here," replied Yvette, refraining from a more exuberant greeting in front of the other security guards in the room. "We have this nutcase locked up in his cabin. I'd like to go over the file on this guy as soon as possible."

"Let's go for it. I can check on the quality of my accommodations anytime," joked Brick as he placed his two suitcases in the corner of Yvette's office.

Yvette and Brick spread the file out on a small conference table. "What really pisses me off is this pervert's attitude. We nailed him cold with the videos he took. The jerk admits it, but he thinks the information he's holding should get him off."

"I understand that Raju hasn't been able to find any evidence in his cabin or on his computer."

"No, and I even went through his service cart just in case he hid a disk or thumb drive in his housekeeping supplies."

Brick and Yvette continued reviewing the case for another hour. Finally, they decided that Brick should have a straightforward talk with Dakila.

Brick and Yvette headed down the stairs to deck three and walked aft down I-95 until they located the corridor that lead to Dakila's cabin.

"Salazar? Security." Yvette inserted her card into the slot, and she and Brick entered Dakila's cabin.

After a brief introduction, Brick made the first move. "Dakila, I am at a disadvantage. Would you tell me your story, please?" he asked in a quiet voice.

"What do you mean?" replied Dakila with a smirk.

Brick grinned. "I understand you like to take naked pictures of the passengers but that you want Officer Fuentes to let you go. Could you explain that to me, please?"

"Well, for starts, this ship owes me! When I want to use the Internet, the ship charges me twenty cents a minute, and the damn thing is so slow. There's also the percentage of the tip fund that we receive."

"Dakila, what I am hearing you say is that you are upset with the *Matisse* nickel-and-diming you to death. Is that correct?"

"Yeah, that is it. You know my brother was on the *Costa Concordia* when the ship sank. I just don't think—"

"Stop. Are you in denial or something? You're ten minutes away from spending the next twenty years in a federal prison filled with two kinds of prisoners—sexual perverts like you and three-hundred-pound psychopaths whose only goal is to fuck you perverts ten times a day. So don't screw with me anymore, Salazar. What information do you have?"

"I want a contract that guarantees my freedom if I give you my information."

"You have to give me something. If you're going to tell me that the ship's navigator is gay, I'm sorry, I just don't give a fucking shit."

"Okay, but I'm not going to give you details without a guarantee."

"Okay."

"The week that we had a code orange because seventy-four cones got the Norovirus, I saw a passenger with a tube of chemicals that I think was used to poison the ship. I know his name."

"Was he in a cabin that you serviced?" asked Brick.

"Fuck you! I want a guaranteed contract!"

"Mr. Salazar, I think you're full of shit." Brick said. Then, without another word, he and Yvette got up and relocked Dakila in his cabin.

Chapter Forty-Seven

"Mr. Batista, my number is by your phone if you need anything." "Thank you. I will be fine." Yusuf escorted the cabin steward out the door. He was anxious to unpack and set up communications with the rest of his team.

Going into the bathroom, he carefully unscrewed the cap on the mouthwash and poured it into the sink. He then pulled out the plastic vials. His big concern was that the liquid would leak into the powder and create a messy paste. He unscrewed the larger tube and extracted the plastic vial that contained the powdered abrin. Satisfied that the powder was dry, he set up the cabin safe and locked up the abrin.

Within thirty minutes, "Fredrick Batista" had retrieved all of the parts and assembled and loaded his 9mm pistol. Because the ship was still tied to the pier, he did not have to log into the ship's Digital Experience to access his e-mail account.

Yusuf was still uncertain as to the timetable for their attacks. He wanted to wait until the ship was between the mainland and Hawaii so as to make it difficult for a rescue or for the ship to receive any outside medical aid. On the other hand, he was concerned that if any members of the team were discovered, all of Nobility's ships would go on high alert. He was now leaning on the next day as the day to disperse the abrin.

One reason Yusuf was in a hurry was he had a funny feeling about the big guy he saw at the San Francisco hotel. After checking into his cabin on deck ten, Yusuf went up to deck fourteen to find some sweets. It was there that he again saw the big American and a lady security officer. He would keep an eye on this man, although Yusuf was not exactly sure why he bothered him.

The 4G feature on his laptop gained him access to his e-mail. The draft copy of his e-mail told the team to be ready for the game to start tomorrow. After a team member read the draft, he was to add the initials of his ship at the end of it. When Yusuf noted that all four ships had read the draft, he would then delete it.

Brick was thinking about the type of approach to use with Salazar when he noticed a text message from a burn phone. Titus. The message was short with only fourteen sets of three digits followed by two words: *code one*. Pulling his first code sheet from his briefcase, he proceeded to look up the words that corresponded to the numbers sent by Titus.

"Baseballfan999 active. Also, I think Chinese are spying on my house. New message tomorrow."

Brick ripped up the code sheet and flushed it down the cabin toilet. He wondered if Dakila Salazar really held the key to the mystery of code orange and if he could lead Brick to baseballfan999.

He dialed the security department. "Yvette, I've got an idea. First, I'd like to have a look at the pervert's computer. After that, will you let Captain Costanzo know that I'll need access to the deck four loading door at three in the morning?"

"Do you want to use his computer here in the security department, or do you want it delivered to your cabin?"

"I'll come to your office. Then I'm going to find some food. Oh." Brick suddenly realized something. "I want Salazar tired when we have our little visit with him at three in the morning. Can you get Raju to walk him up and down the I-95 from ten until we're ready for him? If anyone asks him what he's doing, tell him to say that Salazar is depressed and is on suicide watch. Remind Raju that I just want Salazar pissed off and tired; he is not to waterboard him. Seriously."

"Raju will be in his glory," replied Yvette as she placed Dakila's laptop on the office table.

Brick was busy with the laptop for about an hour. He saved his masterpiece on Dakila's desktop after naming the Word file "For Mother."

"Yvette, now it's his turn. I need this letter translated into Tagalog. Are you up to it?"

"You bet. I can write in Russian, English, and Tagalog, but I only speak Spanish." After taking a look at the letter Brick had composed, Yvette let out a soft "Oh, we're going to be in such deep shit!"

Chapter Forty-Eight

The *Matisse* possessed six large walk-in freezers, and freezer number four was located forward on deck four. The thirty-by-forty-foot freezer was located between dry storage number seven and the fresh flowers storage.

Brick and Yvette moved a case of beef tenderloins so it would serve as a table upon which Brick placed an open bottle of red wine and three glasses. Yvette glanced at the digital panel of the refrigeration control system. "Minus ten degrees Fahrenheit. What a lovely temperature for a wine-tasting party."

"The problem with dealing with sociopaths is that you can't motivate them with emotion. They operate from the lowest rungs of Maslow's hierarchy of needs. They will make decisions only after evaluating the impact on their physiological and safety needs. This jerk doesn't give a shit about love and belonging," expounded Brick.

Just then, Raju entered the freezer room with Dakila in tow. "He is all yours, my friends. He seems very depressed, and I am worried that he is suicidal." Raju then left, slamming the heavy door behind him.

"Dakila, can we serve you a little wine?" asked Brick as he poured some into Yvette's and his glasses.

Dakila did not answer. Instead, he crossed his arms and looked around the meat freezer. "What is this bullshit? You've got no right to bring me here!"

Brick looked at Dakila. "Did you know that a two-inch steak will freeze solid in two hours at a temperature of minus ten degrees? However, that's not true of the human body. When we leave you in here for four hours, you will actually be alive when we return. But the problem is, your lungs will be partially frozen. Salazar, did you know that most cases of pneumonia start in the right lung? That is because the right lung has three lobes and the left lung has only two. You see, we need to have room for our heart. What happens after four hours in here is your alveoli inside your superior lobe will freeze. You'll be alive, technically, but with your alveoli frozen, you will die of pneumonia in thirty-six hours. The doctors will note on your 'cause of death' chart that you died from pneumonia. Natural causes. So what are you thinking?"

"That you are fucking crazy!" shouted Salazar, glaring.

Brick took another sip of his wine and continued. "The problem, Salazar, is that you're worth more dead than alive. Let me explain. A couple of years ago, we had a chef on one of Nobility's ships who went crazy. He started spitting in the food served to the passengers. One time, this nutcase actually poured some of his piss on a platter of veal piccata. The ship was lucky because another crew member observed him spitting on food and reported him to a supervisor. The chef admitted to what he'd done and even confessed to the other bizarre things he did to passengers' food. His explanation was that he heard voices in his head, and the voices told him to defile the food. Salazar, are you still following me?"

"Yes, but I don't—"

"Shut up and listen. When the cruise line discovered what he'd done, it was between a rock and a hard place. If he was arrested and word got out to the press, the Nobility brand would be ruined. Nobody would want to go on a cruise with Nobility, and thousands would lose their jobs. The cruise line called on me, and I flew out to the ship. The following day, there were reports that a chef from one of the main dining rooms was missing. After several more days, it was announced that Bruno Clemente had fallen overboard. Salazar, that ship was the *Bernini*."

"I was on the *Bernini*. I remember when that happened."

"Exactly," added Brick. "Did you ever hear that he had pissed on a platter of veal piccata?"

"No." Dakila rubbed his arms to ward off the cold.

"Salazar, here's the problem: You will not tell us the name of the passenger that we want, and we can't let the story about your taking videos of naked passengers get out to the press. Yvette, would you flip open his computer and let him read the letter he wrote to his mother?"

Confused, Dakila looked at the screen of his laptop and watched as Yvette opened a file on his desktop. He read:

Dear Mother,
Please forgive me, as I have embarrassed you and our family. It is my entire fault, and there is only one way to save our family from the embarrassment I have caused. Please forgive—

Horrified, Salazar said, "I did not write—"

"Quiet, asshole. We're going for a walk now." Brick grabbed his wine glass and Salazar by the arm and walked him out of the freezer and down a passageway toward amidships. Yvette closed the laptop and followed the two men as they proceeded up the stairs to deck four.

At 3:00 a.m., the starboard passageway on deck four was deserted. Walking to the large vertical access hatch, Brick stopped and looked Dakila in the eye. "Salazar, there is no scenario that I'm aware of this morning where you're not going to end up eating shit!"

Brick kept one hand on Dakila's arm and with the other flipped open the security cover plate, exposing the controls for the large hatch. He looked over at Yvette who took a final look at Salazar and walked away with a faint look of false sympathy.

Brick pushed a button. A motor pumped hydraulic fluid into the four slave pistons that slowly raised the four-thousand-pound door. Brick and Dakila stood at the edge of the opened hatch and watched the ocean splash by roughly at twenty knots. The sharp spray of the water rushing by just a few feet below hit them. Brick dropped his wine glass into the water, and Dakila stared as the water violently smashed it, leaving drops of dark red wine that quickly dispersed without a trace.

Without warning, Brick moved on his prisoner. Ten years of judo stepped in. Brick wrapped his arm around Dakila's chest while kicking his feet out from under him. Yelling into Dakila's ear, Brick offered him one more chance. "Just give me a name!" Salazar screamed as he hung half in and half out of the access hatch. His feet were a good two feet below the deck and hanging outside the *Matisse*.

"*Tae! Tae!* Five-oh-nine, five-oh-nine! Okay, Okay! Oh, *Diyos!*" He screamed as a stream of urine ran down his left leg.

Brick dangled him for another few seconds before taking three steps back and brutally depositing Dakila on the deck. Brick strolled over to the control switch and pushed the "down" button for the hatch.

"Talk. What's 509?"

Yvette returned just as Dakila started babbling about Aquarius cabin 509. "Oh, *Diyos, Diyos!* I just wanted to video the combination of his cabin safe. It didn't work, but I got a video of him mixing chemicals as he was wearing some kind of gas mask. You know, the kind that painters use. He was in one of my cabins all by himself. No one was with him."

"A name. Give us a fucking name!" shouted Yvette.

Dakila, soaked and still lying in the passageway by the access hatch, panted and blurted, "His name was Saad! He was an Arab guy. I can't remember his first name. He was in A-509 for sure. *Nangangako ako!* I promise!" Overwhelmed, he passed out, hitting his head hard against the metal deck plates..

The two officers on the bridge noticed the green light reappear, indicating that the deck four loading hatch was closed again. They did not make an action entry when it opened, nor did they make an entry when it closed.

Chapter Forty-Nine

"Rob, sorry to grind on you so early in the morning, but I need some information from Nobility's tech guys."

"Tell me what you need, and I will see what we can do. By the way, did our little pervert give up any information?"

"Yes," answered Yvette. "I think he found some religion last night because he practically knocked himself out to tell us he is sure that a guy named Saad, in cabin A-509, was the cause of all the sick passengers. Can we determine if he used the ship's Digital Experience while onboard? And how fast can we get his picture?"

It took Rob only an hour to reply to Yvette's request.

Brick and Yvette met for coffee on deck five.

"Brick, here's the deal. Spencer said that it's easier to find out about Saad's use of the Digital Experience than it is to get his picture."

Brick was puzzled, but then he was used to bureaucratic bullshit. "When did he think we could get the guy's picture?"

"First, our guy did set up an account with the Digital Experience. He charged his ship account for the purchase of fifty minutes of Internet time. During the fourteen-day cruise, he used only forty-one minutes of the fifty. Rob said that IT told him they needed a couple more hours to dig down to level two and analyze the specifics of his usage."

"Okay, so what's up with his picture?" pressed Brick.

"The passenger card security system and the accompanying data on each passenger are stored in a segregated hard drive. The system that captures the passenger's picture is very old school. It uses the bitmap file protocol instead of .PNG or JPEG, and as a result, the memory storage is enormous. The software that manages the data and matches it with the name of the passengers does not even compress the files. After the guests leave the ship, we download all the files to Florida and wipe the storage clean. When the next three thousand passengers arrive, the hard drive is clear and we start again. Rob claims it'll be later in the day before we can get his picture."

Brick looked at his watch, frustrated. "What did Raju do with our new best friend, Salazar?"

"He made him a deal. He told him that if he forgot his trip to the meat locker and the deck four hatch, he'd let him go to his cabin and change his pants. He also told Salazar that the big black man was fucking crazy, and that Salazar would be smart if he didn't cause more trouble. Raju said he watched you bite a man's nose completely off for smuggling dope onboard the *Degas Under the Stars*."

Brick's eyes grew large as silver dollars. "Where'd he come up with that story?"

Yvette smiled. "I think I told him that when we were hooking up in the holding cell. Just kidding. Raju reads a lot of murder mysteries."

"Looks like we have to cool our heels until we get that info from Florida." Brick leaned back in his chair and folded his arms across his chest. "Let's look at this case from fifty thousand feet and see if we can a better perspective or think of a couple of different angles."

"Okay, where do we start?"

Brick got some paper from the deck five coffee bistro cart. "Three weeks ago, seventy-four people got sick, and both of us are certain it was not the Norovirus. We have a cabin steward who says he saw an Arab guy named Saad mix some chemicals at the same time. My cyber sleuth picks up international traffic about terrorist activity against any cruise ship and hacks into the computer of a guy called baseballfan999. Then this guy is discovered looking for rosary peas, which is the main ingredient of a poison called abrin."

"Then there's that stuff you shared with me about your visit with the FBI," added Yvette. "You said it was the FBI who dropped that crazy hacker name on you, the name you said was used by your cyber sleuth."

"Here's my gut feeling, Yvette. The Feds are wired into this situation. My bet is that the bio-samples were diverted to an FBI lab. What I can't figure out is why the FBI continues to be in such denial about terrorism. When I was in DC, I felt I was being encouraged to pursue the possibility of cruise ship terrorism, but now I'm hit with these roadblocks."

Brick rose from his chair and was just about to tell Yvette that he needed a forty-five-minute power nap when Yvette's two-way beeped. Brick hung around in case it was information from Rob Spencer on the Saad cabin.

"It's a message from the purser's office," explained Yvette. "They just received a call from Nobility in Florida. They were asked to get a message to you. The message says, 'Code sheet two.'"

"If only Titus could be more dramatic. I swear, she thinks the People's Republic of fucking China is camped in her backyard and ready to make her disappear. I'll head up to my cabin and see what's going on. Needless to say, if you hear from Spencer, call me." Brick grabbed another black coffee and hurried to his cabin.

Using his iPad, Brick logged into his e-mail account through the *Matisse* Internet. It had only been two hours since his last log-in yet another five new messages had arrived. Two were from the NRA soliciting funds to protect the Second Amendment, one was a receipt from iTunes, another was a message from Mark Whitfield about a future performance, and the most recent was from Titus.

"Friend, open text. House still being watched. 759, 832, 117, 776, 449, 233, 003."

Brick pulled code sheet two from his file. He figured there had to be over five hundred words on the sheet, and each word was assigned a three-digit number. He was not concerned with the five hundred words; he only wanted to decode seven words. His fingers flew over the columns of numbers until he located number 759.

HIGH SEAS DARKNESS

Then he found 832 and 117. It took him an agonizing two more minutes to decode 776, 449, 233, and, finally, 003. He picked up the phone immediately.

"Yvette, Brick. How fast can you get to my cabin?"

Chapter Fifty

Filling out forms and reports is the nemesis of anyone associated with law enforcement. It does not matter whether one works the street beat out of New York City, is the chief of police in Fullerton, California, or heads security on a major cruise ship. There is always the paper. When public safety software was developed, the paper-pushers figured out a way to double and triple the forms and reports. There might be less actual paper, but all the reports still meant that Yvette spent half of her time filling out what she saw as bureaucratic bullshit fluff. She had nearly finished organizing the reporting documents needed to process Dakila Salazar when she received the call from Brick.

Within seconds, Yvette locked up security, passed the medical center, and was on the elevator pushing the button for the Cassiopeia deck. Using her elevator security key, Yvette was able to override the other floor commands and took an express ride to deck ten.

Brick opened his door, and before Yvette was halfway into the room, he handed her the sheets of names that made up code key two. Yvette looked at the rows and rows of words and then focused on the seven words that had been circled.

"Does this mean what I think it means?" asked Yvette, concerned.

He read the seven words aloud. "'Alarm baseballfan999 active on *Matisse* terrorist onboard.' My cyber tech installed a malware inside the guy's computer that she has been tracking. He is the same person who sent e-mails about terrorism on cruise ships."

"Do you think there could be any mistake? Your tech is saying that the terrorist is on the *Matisse* right now!"

The ringing of Brick's cabin phone interrupted them. Raju was on the other end, asking for Yvette.

"You need to call headquarters. Spencer has new information," declared Raju.

"He had better have the picture of Saad," she said as she dialed the number for the cruise line's director of security. "Rob, Yvette. What did you find?"

"First, you'll have your picture in ten or fifteen minutes. I'll send you both a JPEG and bitmap file. Okay, so here's the good stuff. We worked down another layer on the traffic from the guy in cabin A-509. It turns out that most of the time he was logged into your ships, he was using a Gmail signed in as baseballfan999."

"That means Saad is baseballfan999. It also means that Saad is back on the *Matisse*."

"You're losing me. Why do you think he's back onboard the ship?"

"Another technology source picked up the Gmail ID of baseballfan999, and it's currently being used on our Internet server. Rob, we need Saad's picture now!"

"Fine. I'll see what I can do. Rob, out."

After hanging up the phone, Yvette turned to Brick. "What're we going to do with Saad's picture when we receive it?"

Brick thought for a minute as he paced around his cabin. "First, we distribute the picture to your security team. We don't want every crew member walking the ship looking for this guy. He could be carrying a bunch of that poison. We don't want him to get spooked."

"We need to compare his picture with the database of our existing passengers, but we don't have a software program onboard that can do a facial recognition match," Yvette said.

Sitting down on one of the suite's sofas, Brick closed his eyes for about five seconds. "Yvette, we go manual. We don't have time to download our database to headquarters and have them try some software that would match up our current passengers with this Saad guy. Here's what we do. We shut down the crew's Internet space and fill it with five crew members from the purser's office and five from your department. They'll be the most discreet. That's ten crew members. You and I will make twelve. Subtracting women and children, we only have fifteen hundred pictures to look at."

Yvette jumped up and headed to the cabin door. "I'll swing by the purser's office and then run down to my office. The picture should be in by the time I get there. I'll meet you in ten minutes."

"I need to leave a message for the FBI. They should bring Interpol up to speed and know that we have narrowed down this threat."

After Yvette left, Brick used his Inmarsat satellite phone to place a direct call to Kryss Mitchell.

"This is Special Agent Kryss Mitchell. If you have an emergency, call 911. Otherwise, please leave a message and your phone number, and I will return your call soon."

Shit! For a few seconds, Brick considered hanging up but changed his mind. "Kryss, Brick here. I'm back on Nobility's *Matisse*. We think that a terrorist is onboard. Remember when I told you about that 'baseballfan999' account? He's onboard and could be carrying the poison. Call Interpol and let them know. Call me or e-mail ASAP."

By the time Brick arrived on deck five and entered the crew's Internet facility, Yvette had assembled ten members of the *Matisse* crew and held thirty copies of the photo of Saad.

Raising her voice, Yvette took hold of the group's attention and explained the importance of the work they were about to undertake. "Let me introduce Mr. Brick Morgan. Mr. Morgan is an investigator who is helping the cruise line locate this individual." She then handed everyone a copy of the photo and called on Brick to make some additional remarks.

"Guys, thank you. Here's the deal. The man in this photo is very dangerous. He may have tried to alter his appearance. He might have a beard, or he could've shaved off his mustache. Study the facial triangle—the eyes and the eyebrows down to below the nose. We need each of you to look at about three hundred photos. The ship's database of passengers has been loaded on each of your computers. Yvette will give you specific groups to scan. Remember, we're in a hurry. Skip the children and women, and for now, ignore the white guys. If you see a picture that's close, give us a shout-out. Good luck. And, of course, we're paying you for your time."

Yvette whispered, "Brick, I can't get authorization for that without explaining more to the crew managers."

"Put in on my bill."

The crew member that oversaw the passengers' Digital Experience had helped Yvette load the ship's passenger database into the ten computers in the crew's Internet cafe. During the next fifteen minutes, there were six close matches, but on inspection, none were close enough to be Saad.

Then a woman from the purser's office got a good hit. Both Yvette and Brick agreed that they might have a 90 percent match. The eyes and nose seemed perfect, but the mustache was gone and the guy had a goatee. Yvette wrote down the name and cabin number: Phillip Dariush, B-414. No sooner had she recorded the information on Dariush, a member from her department announced that he had also found Saad.

"Officer Fuentes, look at this guy. The nose and mouth are perfect, and the hair looks very close. Mustache is gone, and he appears to be starting a beard."

Brick made a copy of the passenger's photo and placed it next to the photo of Saad and the image of Dariush. The new suspect was named Fredrick Batista in cabin C-320. Yvette looked at Brick, shook her head, and shrugged.

"Yvette, why don't you do some research on these two. I think Saad could be either one. See if they're sharing a cabin. Whatever you can find. I'll stay here until we've reviewed the entire manifest. My guess is another ten minutes."

Chapter Fifty-One

Walking down the starboard passageway, Yvette passed the medical center and entered the security department. Part of her wanted to charge down to the identified cabins and break through the doors, but she knew it was important to get additional intel before they acted. She was about to access the passenger portfolio for Phillip Dariush when Raju walked up to her.

"He is a red herring. It is all bullshit!" Raju pulled up a chair next to Yvette.

"What's a red herring? What are you talking about?"

"You know, red herring. I have been reading American business and spy books, and he is a red herring."

"Raju, who are you talking about?" asked Yvette.

"Dakila Salazar. The whole bullshit about an Arab who had poison powder was inserted to distract from the original topic. I know of real terrorism. And he just wants us to chase this fictitious Saad so we will forget about his perverted activities."

Yvette considered what Raju said and then reviewed Dakila's description of the video of the man called Saad. "He was very sincere when he described what his spy camera had captured."

Raju jumped up, waving his arms in her face. "It was a confession extracted from torture. You and Morgan tortured him in the meat locker. It is just like your CIA and their waterboards."

Yvette jumped up and went nose to nose with her deputy of security. "What's wrong with you? We didn't torture him in the meat freezer, even though he fucking deserved it. Hell, we even offered him a glass of goddamned wine!"

Raju refused to back down. "Salazar told me you guys did something to his lungs, and that he was going to be dead in two days. I might as well tell you that I have sent an e-mail to Mr. Spencer and informed him that the *Matisse Under the Stars* is a CIA secret-torture facility. I told him that you and Morgan should be arrested, and that I should be appointed director of security." Raju then pushed through the office door, almost running over Brick as he entered the department.

Brick looked at the slamming door and took a seat near Yvette's desk. "What was that about?"

"Later. Did you get any more matches on the photos?"

"No. Let's work up the two guys that we have," answered Brick.

They first looked up the information on Dariush in cabin B-414. "He's traveling with another man by the name of Feroz. They both list their occupations as bankers from California. Their passport details indicate they were born in Iran. Dariush is twenty-eight years old, and Feroz lists an age of thirty-one. They both signed up for shore excursions when we get to Honolulu."

Brick looked at the file. "These guys could easily be a couple of Americans who were radicalized through the Internet. The Honolulu excursions could be a red herring."

"Brick, don't use those words *red herring*. I've had my fill of goddamned red herrings," proclaimed Yvette, pretending to be pissed off. Looking over her notes, she continued. "The information provided from the purser's office seems rather benign. Frederick Batista is a twenty-seven-year-old American. Passport says that he was born in Miami. This is his first trip with Nobility, and he's traveling alone. He's on the Cassiopeia deck, cabin 320. I'd put my money on Batista because he's traveling alone."

"That's logical, but we have to be sure," said Brick. "Look, if my cyber tech is correct, Saad, or whatever his name is, has been sending e-mails while on the *Matisse*. We need to find out if either of these cabins signed up for web access through Digital Experience."

Yvette quickly dialed the number for the manager of Digital Experience. Inna Kozlov possessed extensive computer experience from working for the Russian government. She and her sister were on their second contract with Nobility Cruise Line. "Inna, I need to know if two cabins have signed up for the Internet."

"Miss Fuentes, have we found that man yet?"

Yvette had forgotten that Inna had been part of the photo search group just thirty minutes before. "Not yet, but we are getting close."

Inna entered the cabin numbers into her terminal of paid subscribers. "Ma'am, both cabins purchased plans. C-320 has a 120-minute plan and has used thirty-three minutes. B-414 went with a fifty-minute plan and has used fifteen. It looks like B-414 is logged into the system now."

"Thank you, Inna. If you see any action from C-320, give me a call."

Just then the door to the security department opened, and two men entered and closed the door. Yvette jumped to her feet, taken aback by their presence in this secure area of the ship. "I hope you have a good reason for being in a passenger-prohibited zone," said Yvette as she blocked their path into her office.

"Excuse us. We just thought that you and the big guy could use a little help."

Before Yvette could say another word, Brick was on his feet. "Mitchell, what the fuck are you doing here? Yvette, this is Kryss Mitchell. FBI."

Kryss smiled at Brick. "And this is my partner, Special Agent Nathan King." Kryss extended his hand toward Yvette. "I presume you're the chief of security, Yvette Fuentes."

Chapter Fifty-Two

Only recently has there been a specific *fatwa* with respect to the use of tobacco. Such a legal ruling relaxed some of the rules, as the Quran does not directly forbid cigarette smoking. But there are specific expectations as to using reason and intelligence, and certainly smoking must be harmful.

Yusuf was too nervous to be concerned about a nicotine fatwa at this time. When he traveled as Saad, he learned the hard way about the difficulty of finding places to relax with a cigarette on the ship. So for this trip, he invested in an electronic cigarette kit. Yusuf hoped that a good hit of nicotine would help him with his difficult decision.

He inserted the atomizer in the charging unit while he removed a liquid nicotine cartridge from the box. After inserting the cartridge into the atomizer, he took a long puff on the smokeless cigarette. The rush of nicotine created some light-headedness, but it did help his mind focus on the dilemma.

Yusuf's original goal was to launch his chemical weapon when the ship made it halfway to Hawaii so it would be impossible for help to arrive in time to mitigate the casualties. Through Internet research, he had learned that the abrin poisoning would not start right away but would take place between twenty-four and fifty-four hours after ingestion. The other issue was that the other four ships were on shorter itineraries, so Yusuf decided that today should be the day he would make the Great Satan pay for the deaths of his father and brother.

Another puff of his e-cigarette gave Yusuf a strange feeling of tranquility. Within hours, he would avenge the drone strike that had taken the lives of his father and brother. The anger that he initially felt, especially after seeing the family's mangled truck, transformed into a resolve to not only avenge their deaths but also for him to be an agent of action for his radical Islamic movement.

Both Yusuf and Zaeem were adamant that Israel's presence in their historic homeland was the cause of the world's problems. For many months, Yusuf studied the history of this international injustice. That fateful day of November 29, 1947, was a deliberate attack on the Holy Land. The United Nations' vote of 33-13 partitioned the sacred lands and inserted America's puppet country right in the middle of their home. Today's attack, he expected, would cause the American people to insist that their leaders abandon their military support of Israel. The previous week, Yusuf had read that the US Secretary of Defense had agreed to sell even more missiles and planes to the Zionists. Zaeem had told Yusuf that once Israel was without the United States weapons, the Arab nations would attack and be successful in ripping Israel out of the Middle East.

Before Yusuf could perform the ablution and focus on his daily afternoon prayer, he had to contact his fellow brothers who were on the other ships. If time permitted, he would have preferred to establish a voice communication link with the four other terrorists. A voice link would have allowed him to personalize a motivational message and to reinforce the focus that was necessary for a successful mission. Yusuf figured that he needed a minimum of six hours to coordinate the usage of the Scrabble application chat feature. He was certain that it would have been virtually impossible for America's intelligence agencies to conduct real-time surveillance of a computer game's chat features. Today he would coordinate the attack by posting a final draft on his e-mail account.

The cabin steward had just refreshed the cabin, so Yusuf felt he would not be disturbed for at least a couple of hours. After placing the "Do Not Disturb" card outside the door, he pulled his cabin balcony's French doors shut and locked them and closed the drapes in preparation for his work.

Lifting the cover on his laptop, Yusuf started the process of logging into the ship's Digital Experience Internet. But a sudden epiphany made him close down his laptop. *Maybe he should prepare the abrin before he placed his message on his Gmail account.* Activating his e-cigarette, he sat down on the only chair in the cabin and analyzed again the best timeline. After concluding that he should first get the poison ready and then send his message, Yusuf put the cigarette away and approached the cabin's safe.

The safe door swung open, and Yusuf, using a piece of toilet paper, carefully lifted out the plastic vial and placed it on the bathroom counter. He was determined to use the utmost precaution when handling the deadly abrin, as the inhalation of just a small speck of the powder would cause a violent death. Before he died, Faroug, the traitor, promised that he not only produced the abrin from rosary peas, but he had also used a special chilled grinder to weaponize the toxin. He had boasted that he ground the abrin into a fine powder without creating any heat that would have reduced the toxicity. The most hazardous step would be the transfer of the powder into four separate containers.

Yusuf was not afraid to die, but he wanted to leverage his terrorist skills and kill the largest number of infidels before receiving his rewards for martyrdom. Before packing his luggage, he ordered a new dust cartridge for his mask that would capture a particulate down to .3 microns in size. After attaching the new cartridge, he selected a long-sleeved shirt and a ball cap.

Yusuf tore a glossy sheet of paper from the room service menu, creased it, and placed it on the bathroom counter. He then put on the long-sleeved shirt, the dust and particulate mask, and a pair of disposable plastic gloves. Taking great care, he poured about a fourth of the powder on the creased paper and transferred it to a small vial. He repeated the process three more times and then ran the faucet over the glossy paper and flushed it down the toilet. As he cleaned up, he wondered if he should save one of the vials and, instead of pouring the powder on food, sprinkle it from deck seven over the stair rail and poison the air above the grand atrium on the *Matisse*. He knew that the toxic effect of the abrin would be significantly more effective if his targets inhaled instead of ingested it.

Opening his computer, Fredrick Batista from cabin C-320 logged into the *Matisse*'s Digital Experience. The Gmail log-in appeared much faster than usual. Yusuf left the "Send to" address blank and inserted "God's Will" in the new message subject line. In the message text box, he wrote, "Urgent: we proceed as soon as you read this." He then explained that once a team member logged in and read the draft, he was to add his ship's name to the end of the message and resave the draft. Fredrick then selected "Save Draft."

Inna Kozlov glanced at the time display on her monitor. The last few hours at work reminded her of the computer assignments she had received while working for the Ministry of Agriculture of the Russian Federation. Her primary job description then was to digitize the volumes of data from the soil improvement and fertility projects. Her secondary responsibility was to hack into the computers of potash production facilities and look for black-market activities. Today's excitement from searching for the dangerous passenger gave her a similar rush of adrenaline.

Before she quit her shift at the Digital Experience, Inna thought she would scan the *Matisse* server for any online activity from C-320 and B-414. She knew Yvette immediately needed to know anything she found.

"Officer Fuentes, this is Inna from the DE. Before finishing for the day, I checked the Internet activity for those two cabins."

"Thank you, Inna. Any action?"

"Yes, ma'am. C-320 is currently logged on."

Yusuf closed his computer and prepared for his daily prayers. He was anxious to spread the poison, but he realized that today was certainly not a day to skip his prayers. Prior to logging into the e-mail account, he entered the ship's heading into www.qiblalocator.com and received the direction to Mecca's Great Mosque and the central shrine of Kaada. He quickly performed the ablution to clean his body before kneeling on his *janamaz*, or prayer mat.

When he completed his prayers, Yusuf put on a Los Angeles Angels T-shirt and a plain ball cap and carefully placed the four vials in his pocket. As Fredrick Batista, the occupant of cabin C-320, he opened his cabin door at the same time that Bashir on the *Rembrandt Under the Stars* and Hahid on the *Goya Under the Stars* logged into "baseballfan999" and read the draft e-mail. Yusuf closed his door and quietly affirmed, "Allah, the most merciful, my destiny is in your hands."

Chapter Fifty-Three

Brick was the first to speak. "Are we to assume that you two have not chosen the *Matisse Under the Stars* for your honeymoon cruise?"

"We're as surprised as you to be on this ship. Forty-eight hours ago, Nathan and I were in Montana dealing with a couple of wannabe jihadists who tried to blow up the Yellowtail Dam. We should've been suspicious when the director let us use his jet. We were only there for six hours when Herb Wallace called and said we needed to get on the *Matisse* and support you. Brick, what's so screwy is that the Bureau gave me a hard time for pushing your theory on these guys from Lashkar-e-Aalam."

Yvette started to relax and offered the special agents chairs at the table in the middle of the security department office. "Brick, I think you need to bring them up to date. A lot has happened in the last couple of hours."

"My technology assistant sent me a cryptic message that said the suspect to the poisonings a couple of cruises ago is now on this ship."

"I would guess that your cyber tech is Spindleratchet?" asked Nathan.

"Yes," answered Brick, relieved that they knew but also concerned for Titus's anonymity. "We had to deal with a pervert who was taking videos of passengers, and he provided us with the cabin number of the guy. That's the cruise I was on a month ago."

Yvette placed three pictures on the desk and picked up the briefing. "This picture is Saad. He was the occupant of cabin A-509 on this ship two cruises ago. We matched his picture with all the passengers who are on this cruise. We have come up with these two possibilities. This guy is Phillip Dariush in cabin B-414. Then we have this picture. He is Fredrick Batista in C-320."

Nathan picked up the three photographs and rearranged them in several different orders. "I'll send these to the Quantico lab and have our facial recognition people give an opinion."

"For sure. What do you need from me?"

Nathan grabbed the pictures, walked over to Yvette's desk, and sat down in front of her computer. "Yvette, if you would just log me in and point me to where you have the files saved, I'll forward the three photos right now."

Advancements in facial recognition software like that used by the FBI greatly increased the usage and reliability of the forensic apparatus. First-generation software only utilized the two-dimensional metric geometry of key facial points. The extraction points were the center of the eyes, the tip of the nose and the corners of the mouth. The latest software, third generation, measures the depth of the eye sockets and the prominence of the cheekbones. It produces much more accurate analysis even when the subject is as much as 20 percent off the center view angle. The integration of facial recognition software with iris recognition software is the next facial forensic advancement. Each human eye's iris has unique intricate structures that can be converted to mathematical patterns. The analysis of an individual's eyes can themselves be an accurate method of individual recognition.

Brick got up from the conference table and walked over to a four-drawer file cabinet and opened a plastic water bottle. "I have an idea." He took a drink of water. "Kryss, do the Bureau's code monkeys have the ability to hack into the ship's servers? If we could provide them with settings and access to the RPC port mapper, could they get details of baseballfan999's activity while on the *Matisse*?"

Kryss folded his arms across his chest and thought a moment. "Yvette, how fast can you get me to your Internet center and the crew member most adept with Nobility's IT systems?"

"Brick, if you take Kryss to the Digital Experience, I'll have Inna over there in five minutes."

Within ten minutes, Kryss connected Inna with the best of the best at the FBI's Operational Technology Division. OTD's specialists provide support that includes digital forensics, electronic device analysis, and electronic surveillance to provide a platform for counterterrorism and cyber searches.

Brick and Kryss sat on each side of Inna as she focused on the two monitors that were linked to the *Matisse*'s computers. The monitor on the left displayed a continuous stream of advanced directory symbols, Internet protocol addresses, and a few ISP codes. The three continued to watch as the waterfall of data streamed down the monitor on the left. Occasionally, the right monitor would send Inna a text box asking her to enter a variety of keyboard commands.

"Brick, you're looking at the screens like you have some idea what you're looking at," remarked Kryss.

"No, too advanced for me. But if you look closely, you can see the groups of numbers that signify the IP addresses. Here, look at this group of numbers." Brick pointed. "The Internet protocol address can be either dynamic or static. Dynamic IPs are usually used for voiceover or online gaming. We're looking for a static IP because of baseballfan999's use of Gmail. These numbers are what we are looking for. They're composed of four numbers, and each number is between one and three digits, separated by a dot. Look at this: 74.132.9.809. This could be our guy. What we need your code monkeys to do is to figure out who else is accessing his Gmail account."

Inna threw up her hands and screamed, "*Yebat' my poluchi ill!*"

Kryss, fairly fluent in Russian, understood. "Brick, we hit a home run! She said we got them!"

Inna wrote down the information that Quantico sent her: "Cézanne—cabin B-562, Rembrandt—cabin A-303, Goya—cabin B-213, Lautrec—cabin D-404."

Brick quickly called the security office. "Yvette, is Nathan with you?"

"Yes, the FBI will have their analysis in the next fifteen minutes.

We have the real name of Saad."

"Kryss and I will be there in a minute. We need to open a line of communication with the *Lautrec, Goya, Rembrandt,* and Cézanne."

When Brick and Kryss entered the security office, Nathan and Yvette had already opened lines with the *Goya* and *Lautrec*. She gave phones and numbers to Kryss and Brick, who immediately called the other ships. Yvette was the first to get through to security on the *Goya*.

"This is Officer Fuentes on the *Matisse*. I have two members of the United States Federal Bureau of Investigation with me. Yes, the FBI. This is a terrorism alert. The passenger in cabin B-213 may have a deadly poison. It will be a powder. It's a real WMD. This stuff is deadly. Do not give the passenger any warnings. These guys are martyrs. You're looking for a tube or vial of powder. Be careful."

Within five minutes, Nathan, Brick, and Kryss repeated the warning to the *Lautrec, Cézanne,* and *Rembrandt*.

Brick looked at the three pictures and then at Kryss. "What did you learn from technology?"

"They need," Kryss looked at his Casio G-Shock, "another ten minutes. However, we learned that Saad's real name is Yusuf Al Omar. We received an Interpol Red Notice just a week ago. The French Direction Générale de la Sécurité Extérieure got a tip from a really pissed-off woman in North Africa. Seems Omar killed her husband, so she went to the French DGSE and said this Yusuf guy was a terrorist. The French gave the info to Interpol, and they posted a Red Notice."

Brick opened the small case that he had been carrying and pulled out his Ruger SR22PS and an extra ten-round clip. He slipped the pistol in his back waistband and looked at Nathan and Kryss. "Are you ready to rock 'n' roll? Yvette, you stay here. We need to know what the facial recon guys find out. Kryss, you and Nathan go to C-320, the Batista cabin. I will head to B-414. Yvette, have you seen Raju?"

"Yes, Raju was just here. He looked at the three pictures and ran out the door."

Chapter Fifty-Four

Outside his cabin, Yusuf looked down at the red carpet that designated he was on the port side of the ship. He walked about ten steps when he noticed that the cabin numbers were increasing, not decreasing. *Shit! I'm going the wrong way.* Turning around, he remembered that the lobby for the forward lifts and stairs was adjacent to cabin 300. When he reached the elevator banks, he took the stairs to deck fourteen.

The *Matisse* was considered a class AAA cruise ship because of her hundred-thousand-plus tonnage and distance between decks, which was almost twelve feet. The number of stairs between decks was sixteen, with a switchback after eight. Yusuf was feeling the anxiety of his mission and was having trouble staying focused. He glanced again at the deck sign and started up the stairs to the Bootes deck. After eight stairs, he paused before making the turn for the next set of stairs and forced himself to control his breathing and review his mental checklist. The missing element in his planning was the issue of escape. As he reflected on his commitment to this part of the jihad, and that his fate was in the hands of Allah, he wondered if he should consider taking some of the abrin himself.

He reflected on the April 2013 Boston Marathon bombing and the frustration felt by jihadists worldwide. Yusuf thought that it was a model for all future terrorist activities. Everyone was excited that a little ghost cell could create such carnage and paralyze the northeastern part of America. Then all the air came out of the balloon when the younger brother failed to commit suicide. With his capture, the world news only discussed the brother's dysfunctional family and did not report on the brother's commitment to Islam or the pressing need for an Islamic caliphate. If only they had spent more time thinking about the days after the bombing. They had had months to hide provisions around the city and even plant more IEDs around Boston. Yusuf cringed at repeating their shortsightedness.

He walked up the eight steps and paused on deck eleven, moving to the right when a room service steward passed down the stairs carrying a large tray of food and drinks. Looking at the stairs leading to deck twelve, Yusuf realized how close he was to his dream, yet he was feeling a wave of nervousness. Above was deck fourteen and the Gallery Grill and Food Court where he would release the toxin. He hesitated when he finally came to the realization of his apprehension. It was that fucking Gitmo.

Noting that he was alone, he made his way up the sixteen steps to the Aquarius deck. He walked over to the bank of elevators and pretended to wait for the next lift. The more he evaluated his situation, the more he visualized three possible outcomes. He could succeed in spreading the poison on the food, discard his contaminated clothes, and then return to his cabin. Once he made it back to his cabin, he would have time to destroy any evidence of the abrin. He might even pretend to be sick. If it were possible to escape from the ship in Hawaii, he would return to Mali and begin plans for another attack on the infidels. But if he felt he was going to be apprehended, he could commit suicide, and his martyrdom would assure him the highest level in Paradise, the level of *Firdaws*, which is reserved for prophets and martyrs. He imagined the exquisite gardens, eighty thousand servants, and his seventy-two wives.

But the third outcome troubled him. If he failed to escape and failed to become a martyr, the best he could hope for was being arrested, charged as an enemy combatant, and locked away in the terrorist prison in Guantanamo Bay. Maybe they would first send him to a CIA torture facility where they would hang him upside down for weeks with his head in a waterboarding bucket. Regardless, he would end up spending the rest of his life in Gitmo with his head stuck in a canvas bag. It was too terrible to imagine. Knowing what he had to do, Yusuf took the final thirty-two stairs to the food court.

Upon arriving on deck fourteen, he nonchalantly walked into the men's room and found an empty stall. He stacked three squares of toilet paper on top of one another and folded them into a square. Next, he retrieved one of the vials of abrin and loosened the cap. He took a deep breath and held it before pouring a small amount of the deadly powder into the folds of the paper. He quickly returned the vial and secured the folded toilet paper containing the abrin. If it appeared that he was going to be captured, he would inhale this supply of the toxin. Yusuf was euphoric, believing he had dealt with all the possible contingencies.

He needed to scout out the different foods that would be served that night. He entered the food court buffet and placed his hands under the plastic globe of sanitizing alcohol gel. Keeping his head down, he accepted a white dinner plate from the food court attendant and walked to the hot food stations. He had already decided that he would dump one vial in the large bowl of mixed salad greens.

Yusuf spotted a large serving pan that contained an assortment of vegetables. Wanting to find the food that would serve the most people, he put a piece of chicken on his plate and headed to the soup station. A large kettle of cream of mushroom soup held a minimum of three gallons. *Perfect*, he thought as he added two cookies onto his plate of chicken. After placing a tablespoon of rice on his plate, he left the food court and located an empty table with a clear view of the buffet.

While Yusuf nibbled at his plate of food, there were four separate log-ins to his "baseballfan999" account. As instructed, each member of the terror cell placed the name of his ship at the bottom of the e-mail draft and resaved it.

Thinking that he would make his move in the next ten minutes, Yusuf sipped some tea and watched as more and more passengers came to deck fourteen for dinner. Recognizing one of the girls from the Mark Hopkins Hotel in San Francisco made him realize how long it had been since he had been with a woman. Months ago, when he and Jari buried the body of Faroug, Jari was adamant that they drive over to Faroug's apartment and rape and kill "that bitch Maali," Faroug's wife. Jari blamed her for creating all the problems for their cell back home. Yusuf had talked him out of raping and killing the woman. Now he wondered if she would make a good wife—once he reeducated her, of course.

Yusuf left his plate on the table and walked to the food court entrance. He discreetly touched his pocket, satisfied that all four of the plastic tubes were accessible. There were three passengers ahead of him as he waited to sanitize his hands and take a plate. Just before reaching the alcohol gel, he noticed a member of the security detail looking at him. Another crew member suddenly handed him a plate as he entered the food court. Pretending to look at the cookies, Yusuf looked back in the direction of the security man and noticed that he was gone.

His right hand fingered one of the vials as he headed toward the kettle of soup.

Chapter Fifty-Five

"Mr. Director, I have the secretary of DHS on hold."

Damn, Alexander Zittel thought. *The last thing I wanted today was a conversation with that dog's breakfast of a woman from Homeland.* He believed that the whole department was a joke, and worse, that the president had appointed a reject from the Senate to be its secretary.

"Alright, put her through, and tell the deputy director to get over here." Ace reached into his desk and pulled out a digital micro-recorder, placed it near his speakerphone, and pushed the record button as he answered.

"Madam Secretary, to what do I owe the pleasure?"

"Ace, madams run whorehouses. I prefer Maxine, thank you. I just got a call from Vic Bodner, and he was pissed. He said the president went ballistic this morning at the daily briefing. His Homeland Security advisor added the activity on that cruise ship to the PDB."

The President Daily Brief is a top-secret, written document that is prepared for POTUS six days a week. Prior to the reorganization of the intelligence community after September 2001, the CIA prepared the PDB. Today, the fifteen-to-twenty-page document is the responsibility of the Office of the Director of National Intelligence. The PDB compiles the highest levels of intelligence analysis, including issues of international security and current covert operations.

"Maxine, what did the chief of staff think the president found so upsetting about our operation on the cruise ship *Matisse*?"

"This morning's PDB contained six intelligence issues, and two were related to Lashkar-e-Aalam. First, there was some intel picked up by NSA—some cell phone intercepts forwarded from one of our subs. Then they briefed him about the FBI working with an ex-Justice

Department employee on possible terrorism on the high seas. Bodner says that the president feels it's premature to use the term *terrorism* in the PDB."

"Jesus Christ, Maxine, what does he think using a weapon of mass destruction against four thousand people is? Do you think we should label the threat as some crew member's ocean discontent with a passenger?"

Deputy Director Elizabeth had quietly entered Ace's office and had listened for the last five minutes. She wrote a note suggesting that they get the chief of staff on the phone.

"Secretary, this could become a very big expansion of the abilities of terrorists. If your department and mine are supposed to sit on our hands, I think we need to hear it directly from either the chief of staff or POTUS. Do you think you can get Bodner on a conference call with us?"

"I'll call Vic back. I spoke with him just ten minutes ago. Give me a second," replied Maxine.

"Liz, what are you thinking?" asked Zittel.

She paused for a few moments. "We're walking the fence between plausible deniability and covering our asses. Let's squeeze the COS and see how far the president wants to push this issue."

"Mr. Zittel, the DHS is back, along with the White House," interrupted Ace's assistant.

"Thank you. Plug them through."

"Director Zittel, this is Maxine, along with the president's chief of staff."

Ace gave Liz a look that said, "Get ready for the fireworks."

Ace jumped in with the usual round of cordial banter. "Vic, thank you for adjusting your schedule so you could join the secretary and me. We had been discussing the developments taking place on the cruise ship *Matisse*. I understand that Director Copper included our operation on the ship in this morning's PDB?"

"Yes, that is correct, and I might add that the president was caught off-guard. Ace, here's the problem. The president was planning to make a major policy announcement this week with respect to Operation Bridgewalk. He's been laying the foundation with the Muslim community for months, and now he fears that your Bureau's escapades on the ocean will ruin his communiqué."

"Maxine, jump in anytime you want, but, Vic, I have a question. What exactly did Copper say was going down on the ship?"

"The PDB said that the FBI was working with Morgan Maritime Investigations on the cruise ship because the FBI suspected a passenger with ties to a terrorist cell from North Africa was going to poison the ship. The president is sensitive to the apparent rush to classify every nutcase as a militant Islamist."

"Vic, the intelligence community now has assets on the ground in Mali. The NSA trapped cell traffic, and both Morgan and the FBI have intercepted e-mails that spell terrorism with a capitol T."

"Ace and Maxine, we have to keep the lid on this situation. The president directed me to instruct both DHS and the FBI to keep this problem off the grid. I might add that he ordered the secretary of the navy to have a fast-attack sub shadow the cruise ship. If it turns out that the ship is loaded with small pox or something worse, we cannot let it arrive in Hawaii."

"Bodner, what I hear you saying is that the president of the United States ordered the navy to put a Mark 48 ADCAP torpedo into the side of a cruise ship so he could announce Operation Fucking Bridgewalk. Is that right?"

"Ace, calm down. He did not say it exactly that way, but remember, these ships are not registered in the United States. They always have a flag of convenience."

Ace took a deep breath and looked at Liz, who gave a thumbs-up. "Maxine, this is Ace. What do you need to do at your end on this?"

"DHS is very compartmentalized on this situation. We can sterilize our documents and communication yesterday, if you know what I mean."

Liz passed her hand across her throat, signaling to signal Ace that he had them where he wanted and to end the call. Ace nodded.

"Vic, I do not want to speak for Maxine, but the FBI knows its marching orders. We will keep the White House informed of any developments on the high seas."

After disconnecting the conference call, Ace leaned back in his chair, put his Gucci loafer-clad feet up on the corner of his desk, and closed his eyes for a full fifteen seconds. He knew he was not the first director of the FBI to get such orders. But was this really happening? Finally, he said, "My God, Liz, did you hear what I heard?"

"Yes, Ace. The president of the United States would kill four thousand people so he can build his fucking bridge to Islam."

"One more thing. What do you know about this guy Morgan?"

Chapter Fifty-Six

Titus felt she was missing something. She had finished her second cup of coffee and was deep in thought over how to advance her infiltration of baseballfan999's computer. If there was a way she could bypass the firewalls and break the encryptions to Nobility's servers, it would be easy enough to access the simple mail transfer protocols. It was not that the system was impenetrable or was even all that secure compared to other corporations she had hacked. But she knew she was being watched, and that she needed to do this quickly without leaving a trace, lest the powers-that-be turn more of their attention to her cyber activities. She had already defeated the most preliminary of obstacles toward accessing Nobility's file transfer protocols. If she could get inside their main server, she could discover exactly who was on the other side of those communications with baseballfan999.

Dumping the remains of her coffee down the sink, Titus decided to unwind in her small home workout center. She started with some upper body work. After working her way from twenty-pound dumbbells to twenty-five, she tried three sets of ten with a pair of thirty-pounders. She adjusted the back of her weight bench to forty-five degrees, spread her bare legs on each side of the bench, leaned back, and started her first set of ten dumbbell bench presses with the objective of developing the upper regions of her pectorals. .

As she started the last set of presses, a thought hit her. Dropping the weights, Titus jumped up from the bench and ran to her computer station. *Maybe I don't need to hide my digital footsteps as much as I need to make someone else's more obvious,* she speculated.

Within half an hour, she had hacked into the home desktop computer of Rob Spencer and was well on her way into the labyrinth of codes that would lead her to the hard drive of the *Matisse*'s Digital

HIGH SEAS DARKNESS

Experience. As Titus was scanning the IP addresses of the passengers, she heard a noise.

Earlier in the day, she had increased the motion sensitivity of her CCTV monitors. Even if an object were out of the video reception angle, the motion sensor would still give an audio reading of a possible intruder. This was the fourth night in a row that her equipment indicated an intrusion. She was not sure what pissed her off more—having someone dicking around on her property or having to put on some clothes.

She pulled on a pair of jeans, a dark sweatshirt, and a pair of tennis shoes. *Fuck the socks,* she thought. Titus walked into the kitchen and grabbed a bandolier that contained a dozen twelve-gauge shotgun shells and slipped it over her shoulder. With her Remington 870 in hand, she opened the door to the basement and proceeded down the stairs. The sixty-year-old house had three doors that allowed an exit from the home. What nobody knew was that Titus had rigged a basement window with a quick release that allowed her to climb through the window into a ground-level window well that served as a small bunker on the west side of the house.

Titus crouched silently in the window well and allowed her eyes to adjust to the darkness. She aimed her pump-action shotgun at a Japanese laceleaf maple tree that was about twenty feet from the side of her house. The chamber of the 870 was empty, but the shotgun's magazine contained four shells. The first was a tactical buckshot load with reduced recoil. The next three were Winchester PBX1 shells. The specially designed shells contained a load of three "00" buck pellets and a one-ounce slug. She deliberately left the chamber empty so as to retain the effect created when she chambered her first round. No intruder or burglar could mistake the distinctive sound of a shell being cycled into the chamber of a pump-action shotgun.

The laceleaf maple had enough open space that Titus could make out the shape of someone or something hiding on the other side. She figured it was now or never. Titus did not think the intruder was part of a terrorist cell, but she was suspicious of the Chinese and their commitment to controlling cyber activities.

Quietly, Titus stood up in the window well. She pushed the stock of the shotgun into her left shoulder and used her right hand to pull back on the fore-end. The sound of the shell moving from the magazine into the gun's chamber was much louder than she expected.

"Okay, motherfucker, the next sound you hear will be your last!"

"Wait!" a panicked voice shouted from behind the maple.

Titus was so focused on the silhouette behind the tree that she did not pick up the movement next to her. In a fraction of a second, a cold hand reached across her chest, grabbed the barrel of the Remington, and jerked it up and out of her hands. For the first time, she truly felt naked.

Chapter Fifty-Seven

Brick, Kryss, and Nathan all ran out the door of the deck four security office.

"Let's take these service stairs to deck five, and then we can locate the amidships stairs and elevator lobby," instructed Brick as he pointed to a gray interior door.

Once the trio was on deck five, they located a service door and entered a populated passenger hallway. They quickly maneuvered through dozens of passengers before arriving at the atrium-level bank of elevators. Brick glanced at the elevator locator lights and determined that the closest one was still on deck seven. "The stairs'll be faster!" said Brick as he led the way.

Thirty-two steps later, they checked the location of the elevators. A lift had just arrived at their deck seven location.

"Brick, you need to get to deck eleven. We're going to ten. Let's grab this car," said Nathan. When they leaped into the elevator, they found a family of Japanese passengers who spoke limited English. Nathan flashed his credential and badge wallet and motioned for them to move to the back of the elevator.

The car stopped at deck nine, but Kryss quickly reclosed the door. At deck ten, the trio shot out of the lift, and Brick ran to the stairs. It took him about fifteen seconds to find himself on the Bootes deck. Cabin 414 would be on the port side and a few cabins toward the bow.

Brick stopped at cabin 414 and reviewed his approach. After removing his pistol from his back holster, he inserted the keycard into the cabin's lock. Knowing that the terrorist might have the abrin within reach and throw it in his face meant that Brick would need to move quickly. When the lock clicked open, Brick rushed in with his gun ready.

Years of law enforcement experience kicked in with Brick evaluating the situation in a fraction of a second. He found one occupant reading on the bed and the other sunning on a chair out on the balcony.

"Hands! I want to see hands!" Brick held the gun in full display.

Both men raised their hands. They watched in shock as the six-foot-four man took over their cabin.

"Who is Phillip Dariush?" demanded Brick.

The man on the bed kept his hands raised. "I'm Phillip. Who are you? Is this a robbery?"

"Look, guys, work with me. We got a report someone may have planted a device in your room. Let me make sure that you are safe."

"Is this a homophobe thing? We're just on our honeymoon." Phillip was clearly confused and concerned. "We heard cruises were supposed to be safe."

"Better safe than sorry. I'm Morgan with ship security. Stay right there, and I will make sure there's no danger in your room." Brick did a quick search of the room and asked the occupants to open the safe.

"It's open. We've never used it," replied the other man.

"Look at this picture. Have you ever seen this guy?" Brick held out a photo of Yusuf Al Omar.

"Looks like an Arab. We are Prussian, but we have not met that many people yet. This is our first cruise."

Brick's cop instincts told him that this was a false alarm, so he decided to reduce the bad press or litigation that could result from barging into their room and do a little damage control.

"Guys, sorry for busting in with guns drawn on your vacation. Nobility always puts the safety of passengers first. I'll make sure that your purser's charge is cleared and that you get a chance to meet Captain Costanzo. Is that cool?"

"I—" stuttered Phillip.

"Great. Congratulations. Happy honeymoon." Brick quickly closed the cabin door. Tucking his gun back into the holster, he and headed to the stairway to the Cassiopeia deck to locate Kryss and Nathan.

After Brick left the elevator, the FBI agents ran to cabin 320. With their Glocks pulled, they prepared to enter the cabin.

Nathan followed Bureau protocol and announced prior to entering, "FBI! Open up! Open up! FBI!" and inserted the keycard that Yvette had given him. Once it clicked, Kryss pushed on the door and flew into the cabin. He went left and cleared the closet and bathroom.

"Clear!" yelled Kryss as Nathan continued into the main room. Seeing it was empty, he continued to the sliding doors and cleared the balcony.

"Fuck, this room is hot. Whoa, Kryss, we got shit on the bed!" proclaimed Nathan.

Kryss took one look at the bed and backed up. "Call Morgan on the radio, and cover your mouth with something. That shit could be anywhere, and it's deadly!" Kryss used his free arm to cover his nose and mouth.

Kryss moved toward the door just as Brick arrived, stopping him from entering the room. With his mouth still covered, he got Nathan's attention. "Let's find some towels to protect our lungs. We don't want to breathe any of that toxic crap."

Brick held his breath and took a quick look into the room before they locked the door.

Once out in the hall, Nathan grabbed an assortment of towels from a service cart and returned to the cabin.

"I saw a gas mask. What did you guys see?" asked Brick as he placed a hand towel over his face.

Nathan, also wrapping his face in a towel, replied, "I saw a gas mask, at least one extra mask filter, and a pair of rubber or latex gloves."

"When I cleared the closet and bathroom, I noted that the safe was open, and I might have seen a test tube or something similar in the sink. I was in and out in a few seconds, though," explained Kryss.

"Fine. We give the room a fast toss and then go find the fucker," advised Brick as he reentered the cabin. He went into the bathroom while Kryss and Nathan looked at the gas mask and some scattered clothes on the floor.

"Guys, there's a plastic tube in the sink, just as Kryss said. I bet we'll find residue of poison inside. I think this case is now in your wheelhouse, but I suggest we call Yvette, update her, and then go find our terrorist."

Nathan grabbed the gas mask from the bed, and the three men regrouped out in the hall.

"Let's work together on his," said Kryss. "Brick, you know the layout of this ship better than Nathan or I do. What do you think?"

Brick thought for a few moments. "First, we have Yvette get an armed security detail to secure this cabin. We don't want the terrorist to return or housekeeping to access the cabin. Next, the ship's security team should head to engineering and guard the ship's water system. And finally, the three of us and Yvette need to search this ship until we locate this guy."

Nathan was the next to interject. "Do we want the captain to sound the general alarm and confine all passengers to their cabins?"

"I'd hold off on that. The ship's alarm would alert the terrorist that we are onto his plot, and he might panic and start dispersing the toxin," answered Kryss. " Nathan, you go to deck fourteen, secure the food court, and search that area. Brick, I'll try to find the engineering space and look there."

"Okay, I'll drop down to decks five, six, and seven. They're the most populated with passengers. Be sure to keep your two-way radios on channel three," directed Brick as he removed his Ruger from its holster and cycled a shell into the chamber. Just as he returned it to his holster, all three two-way radios came alive.

"Brick and FBI, Fuentes here. Reports of disturbance at food court on deck fourteen. I'm heading there now."

Chapter Fifty-Eight

Using the plate to hide the first vial, Yusuf continued walking to the kettle of cream of mushroom soup. He pretended to look at some pasta, which gave him a chance to look back at the food court entrance and scout for the security department guard. Not seeing the man, he continued toward the soup station.

Yusuf was not sure of the solubility of the abrin. He wondered if the powder would float to the surface of the soup or if it would dissolve quickly. But it might not matter because this batch of abrin was highly concentrated, and the chilled grinding process had weaponized the toxin into a super-fine powder.

He picked up a soup bowl and placed it on his dinner plate as his thumb flipped off the tube's lid. While shifting the plate and bowl to his left hand, he poured the poison into the kettle. Pretending to fill his bowl, Yusuf used the large spoon to mix the toxin into the soup, looking around nervously for the guy from security who was hanging around the food court.

"Mom, that's cream of mushroom soup. Will you help me get some?" said a little girl.

Yusuf looked at the child and for a fraction of a second felt a hint of concern for the little girl. But that was immediately replaced with memories of his father's mangled truck. Yusuf was not only motivated by the desire to drive the infidels from the holy lands, but he also was committed to punishing the American people. It was the leadership of America that was directing the atrocities against Muslims. In a democracy, the people elect the president and members of Congress. Who were they to have so much when he and his family had so little? It was only right that they should suffer before they die.

Three large serving trays were seated in a steam well. Mixed vegetables filled the first tray, broccoli filled the second, and stewed tomatoes filled the third. Yusuf carefully opened the second tube of toxin and was spreading the poison on the mixed vegetables when he again noticed that he was being watched. This time, by a ship's officer. Yusuf's first reaction was to leave his plate and run from the food court. Instead, he took a deep breath and walked over to the salad bar where about a dozen passengers were in line to enter the buffet, waiting to pass their hands under the globe of sanitizing gel.

Yusuf was anxious to disperse the third vial of toxin and shake the last of it over the fancy, three-deck atrium that was located amidships. He placed his still-empty plate on the three stainless steel rails that were in front of the assortments of salads and dressings at the salad bar. He reached for the tongs with his left hand while he carefully palmed tube three in his right. Just then, he saw both the deck officer and the guy from security standing at the buffet exit, and Yusuf was certain that he was being watched. Panic overtook his usual sense of confidence, and he froze. He locked eyes with the puzzled security officer.

Suddenly, Yusuf dropped both the salad tongs and vial and ran toward the entrance. The crew member who was handing out the plates jumped out of the way and crashed into the big globe that held the hand sanitizer, knocking it to the floor. The crash scared the little girl who was carrying her bowl of poisoned soup, causing her to drop it.

Immediately, the crew called security. Yusuf knew that safety was only fifty feet away. Despite his concern over the loud crash of the dishes, he was afraid to look back to see if he was being followed. Instead, he dodged and bumped through seven startled passengers and focused on getting to the stairs that would lead him to safety. He stumbled briefly as he pushed people and obstacles out of his way. He knew word would quickly spread throughout the ship.

Within a few moments, Nathan appeared. He had run through the Galileo pool area and Big Dipper Bar, almost slipping when he approached the entrance to the Gallery Grill and Food Court. He nearly ran over the deck officer who was still on the ship's wall phone, talking to security. Nathan pulled out his credentials. "What's happened here?" he shouted.

"I just called security. We were watching this guy in a red-and-blue shirt acting strangely in the food buffet. It looked like he was messing with the food, and just as we got closer to question him, he freaked and ran out and headed in that direction."

"Call security, and then secure the food court. Shut it down, you understand?" ordered Nathan. "But first, have you seen this man?" He held up the picture of Yusuf.

"Yes, yes, that's the man!"

Nathan ran into the buffet while putting on the gas mask he had taken from cabin 320. He ran from person to person, knocking plates out of their hands. "Poison! Poison! Poison! Get away from the food!" Shocking the kitchen staff working the buffet, he yelled, "Poison! Walk away from the food! Do not touch anything! Emergency! Danger! Get off this deck!" Within ten seconds, no kitchen crew member was in sight.

Still wearing the gas mask, Nathan ran from table to table, pushing plates onto the floor. Not seeing any crew members, he recruited three college-aged Americans to help him pile chairs and tables in front of the access points to the food court. He then moved about twenty feet away from the food court and removed his mask.

"Channel three, Nathan King. Suspect wearing red-and-blue long-sleeve shirt. Ran down aft stairway. I need help securing food court. Out!"

Nathan took a deep breath and tried to size up the situation. He determined that the food had just been poisoned, but he was not in a position to chase after the poisoner. Brick and Kryss would have to take point. Nathan needed to come up with a plan to save as many lives as possible.

HIGH SEAS DARKNESS

Just then, a member of Yvette's security department arrived and asked how he could help.

"I need some paper and pens or pencils. Do not touch any food or go into the food buffet."

The man ran off, and Nathan climbed up on a table.

"Quiet, please! Quiet, please! My name is Nathan King. I am a special agent with the United States FBI."

A middle-aged man jumped up and yelled, "Are we being hijacked? What's happening?"

"Sit down, sir, and I will explain. Please remain calm, and we will be able to save lives. If you panic, people are going to get hurt. Listen up! There is a possibility that the food in the food court has been poisoned."

Several passengers jumped up and started yelling questions. Nathan barked at them, "Wait! I'll answer your questions in a few minutes. But listen now. If you ate any of the food from the food court in the last twenty or thirty minutes, raise your hands. Let me repeat, only raise your hand if you ate any food." About fifty people raised their hands. "Those of you who did *not* eat—*only* those who did not eat any food—go to the door that leads to the pool. Stay in that area until we get your cabin number. Then please leave deck fourteen."

The security guard followed the group who had not eaten to get their names and cabin numbers. Nathan grabbed the pencils and paper the guard had left.

"Listen up!" yelled Nathan, still standing on the table in the middle of the dining area. "If you feel ill—fever, stomachache, anything—call the sick bay. I need you to write down your name, cabin number, and what food you ate. This is important. When we find out what food was poisoned, we will let you know that you are safe. Again: name, cabin, and food you ate. Now repeat, please: name, cabin, and food you ate. What do I want?" Nathan cupped his hand to his ear while half the small crowd repeated back his instructions.

Nathan jumped off the table, put on the gas mask, and made a path through the pile of chairs to reenter the food court. Not sure what he was looking for, he carefully stepped over the broken plates and spilled food and examined the crime scene. He was just about to leave the area when he spotted a vial resting on a bed of romaine lettuce.

"Channel three, King on deck fourteen. Ninety percent sure that the suspect poured poison on food. I will join the hunt in five minutes. Out!"

Chapter Fifty-Nine

The *Goya Under the Stars*' next port of call was the Bahamas, the second stop on the southern Caribbean cruise. Yvette's emergency call to the *Goya* was routed to Rickie Nooner the *Goya*'s chief of security. Yvette explained that the occupant or occupants of cabin B-213 might be carrying a dangerous poison powder and have plans to kill hundreds of passengers.

After Security Director Nooner hung up, he placed a call to Rob Spencer. Nooner had only been the head of the security department for one year. He signed his contract with Nobility as soon as he retired as chief of police in Eugene, Oregon. He wanted to be finished with all that stress.

Rickie wife had died from cancer just one year prior to his scheduled retirement. He felt it was good fortune to have a new job where he could get away from the memories, use his knowledge of public safety, and also go on yearlong cruises. However, after receiving the call from the *Matisse*, Rickie was having second thoughts.

Nobility's headquarters confirmed the authenticity of the call from Yvette and instructed him to secure cabin B-213. Rickie met three members of his team at the *Goya*'s security department so they could access the arms' locker. Simultaneously, the assistant director of security informed the *Goya*'s captain of the emergency. Rickie and his team then went directly to the cabin on deck eleven.

When Rickie quietly opened the cabin door, the four armed security personnel rushed inside. They found the suspected terrorist prostrate on a mat in the middle of the cabin. Zahir Ahmed Hahid paused in his mission to partake in prayers before fulfilling his obligation to

Lashkar-e-Aalam. The retired chief of police spotted four plastic tubes and a gas mask on the bed.

The *Lautrec Under the Stars* left Los Angeles on schedule and was heading south for its rendezvous in the Panama Canal. Security found Mullah Saleh Rahim seated in front of the "Wheel of Fortune" dollar slot in the ship's casino, trying to hit the "spin the wheel" payoff. During interrogation, he spent several hours claiming he did not understand English. After being handcuffed and shown the poison in his cabin, he said that it must belong to the cabin steward. The security team apprehended Rahim before he had a chance to distribute the abrin.

Mike Chopra was talking to his deputy director of security when he received the alert call from the FBI agent. The first thing he did was open the locker that contained their small arms. The *Cézanne* was in port at Puerto Vallarta, and most of the ship's passengers had not yet returned. Given the less-strict security requirements in Mexico, more cruise personnel were able to leave the ship, making PV a port where the ship largely emptied out. When Chopra and his two other security guards barged into cabin B-562, they found Muhammad Bin Attash watching porn on his laptop. When the three men rushed into his cabin, Attash reached for a vial of the toxin. Chopra then emptied his magazine of 9mm bullets into Attash.

Four thousand miles east, the *Rembrandt* left Antigua and was en route to Saint Lucia. To Muhamed Bashir, the message he received from Yusuf seemed like bullshit. He asked himself, *What is the big rush?* He was on a Caribbean cruise and was determined to see Barbados and maybe even Saint Thomas, one of the US Virgin Islands, before he completed his mission.

Bashir planned to hit on the flirtatious Mexican girl who worked at the wine bar on deck five. He was on there when *Rembrandt*'s security department entered his cabin. Armed with the ship's universal code that opened all cabin safes, the director of security opened his safe and discovered four empty vials and a larger tube filled with a cream-colored powder.

The purser's office called the security department, telling the director that cabin A-303 had just made a charge for wine on deck five. Within three minutes, Muhamed was tackled, handcuffed, and looking up from the floor at the Mexican girl he had wanted to fuck. She pointedly looked away.

Herb Wallace joined Robert Spencer in his office at the headquarters of Nobility Cruise Lines. The FBI was anxious to retrieve the poison so their Quantico lab could start a chemical analysis. Rob was trying to maintain five open lines with his ships, doing his best to assess how much of Nobility's fleet was targeted. The initial reports indicated that one terrorist was killed and three were in custody. Disturbingly, there was still no information from the *Matisse*.

"Rob, this could become a jurisdiction circus," said Herb. "Your people shot the guy on your ship that has a Bermuda flag while it is moored to a Mexican pier. As far as the Bureau is concerned, we need pictures and fingerprints of the body, but we're not going to go ballistic if the Mexicans want the body. But we need to make sure that your team on the *Cézanne* uses hazmat procedures to secure the toxin. We need to keep the poison locked up until I get my people down there. Quantico is standing by to study the toxin once we get it to them."

"Assistant Director Wallace, what is your estimate of when your people will be able to get to the *Cézanne*?"

"Two agents are on a plane as we speak. San Diego to PV is about a three-hour flight."

"Shit, finally! A text message from the *Matisse*. 'Yusuf Al Omar is loose on the ship after dispersing poison at food court. Agents King and Mitchell in pursuit with Brick Morgan,'" reported Rob as he showed Herb the message.

"Your *Matisse* is only a day and a half out of San Francisco. It would make more sense to turn around and head back to California than continuing to Hawaii. Rob, if the *Matisse* can get back within 180 nautical miles of California, we can get a helicopter on her deck."

While Rob and Herb waited for more information from the *Matisse,* another FBI agent handed Herb a message.

Herb read the message and smiled. "I think this is good news. It seems the Policía Federal Ministerial took control from the Jalisco State Police, and the *Federales* do not want the body. I figure they made a business decision. With no potential revenue or opportunity for bribes, and lots of paper work, they would rather we took care of it."

The phone rang and Rob answered. After listening for a minute, he hung up.

"A new problem. Nobility's fleet operations just received a call from Captain Costanzo. He is turning the ship and returning to San Francisco. He just received a report of gunfire belowdecks."

Chapter Sixty

At this point, Yusuf knew it was not about escaping; it was about how to maximize the potential of his last tube of abrin. His plan was to empty his M&P9 pistol into as many infidels as he could before sniffing the last of the abrin and heading to Paradise.

He skipped half of the stairs as he flew from deck fourteen down to deck twelve. Nobody was in the lobby on the Aquarius deck, so he ripped off his long-sleeved shirt and tossed it into an empty elevator. He needed to get away from the aft stairway, so he used the blue-carpeted starboard hall to walk quickly to the amidships stairway, where he proceeded down to deck eleven.

Yusuf realized that he was just one deck above his cabin. What were the chances that he had been identified when he ran from the food court? Certainly, the two crew members who had been watching him had gotten a good look at him. But then he had been wearing the blue-and-red shirt along with sunglasses and a ball cap. *Shit, I am still wearing the hat! If I drop it now, they'll know I was on the amidships staircase.* Stuffing the hat into his back pocket, he decided to take the stairs down to deck eleven to see if he could access his room.

Once on the Cassiopeia deck, Yusuf casually walked to the portside hallway and peered forward. Although it was only a quick glance, he took a clear mental snapshot of the commotion outside his cabin.

What is the American phrase? Yusuf wondered. Suddenly, he remembered the term— *game changer.* The options that he contemplated earlier had narrowed considerably. There was nothing to be gained by trying to figure out how he was identified. The three guards standing in front of his cabin was enough proof that he was now a wanted man. Yusuf figured there was zero chance he could get off this ship alive, yet he was not willing to make their search for him a cakewalk. If he was going down, it would be after committing the maximum amount of collateral damage. He wanted to make sure the Americans remembered his name and the pain he had caused.

He needed a safe place to think of a plan, some spot on the ship where he would not be seen for a few hours. He walked forward on deck ten as casually as he could. He passed a food tray that had been set out to be picked up by room service. Grabbing three oranges, he continued to the forward stairwell as he attempted to juggle the oranges. A middle-aged couple came out of their cabin and started walking toward him.

"Great job. Are you part of tonight's show?" they asked as they passed.

Yusuf smiled and employed his questionable British accent. "Why, yes. I'm in training, thank you."

After they'd passed, Yusuf considered his next steps. He recalled that a bar on deck six remained closed for most of the day and did not open until seven, maybe eight at night. That would give him at least an hour. He avoided further contact with passengers until he stepped from the stairs onto deck six.

He ditched the oranges on the stairs and walked along the starboard side of the *Matisse* in the direction of the Luminosity Bar. The bar's open architecture lacked a door. A quick look confirmed that it was closed, and he noted that the huge back bar was secured with a copper-colored grate. Yusuf ducked into the bar and, when he was sure he was out of sight, climbed over the bar and lay down out of sight. After taking a few deep breaths to calm down, he checked for the folded paper that contained the abrin. Next, he removed his 9mm pistol and chambered a shell. *Let them come . . .*

Channel three barked team locations, but there were no reports on the location of the terrorist.

Raju finally checked in with Yvette, letting her know that he had cleared deck seven and had just arrived on deck six and was starting with the stern. Once he searched deck seven, he quickly returned to his cabin and armed himself with his Gurkha knife. He placed the large combat knife in its sheath and slid it into the front of his pants.

Raju entered the Equinox Disco and quietly walked about one-third of the way down the center aisle. The disco was used as an entertainment center with a large stage, and after midnight, its large dance floor served as a disco. The massive bar situated against the port bulkhead served wine, beer, and cocktails. Raju stood still, listening for any sound that might provide a clue to the location of Al Omar.

Two members of the *Matisse* security detail had been glued to the eight monitors displayed on the starboard wall of the security office that received feeds from fourteen hundred CCTV cameras mounted throughout the ship. One of the monitors showed Raju standing in the middle of the Equinox Disco on deck six. As if on cue, the former Indian Gurkha looked up at one of the dark ceiling-mounted cameras and gave a nod as if to say, "We are going to catch the bastard."

The hunt always triggered Raju's sense memory. He could almost smell the moist, floral mist that radiated from Sri Lanka's Dunhinda Falls. For a moment, he was transported back to Badulla, Sri Lanka, and his Gurkha deployment during the Sri Lankan Civil War. Raju would never forget his discovery of a mass grave that contained the bodies of hundreds of women and children. The memory brought him back to the reality of the current situation. Onboard his ship was a militant Islamist who was determined to also kill women and children. Raju briefly touched his knife and continued searching the disco.

Chapter Sixty-One

The Bella di Buco was one of the *Matisse*'s specialty restaurants, and because it charged each passenger an extra twenty-five dollars, it served as a great revenue driver for the ship's bottom line. Yvette thought the busy Italian restaurant was a less likely place the terrorist would hide, but she wanted to double-check anyway before continuing her search of deck six.

Dressed in her officer whites, Yvette casually walked in and sat at a table for two that was in the middle of a reset. Law enforcement professionals develop great instincts, and her study of the Bella di Buco told her that this was not the hiding place of Yusuf Al Omar. After a few minutes, Yvette left the restaurant and moved her search farther toward the bow.

Brick and Kryss met in front of the casino after Nathan and Kryss had cleared deck five. Nathan wanted to return to the Galaxy Grill and Food Court on deck fourteen, so Kryss went to deck six to join Brick.

"Brick, let's clear the casino and then continue aft, going shop by shop," suggested Kryss as they looked down the various rows of slot machines.

"The problem is, we don't know what he's wearing. We know he ditched the ball cap and long-sleeve shirt. The good news is, we now have two pictures of the guy, and there are at least a dozen of us looking for him."

"My concern is, what if he breaks into a cabin and holds a couple of passengers hostage?"

Brick headed into a perfume and purse shop when Kryss said he needed to check in with Herb Wallace. Kryss used his cell phone to link with the *Matisse* satellite service and connected with Wallace to provide him with a status report. After Brick made certain that Yusuf was not in the perfume shop, he and Kryss moved quickly in the direction of the Luminosity Bar on deck six.

Between the Bella di Buco and the Luminosity Bar stood a series of panels that displayed thousands of photographs of passengers. At different venues on the ship and some port areas, several *Matisse* photographers captured moments for an album of memories to be sold for twenty dollars each. The day after a port-of-call or formal dinner, thousands of new pictures appeared on the dozens of floor-to-ceiling panels. Yvette took her time, making sure that Al Omar was not hiding among the passengers looking for their photos. She occasionally retraced her steps to ensure that he did not slip into any areas she had previously searched.

While systematically looking around the photographic department, Yvette ran into Raju. "What areas have you covered?" she asked him.

"I covered deck seven and have just left the Equinox," he answered.

"Raju, are you carrying your big Gurkha knife?"

"Yes, and when I find him—and I will—I am going to cut off his head with one swing of my friend."

Yvette smiled at her eager deputy. "Why don't you check out the restroom by the restaurant, and I'll finish up here and continue sweeping forward."

Brick and Kryss split up as they arrived at the Luminosity Bar. Brick went left to examine some supply rooms located across from the bar while Kryss went right and entered the apparently empty bar.

Walking past the long bar, Kryss glanced up at the massive display of whiskeys displayed on the back bar. What a shame that a security screen kept all the bottles out of reach, he thought. The whole lounge was dark, and the FBI agent had no clue where the lighting panel was located. Touching his service piece for security, he headed to the stage area, planning to inspect the lounge from the back of the stage and confirm that it was empty after he looked under the dozen or more tables. His search was almost complete when he heard a small distraction coming from the far side of the lounge near the bar.

As the tall man with short blond hair carefully looked under tables one by one, Yusuf crouched no more than twenty feet away. It appeared that Kryss was advancing in his direction. The floor behind the bar had been Yusuf's hiding space for the last thirty minutes. During that time, he had formulated an idea that might buy him some time and possibly provide him a way off the ship.

Yusuf was certain he could access the engine space by running to a stairwell and proceeding to deck four. He was confident that if he traveled aft on deck four, it would lead him to the ship's engineering space. He visualized capturing an engineering officer and using him as leverage for transportation off the *Matisse*. But his dreams of a safe escape had been interrupted by the sound of someone entering the lounge. Now, Yusuf carefully grabbed his pistol and discreetly peered over the edge of the sky-black granite bar top. *If he was going to make his move, it had to be now.*

Yusuf put his foot in the liquor well, flipped himself up and over the bar, and found himself standing merely fifteen feet from the exit and twenty feet from the tall man. Operating on pure adrenalin and an instinct for survival, Yusuf turned toward Special Agent Kryss Mitchell and fired one shot in his direction. Yusuf heard the man cry out and hit the ground hard.

Still holding his pistol in his right hand, Yusuf ran out of the bar and turned toward the stern of the ship. As he started aft, he froze at the sight of a woman officer twenty-five feet away heading in his direction. As if in slow motion, Yusuf raised his right hand and aimed the gun at the chest of Yvette Fuentes. Placing his left hand under the grip of the 9mm pistol to provide additional stability for his shot, he would squeeze off just two shots and continue his dash to the engine room. Yvette saw his right index finger pull the trigger once and then twice, unleashing two 9mm slugs toward her.

Returning from his inspection of the restrooms, Raju heard the single gunshot from the Luminosity Bar. As he turned in that direction, he saw the terrorist aim his gun with Yvette as the madman's target. Without hesitation, Raju Kumar Marwah stepped forward and absorbed both of the 120-grain hollow point bullets into his chest.

His right leg started to buckle, but Raju defiantly righted himself and yelled, "*Kafar Huna Bhanda Marnu!* Better to die than live like a coward!" Raju reached for his knife as he took a step toward the terrorist. Then both legs gave out, and he collapsed on the deck between Yvette and Al Omar.

Yvette went for her own weapon. When Yusuf realized that he had missed his intended target, he again raised his gun toward the woman to take the killing shot.

"Do it, you bastard. Let's see who wants it more," Yvette hissed.

Yusuf yelled, "*Allahu Akbar!*"

The sound of gunfire echoed throughout the *Matisse*.

Brick did not hear the first shot in the Luminosity Bar, but he did hear the two following shots as he was closing the door to a supply room. He left the bar, his pistol already drawn before he could fully process the sequence of events.

Brick saw Raju fall and Yusuf Al Omar raise his gun in the direction of Yvette. In a fraction of a second, Brick aimed his Ruger for a headshot. Just as he pulled the trigger, he lowered the pistol and focused on the hip of the terrorist. Three quick and accurate .22 hollow points shattered Yusuf's upper femur and blew out the acetabulum of his pelvis.

As Yvette ran to Raju, Brick rushed to Yusuf and slammed his foot down on the terrorist's wrist, causing the gun to dislodge and breaking his bones. Brick then spotted Yusuf pulling something from his pocket with his other hand and attempting to place it in his mouth. As another .22 caliber bullet shattered his other wrist, a small piece of folded paper fell from his fingers only inches from the screaming jihadist's face.

Chapter Sixty-Two

When the phone rang in the Florida headquarters of the Nobility Cruise Lines, Kryss patiently waited for Rob Spencer to answer his phone. Rob answered and then handed the phone to Herb.

"Boss, the Bureau owes me a pair of slacks," announced Kryss as he propped his leg on a chair. "That bastard got lucky and nicked my thigh with a 9mm. Nothing broken, just a clean through and through and a lot of antibiotics and Super Glue."

For the next thirty minutes, Kryss brought Herb up to date on the events that led to the capture of Yusuf Al Omar. "I was dragging my shot-up leg out of the bar when I saw the ship's deputy security officer jump in front of two 9mm bullets that were targeted for the ship's chief of security. One bullet hit him under his armpit, broke a rib, and exited his side, just missing his liver and spleen. The next bullet was a gut shot that ricocheted off some big knife he had in his pants. But the doc on the ship says he will make a full recovery. But they're gonna need a lot more Super Glue after using it on his bullet holes too."

Rob jotted down notes and began e-mailing Nobility's PR team to get out in front of this incident as Herb continued listening to the report. Herb then requested to speak with Brick.

"Brick, Herb Wallace, FBI."

"Hello, Assistant Director Wallace. I want you to know that Nathan and Kryss did a great job cracking this case."

"Bullshit, Morgan. The director sends his best and wanted me to call you directly. It seems that the sample we retrieved from the *Cézanne* in Puerto Vallarta tested positive for a deadly toxin called abrin. Very concentrated and partially weaponized. The director wants you to know that your tenacity and wisdom will be rewarded. He will personally call you when he is finished with some issues at the White House."

"Thank you, sir, but—"

"Morgan, one more thing. It seems the Seattle FBI encountered your trigger-happy friend in Fircrest, Washington, near Tacoma. A Miss Titus, whom we had under protective watch, almost shot one of our agents with a shotgun when they intervened."

"Is she—?"

"She's okay. It took some calming down and a lot of assurances on our part, but I understand they are now best of friends, and she is teaching the special agents how to become cyber-hackers. Apparently, she thinks they have to be naked to learn her tricks. Seriously, though, the nation owes you more than a token of gratitude."

As Brick continued his conversation, Yvette e-mailed Rob with a summary of the medical status of the passengers who were on deck fourteen. She knew that whatever came next, the list of casualties deserved to be at the forefront of the news.

Chapter Sixty-Three

An hour later, the news had reached Washington DC. Senate Minority Leader Michelle Murphy walked into the office of Speaker of the House Martin Daniel.

"Michelle, he should be here in the next fifteen minutes."

For the last month, Murphy and Daniel had been discreetly working with one of the most powerful men in Washington on a plan to detour the disastrous direction that the country was headed. They readied themselves to confront the most powerful man in the world. The Speaker's assistant opened the door to the Speaker's inner office and announced, "Mr. Speaker, the director of the FBI."

Alexander Zittel entered the Speaker's office and gave both Michelle and Martin a victorious handshake. Martin was the first to speak. "Director, the last few months have been hell, but the pressure placed upon you and the FBI must have been enormous."

With a modicum of humility, Ace relaxed in one of the Speaker's chairs and confirmed his observations. "The most difficult aspect was pretending to the FBI leadership team that I was buying into the president's philosophy of denying that terrorism was a threat. It was killing me, yet it was necessary to buy us the time to get enough solid evidence so he could not pull that 'plausible deniability' bullshit. I knew I was losing credibility with the agents, but if I'd pushed back with POTUS too early, we'd have a new FBI director today.

"We are due at the White house in forty minutes. I understand that the president is extremely pissed that we busted his schedule today. I also requested that the secretary of Homeland Security attend. My friends, the fireworks begin in thirty-nine minutes."

Ten minutes before their scheduled appointment, Director Zittel's car pulled up in front of the West Wing canopy, and the three got out and walked to the security table and the waiting Secret Service agent. Just then, Secretary Maxine Johnston's car drove up, so Ace, Michelle, and Martin waited by the door for her to check in.

Once inside the reception area, Maxine pulled Ace aside. "I sure the fuck hope you know what you're doing. Do we still shoot Americans for treason?"

"Ask me in ten minutes."

The chief of staff eventually met them and escorted everyone to the Roosevelt Room where he announced that the president would be with them in a few minutes.

The president arrived shortly and took a seat at the end of the table closest to the door. As was customary, everyone stood when POTUS entered the room and waited for the sign to sit down.

"My God," joked the president. "We have both chambers of Congress, the FBI, and DHS in here. Who's running the government?"

Ace was the first to speak. "Mr. President, we want to thank you for meeting with us on such short notice."

"What's up, Ace?" asked the president as he seated himself.

"First, let me acknowledge that because of the nature and seriousness of this meeting, a video message has been prepared by Martin, Michelle, and myself. That video is in the hands of my deputy director and will be released to the press if any of us do not return to our office within two hours."

"Vic, what the hell is this all about? I don't have time for threats and grandstanding."

"Mr. President, I have no idea. But I think we should hear what they have to say," answered the chief of staff.

"Mr. President, we would like to present, for your consideration, a different approach to Operation Bridgewalk." Ace Zittel passed out a white paper containing expanded bullet points that provided an overview of the group's position.

"We have been at war for over twenty years with militant Islamists. In 1993, Ramzi Yousef set off a bomb in the parking garage below Tower 1 of the World Trade Center. In 1998, our embassies were attacked, and then September 11 and the 2001 attempt by the shoe bomber to blow up a plane and Boston and so forth. The reality is that some radical Islamists want to spread the Muslim faith throughout the world. Some of those people are militant, meaning they will use whatever violent means they have to remake the world into a caliphate. Mr. President, these extremists will not be deterred from their goal."

Ace paused and let the group catch up to where he was with respect to his handout. "We have all seen the research of attitudes that deal with our Muslim population in the United States. We can argue percentage points, but the facts are that most Muslims are wonderful people and just want to be good Americans, participate in the American dream, and practice Islam in peace."

The president jumped in. "I'm not naive, Zittel. I know the numbers. That's my whole point. We can't keep punishing 90 percent of them and then act surprised when a small but vocal minority causes trouble. If we want to stop the violence, we need to make a genuine effort to reach out."

"With all due respect, sir," Ace interjected, "the militant Islamists will not stop their jihad because we are nice to our Muslim community. Here is what we must do. The first thing is that you, Mr. President, must tell the American people that we are at war. You must tell our country that a small but violent percentage of our Muslim countrymen want to destroy our country. We have to stop sticking our heads in the sand under the doctrine of so-called political correctness."

The president caught Maxine Johnston, Martin Daniel, and Michelle Murphy all nodding in approval.

"It is critical that we clearly explain the difference between Islam as a practicing religion versus the skewed ideology that pushes the

United States toward a caliphate, or constitutional theocracy. The nation needs to understand that there exists a clear difference between a Muslim who just wants to practice his faith and the nuts, the radical Islamists, who want to violently overthrow our government, eradicate our culture, and replace both with an Islamic government. Once we have bifurcated the issue, we can explain that we are at war with militant Islamists, but not with Muslims or their religion.

"Mr. President, this message must be repeated over and over. We are supportive of the religion of Islam and those who practice it, but we will not tolerate a group that wants to overthrow the government of the United States. When a person or group wants to overthrow the government, they are classified as enemies of the state, whether external forces or internal traitors.

"Once we are honest with our people, we have to announce an aggressive plan to deal with the radicalization of our children. When we speak of our children, I am talking about our Muslim youth, sixteen through twenty-five, who are exposed to a brainwashing ideology that is being taught in some of the mosques. We will meet with each imam in every one of the two-thousand-plus mosques in the United States. We will give each one a grade: A, B or F. We grade restaurants in this country depending on how many cockroaches they have. It is time we grade the mosques. If they invite speakers that profess an ideology that is anti-American, they will get an F. If they get an F, they can kiss their 501(c)3 or their 501(c)4 status good-bye. We cannot let our young children become radicalized by a minority group who are hell-bent on destroying our way of life."

Zittel paused long enough for a sip of water, but not long enough to lose the group's attention. He continued.

"The third leg of Operation Bridgewalk has to do with assimilation. When a group of foreign culture assimilates into society, a country becomes stronger. We have to differentiate between Islam as a legitimate religion that can stand next to our Catholics, Jews, and

Lutherans versus an Islam that wants to be the main ideology of our nation's government. This is the key point: any initiative or philosophy that advocates replacing the constitution of the United States with an Islamic state must be considered treason."

The president appeared dazed for a moment. Those assembled were not sure if he was seriously considering their points or having them tossed out on their political asses. Then he looked at his chief of staff and finally at Ace and Maxine and said, "Why would I want to go along with this aggressive position?"

"Mr. President, I have one more item I would like to share." Ace handed him a folder labeled "Top Secret: President's Eyes Only."

There was silence in the room for several minutes while the president read the contents of the folder. After what seemed an eternity, the president stood up and slammed the folder on the mahogany conference table. "What is going on here? Where did these confidential conversations come from? Vic, who recorded these meetings and conversations? These conversations are executive privilege."

"Mr. President, this file contains seventeen different transcripts of meetings and calls where you directed the FBI and DHS to lie to the American people. This last transcript details your deployment of a United States submarine to shadow and possibly sink a cruise ship, with a complement of over four thousand people, for the purpose of hiding an act of terror. Today, our country was attacked by a spinoff of al-Qaeda, a group called Lashkar-e-Aalam. Five terrorists tried to kill thousands of passengers and crew members while the White House told me to downplay it, to call it 'ocean animosity.' Sir, the Speaker of the House, the minority Speaker of the Senate, and I, the director of the FBI, are prepared to hold the largest press conference this city has seen, and we will make public every one of these transcripts. The 'nuclear option' you hear so much about will seem like a firecracker to this atom bomb."

"So if I don't concede to your plan of effectively profiling one group, a plan that tramples on some of the most basic rights of our American citizens, you'll bring this administration to a halt? Forgive me, lady and gentlemen, but that's bullshit. You're in my house now, and I won't be bullied by your partisan politics. Your agenda comes from the right place, but I'll be damned before I see you target any religion, ethnicity, sexual orientation, or whatever else in the name of national security. It was wrong when the Nazis did it, and it's wrong now."

"Nazis?" cried an angry and insulted Zittel, "Fine. I guess we'll see you on every station from Fox News to PBS tonight!"

"I'm not finished," said the president. "To be clear, radical Islamic terrorists are a problem. There, I said the word for you. *Terrorists*. They want to destroy our way of life. But radical Catholicism or overzealous nationalism are just as dangerous. I make the best decisions I can for the good of this country. I won't apologize for that. Yet I recognize that the protection of the American people must always come first. I think we can reach a compromise that serves the needs of all the citizens of our great nation."

Three hours later, all the major broadcast and cable networks had preempted their normal schedules for an urgent message from the White House. The James S. Brady Press Briefing Room was packed with the press corps to observe a live feed of the president's address. Monitors were set up in the Roosevelt Room and Cabinet Room. Three cameras were positioned in the Oval Office; the secretary of state, vice president, and the First Lady were with the president in the Oval Office.

The president took a seat behind his desk. Someone appeared with a brush and applied some makeup and straightened his tie. The White House director of communications held up five fingers, then four, three, two, and finally pointed one finger at the president.

"My fellow Americans. Today our country bore witness to high seas darkness. A group of radical Islamic terrorists attempted to enact a coordinated plot that would have killed over twenty thousand passengers and crew members on five different cruise ships. Those ships carried men, women, and children from dozens and dozens of different countries. Those five ships carried men, women, and children representing Christianity, Judaism, Islam, Buddhism, and Hinduism, to name a few. Americans, enough is enough!

"Tonight I am announcing Operation Bridgewalk. My administration will work hand in hand with the leaders and followers of Islam. I ask all Muslims to throw away the attitudes of apathy and denial and have the courage to rid this cancer from their religion, to confront the radical elements in their mosques, and ensure that their imams do not preach anti-American messages. For those American Muslims who are uncomfortable with this message, I have one question: Is your current strategy of denial working?

"My administration recognizes that the contemporary cultural climate is filled with difficult decisions. It's easy to blame, to hate, to threaten—that's why our enemies do it. But there is no place for that kind of cruelty in our country, in our world. As part of Operation Bridgewalk, I am renewing America's commitment to showing the world a better way. Make no mistake. Those who enact terror will face the swiftest of justice. Whether domestic or abroad, violence against Americans is always an act of war.

"But war takes many forms. I confess, on behalf of my administration, on behalf of Congress and the FBI and Homeland Security and more, that we failed in building bridges to those parts of our country and our world where Americanism seems anathema. We allowed a cultural war to go unopposed, and this left our republic vulnerable. No longer will we tolerate those who carve out divisions in attempts to tear at the fabric of our society.

"Operation Bridgewalk will tackle two fronts. While continuing America's commitment to aggressively thwarting terrorist actions, I am funding a new initiative to train American citizens to become ambassadors and teachers of what Americanism means to us. These new professionals will enter communities at home and abroad in order to battle the propagandistic attacks on Americanism that are the sources of terror. Yes, this will involve reaching out to religious and social factions that may not resonate positively among most Americans. However, I believe this most recent terrorist act provides Americans an opportunity to embrace the diversity that makes us strong. The future soldiers of terror are those youth led astray by radical teachings that preach violence against us. There is still much to elaborate on Operation Bridgewater, but please, my fellow Americans, recognize this strategy as a means of arming America both militarily and ideologically."

The president of the United States continued for another forty minutes, detailing carefully negotiated versions of the initiatives that Ace Zittel had presented earlier in the day. Then he pushed back his chair and stood up behind his desk. The cameramen adjusted their cameras to accommodate his new position.

"Finally, I must thank the courageous men and women who thwarted the terrorist plots. This group, representing multiple nationalities, came together to show the rest of the world that terrorists will not be tolerated. Today, our great nation is in debt to the vigilance and tenacity of these people, especially one determined American citizen. This private citizen, along with the FBI, stopped an attack of unprecedented proportions. I personally want to thank Brick Morgan of Morgan Maritime Investigations. Next week, I hope to see Mr. Morgan at the White House where I will present him with the highest award that can be presented to an American citizen, the Presidential Medal of Freedom."

Epilogue

Brick's Mark Whitfield CD played quietly in the background as he sat with his new Stephen Marchione guitar. He arrived home from his recognition at the White House to find it waiting for him, signed by Whitfield himself. As decadent as a vacation seemed to Brick given his busy work schedule, the last two weeks almost buried him in an avalanche of calls. He appreciated all of the attention for Morgan Maritime Investigations, but he was content to let the messages pile up for a day or two. He felt he deserved to quietly celebrate his return home with his new guitar and a couple of double cheeseburgers from Frisko Freeze. He was determined to finally make time to learn some new cords, even though he found his mind still juggling thoughts of the *Matisse*.

He had just heard that Carolyn Luna's settlement went through as planned. By now, she and her friend would be enjoying their much-deserved perfect Caribbean cruise on the *Gauguin Under the Stars*. She sent her appreciation as Carolyn and Yvette continued to stay in touch by e-mail. Yvette was always better with victims than anyone Brick knew.

Yvette certainly made her voice known in the aftermath of the crisis on the ship. The hazardous material specialists, the Department of Homeland Security, and a team from CDC were able to clean and release the *Matisse Under the Stars* in three days. With Yvette's urging, Nobility Cruise Line offered exceptional flexibility and generosity to their passengers in light of this incident. About 70 percent of the passengers agreed to stay on the *Matisse* and continue the Hawaiian cruise. The remaining passengers received credits for comparable cruises, plus their incidental charges were absorbed by the cruise line.

Rob Spencer appreciated Yvette's leadership and loyalty to

protecting Nobility's interests throughout the affair. He offered Yvette a substantial promotion and the opportunity to transfer to Nobility's home office. She gratefully declined and, in an act of perhaps playful defiance, she signed on for another contract on the *Matisse Under the Stars*. He could not say he was surprised with Yvette's decision since this whole episode gave her the visibility to make the changes she really wanted to see at Nobility.

Before long, Yvette contacted Brick through his personal e-mail, reminding him that he was always welcome onboard. He noted that her e-mail did not mention missing her old assistant Raju. Brick had already heard from Rob that Raju's bullet wound was healing well, and that he would be able to return to duty in three weeks. But this time, he would join the *Bernini Under the Stars* as chief of security. Raju's Gurkha knife, and its dent from the 9mm bullet, would soon stand prominently on his new office desk. Yvette did, however, make sure Raju's new position contracted him to the ship with Nobility's only female captain and female cruise director. It seemed like the least she could do after how he worked under her on the *Matisse*.

The ship's passengers suffered minimal effects from the abrin. When the *Matisse* was within 180 nautical miles of California, three Blackhawk helicopters dispatched a team of medical specialists and a dozen FBI agents. Nathan King's effort to secure a list of foods that had been eaten was credited with saving many lives. The CDC cited his fast action of running through the food court and pushing plates of poisoned food to the floor as genius. Both he and Kryss Mitchell, largely healed from his own wound, were honored by the FBI and also received congressional recognition from Speaker of the House Martin Daniel.

When Brick went to the White House to receive his Presidential Medal of Freedom, he found that the Nobility episodes caused other changes in Washington. Liz Monroe insisted that he visit her new office as the newly appointed secretary of the Department of Homeland

Security. It seemed that Maxine Johnston suffered the brunt of Ace Zittel's machinations with the president and vacated the position unexpectedly following the announcement of the president's new plan. Liz expressed that if he wanted to return to DC, Brick could easily be the next director of the CIA's National Counterterrorism Center. Politely, Brick declined. They both knew he would never be happy with a desk job. But he requested that Liz always keep a bottle of great bourbon in her bar in case he stopped by.

Maxine's ousting caused very few ripples. Within weeks, Alexander "Ace" Zittel celebrated the outcome of his showdown with POTUS by ordering another pair of Gucci loafers. He felt it was important to continue demonstrating both dignity and respect for the president. Ace knew he had won, and that was all he needed, although he continued to play his own game. The biggest challenges he faced now were replacing that new wildcard Liz Monroe and working his agenda with the NSA's data-mining facility at Bluffdale, Utah. Ace remained committed to eventually implementing his Black Owl project.

Brick knew that Titus would, of course, remain vigilant and likely keep her cyber-eyes focused on Zittel's new enterprises. She enjoyed her exciting experience with the FBI and was grateful that her backyard encounter was between her and the Feds and not Chinese super-assassins. Unknown to Titus, the Bureau had placed her under protective custody because of the vital work she was doing on the Lashkar-e-Aalam project. Zittel recognized that the restrictive laws of privacy made it more prudent to let a private citizen like Titus hack into various e-mails and computers rather than jumping through the hoops with the FBI attempting to obtain permission under Title III of the Wiretap Act or a court order under the Foreign Surveillance Act.

The two special agents had found several reasons to move into Titus's home and continue their protective custody. Titus intimated to Brick that she enjoyed the company of her visitors; however, she soon realized that she was on the government's radar now. Brick knew she much preferred to live underground. Unexpectedly, her place suffered a gas leak and a subsequent fire that left little evidence that the hacker named Titus ever existed. A month later, a tall, leggy blonde with no last name bought a big condominium at Point Ruston near Point Defiance, just outside of Tacoma, Washington. Ipé was back in business.

Brick triumphantly hit a difficult F chord correctly for the first time when he thought of the terrorists that he helped bring down. His last-second decision to keep Yusuf alive left the would-be jihadist largely crippled with a bullet still lodged in his pelvis. Yusuf still did not know what happened to his appointment with those seventy-two virgins and the rivers of wine. He was so close to opening that folded paper with his passport to Paradise. Today, Yusuf Al Omar feels abandoned and alone at Camp 3, as many of the detainees have been transferred to other facilities because of Gitmo's slow closure.

Kryss Mitchell recounted that the rest of the Lashkar-e-Aalam cell crumbled under its own zealotry. While awaiting word on the cruise attacks, Zaeem received an urgent call from the Maali, the widow of his chief chemist, Faroug Hasan Ahmed. She indicated that she discovered some secret papers in Faroug's desk. Zaeem planned to kill her instead of paying her off when they met in the southwest corner of the produce market. But as he drove into the market, his car was riddled with bullets from three AK-47s.

Brick's practice session was interrupted when he noticed that Fox News was announcing an alert about the president. After pausing the CD, Brick turned up the volume just in time to hear the anchorman transfer the transmission to the White House. The president appeared once again seated at his desk in the Oval Office.

"My fellow Americans. Two weeks ago, I announced my commitment to aggressively eradicating terrorism from the soil of the United States of America. Today, I am even more committed to Operation Bridgewalk than ever before. Our great country was built on the assimilation of dozens of diverse cultures, and in the future, we will look back and be grateful for the contribution of our valued citizens of different races and religions. Friends, I want to commit my full attention to the success of Operation Bridgewalk. Therefore, I have decided not to seek, or accept, the nomination of my party for another term as your president."

Brick turned off the television, grabbed a beer, and went outside to watch the sailboats navigate the waters of Puget Sound.

CPSIA information can be obtained at www.ICGtesting.com
Printed in the USA
BVOW03*1605220614